THE SILVER CHAIN OF SOUND

THE SILVER CHAIN OF SOUND

Short Stories

by

HENRY TEGNER

A CIP catalogue record for this book is available from the British Library.

ISBN 978-1-9989947-0-0

Book layout and design by Clare Brayshaw

Cover image painted by Henry Tegner

Prepared and printed by:

York Publishing Services Ltd
64 Hallfield Road
Layerthorpe
York YO31 7ZQ

Tel: 01904 431213

Website: www.yps-publishing.co.uk

For Agnes
Whom Most I Love

CONTENTS

ACKNOWLEDGEMENTS

With special thanks for my friends from the writing group – Shirley Hughes, Blanche Sears, Brigitta Ansdell-Evans, Kerry Beckett, Ted Aves and Robert Lentell. I have learned much from them and benefitted greatly from their wisdom, advice and encouragement.

ABOUT THE AUTHOR

Henry Tegner is a retired general practitioner. He lives in Wiltshire with his wife, Agnes, to whom this book is dedicated. They have three adult children and five grandchildren.

He and Agnes share many interests, and memories going back for over fifty years. It is with some sadness that they reflect upon the certainty that the time left to them is far less than the many decades they have been together, and such time as they have is precious.

Sometimes, with a smile to each other, they imagine themselves as Philemon and Baucis, who, on hearing the knock upon the door, make welcome the two wayfarers who face them over the threshold.

THE SILVER CHAIN OF SOUND

'Bill – please switch that off!'

We were approaching a junction and I needed to concentrate. 'Lost your taste for the classics?' My remark was abrupt, but Mary seemed not to notice.

'No. Of course not. It's a lovely piece. Reminds me of … but they play it at least once every day on this channel. One day they'll play it to death.'

I could see her point. It was an 'easy listening' station that certainly didn't set out to challenge. I moved my hand to the console and turned it off.

Mary fell silent as I negotiated the traffic at the edge of the town. As we dropped speed on a quieter, country road, I found myself moved to take up the conversation again. I wanted to counter the terseness of my words a few moments before. If anyone needed gentleness at this time, Mary did.

'Reminds you of something, you say … or someone?'

I sensed her brief nod. 'Yes. Benbo. It reminds me of a special time with Benbo. So when I listen to it, I have to be in a particular sort of mood. And alone.'

'Was it a favourite of his?'

'Well, yes. But you could say it's everyone's favourite. That's why the wretched station plays it as often as it does. But it was more than that for Benbo. It was the … an association it had for him.' She paused. It seemed that, for the time being at least, she did not want to say any more. Perhaps the situation was not right, focused as we were on the journey.

We said little more for the rest of the drive. We were both lost in our thoughts, I guess, and in our grieving. She for her husband and I for a much-loved younger brother. Ahead of us lay the painful task of going through his papers and other more personal belongings. He had been a man who loved life and thrilled to the beauty and mystery of the world. I knew well that what he had left behind him would reflect this. Mary would need all the support I could give her. They had adored one another. Yet the knowledge that he had so little time left had provoked no bitterness in him. His only sorrow was in his anticipation of the grief that lay ahead of her.

We arrived at last at the small cottage that had been their home and lost no time in getting to work. The music on the radio stayed with me as we worked and sorted together in silence. I could only begin to guess the pain it cost her. But she kept her dignity throughout, with no outward sign of her grief. When at last she spoke again as we sipped coffee on her patio it was clear that her mind had been caught up just as had mine. It was as if our exchange in the car had happened only moments ago. She resumed our conversation as if the intervening hours had never been.

'It was the day you went whale-watching, off the peninsula on the south-east coast. Benbo hadn't the strength to join you. He said the drugs were making him quite sick enough without the effects of heaving around on an open boat.'

'Yes. I remember. The gale had blown itself out overnight, and it was a fine day. But the sea was wild enough. We did see the whales, just for a very few minutes, and they were miles off. It's not something I'd do again in a hurry.'

'I never told you what Benbo and I did while you were out there.' Her expression spoke of a treasured memory.

I waited. I sensed that she wanted to share something with me. But she didn't speak immediately. Instead she went inside to her desk and took from it a disc. I had a feeling that it was the Vaughan Williams, and I was right. She took it to the player and adjusted the volume. This time we sat together in silence for a quarter of an hour and heard it right through to its last, vanishing cadence.

Mary began to talk again. Softly and lovingly. 'It cost him such an effort to walk even the half mile on to the meadows that surround the light-house. He was so frail and slight that I could almost have carried him. But at last we got where he wanted to be. It was a place he'd always loved. In those few years we had together we never once missed the chance to visit it. It became a sort of pilgrimage. And I think he knew that this time would be the last. I sat on the grass and cradled his head on my lap, running my fingers through the little that was left of his hair. Desperately ill though he was, there was a sense of excitement and anticipation about him. And then we heard it at last. A sound that he thought – we thought – was one of the most thrilling and uplifting in this world. His eyes closed, but the look of ecstasy on his face was something that I will keep with me for always. Dear Benbo – his sight was almost gone then. But even I could not have seen what I knew he would have sought in the sky, so vanishingly small it had become. "Poor old Bill," he murmured. "He must be as sick as a dog out there. And how could whales – all the whales in the ocean, compare with *that*?"'

'He always saw the best in the smallest things. He had a gift for it'.

'Uh-huh', Mary nodded. 'The smallest of things. And on that afternoon it was in the song of the smallest of birds that I think he had his first glimpse of heaven'.

* * *

He rises and begins to round,
He drops the silver chain of sound.

From George Meredith (1828-1918)
The Lark Ascending.

ISOLDE

Blessed morphine … the pain is receding. Sister looks down on me and smiles.

'Are you feeling more comfortable now, Hector?'

I nod and murmur my thanks. They are universally kind here at St Anthony's. She leaves the room softly. I fall into a light sleep.

Time passes. Minutes, perhaps half an hour or so. Suddenly I am wide awake. Someone is standing at the end of the bed. A girl in uniform, a care assistant, I guess. I think I have not seen her before. Yet there is something almost familiar. A memory …

'Hello Father,' she has a faint accent. I think it may be German. They must have told her who I am, though soutane and surplice are locked away in the cupboard by the door. Probably they will remain there. I think I shall not robe for Mass again. 'Sister asked me to come and see how you are.'

I peer at her, squinting a little to try to make out her name badge. There is something about her hair – a chord of music drifts through my head. Debussy – *La fille aux cheveux de lin*. And her eyes – she smiles with her eyes.

'My name is Isolde ...'

Yes. Of course. Your name is Isolde. I begin to wonder if I am dreaming.

* * *

Her name was Isolde. I can remember when we first met. It was on a river boat, hired for a party given by the parents of mutual friends. She told me that her father was in the Swiss diplomatic service, on a posting to London. She was a few months past her seventeenth birthday, and I just a year older. Her English was near perfect, yet she seemed somehow to be out of place there. Because I was inclined to shyness then, we stayed talking together, perhaps finding security in each other's company. And I think by the end of that evening, several hours later, that I was already in love with her, that I had moved into another place, irrevocably. There was to be no returning.

Our loving had innocence about it. For the age of free love had not yet dawned, although it was near, and would in the not so distant future affect us in very different ways. Then there were codes of behaviour and unwritten rituals to be adhered to. Yet I cannot imagine otherwise than that our hand holding and gentle caresses were any less exquisite.

As the weeks went by we met often. We would take the train out of London to be in places where we could be alone together and delight in each other's company. Yet even then we knew that our time together must draw to a close. Isolde had gained a place at the University of Lucerne to read English Literature, and would be leaving England in the autumn. At the same time her father's posting would end and the family return to Switzerland. I suppose I had hoped that I might visit her there, perhaps at Christmas, but I perceived a barrier:

Isolde's family were strict Lutherans and I was a Catholic. And besides I was … I am, black.

One day late in the summer, as we lay on the grass beside a wide estuary in Kent she raised herself on one elbow, looked down on me with those smiling eyes and put her forefinger to my lips. I had voiced my sadness at the thought of our parting, wondering when we might, eventually, see each other again.

She said, We will write. Often. Then we will see!

Perhaps even then she knew that her future and mine were set upon different courses. I think that was because she knew me better than I had ever realised, better even than I knew myself.

A great flock of geese rose from the mudflats below us, scattered across the sky and then drew together again forming into a ragged skein, and made eastward to the sea. Isolde turned to gaze after them, and I sat up to watch with her and listen to their cry.

There was something unworldly about the beauty of their calling and their measured wing beats. I whispered, What is it …?

She began to murmur, to half chant what I took to be verse. I did not recognise it:

I saw the geese …
And I wondered at the unencumbered grace of that formation
As it curved sunward. And when they lost themselves
In the fierce glare, and then gave voice, it was as though
They passed beyond the confines of this world.
For I thought I heard that morning
Not the mournful cry of marsh fowl
But echoes of another firmament. I heard, it seemed to me …

Her voice faded. I wondered if what followed was lost to her. But then she turned to me with a look of expectation. I must have read it, or something like it before, because the words came to me quite effortlessly and to my complete surprise:

> *… I heard, it seemed to me*
> *The sound of trumpets at the Gates of Paradise.*

Yes! That is it, exactly! And she leaned over me and kissed me.

Two weeks later she took a flight with her parents to Geneva. I never saw her again.

* * *

Isolde has been a regular visitor to me over the past few weeks, since that first time when she stood at the end of the bed as I drifted out of sleep. I believe that the child has become fond of me. This evening, long after she should have gone off duty, she is sitting with a pad in the chair to one side of bed, sketching the biretta placed on the bedside locker.

She is silent, and I say to her, 'Why do you stay on here? I am sure you have friends you would sooner be with.'

She shakes her head. 'They can wait. They have time enough.'

'Unlike me?'

She makes no direct response to my question. 'If you must know, I feel ashamed to think that you – Father Hector Ademokun of the mighty Roman Catholic Church – have not had a single visitor since first I met you.' She smiles. 'I am trying to make up for the failings of my fellow men and women!'

Isolde knows something of my past. She knew very soon after our first meeting that, half a century ago I had loved the woman who was her grandmother more than I have ever loved anyone since. And she is the only other living soul who *has* known this. But does she know that her grandmother – dead these last five years – has never, for one single day, been absent from my thoughts? Nothing can change that. Not even my faith, or the crumbling remnant of it that still lingers.

She told me that the Isolde I had loved never married. Swept up in the movement towards free love and the illusion of freedom, she became pregnant when in America, shortly after graduating. She returned home to a shocked and reproving family and gave birth to a girl who would one day become Isolde's – this child Isolde's – mother. She spent much of her life as a recluse, writing – quite successfully – and painting.

'I really miss her. She was a lovely grandma to me. When she died, she left me a painting, one of her best. I think it is perhaps the most precious thing that I own.'

'What is the painting of?'

'A flight of geese. They are flying towards the sun across a glittering sea. I think … sometimes I think that it is a vision of heaven.'

* * *

I am very near to the end now. The staff here at the hospice are beyond praise. I have no pain and I am sometimes even comfortable. As I said … blessed morphine!

Isolde has come to see me, as she does several times a day now. She pulls the chair close to me.

'Father – I am … I am going away for a few days. Home. To Switzerland. So I thought I'd come … come to say goodbye'

She takes my hand. I turn to her and I know that a tear is rolling down my cheek. I will never see her again.

'You have been so very, very good to me. I ask myself, why?'

She does not answer immediately, but instead says:

'Grandmother … grandma, loved you so, so dearly.' And then, 'you *know* why I …' and her voice catches and falters.

I think I am falling into a dream. Perhaps my last. She leans over me, and her beautiful flaxen hair falls across my face. Her lips brush my forehead.

And at last I know that we never lose those we love, because we see them for ever, deep in the eyes of their children, and of their children's children. In this knowledge I find solace that sweeps away the sorrow and regret that had accumulated so relentlessly for me over the years. I am at peace.

Outside in the park, where I am told there is a wide lake where waterfowl nest and find sanctuary, I hear the cry of the geese. And their calling reaches a crescendo, like a mighty fanfare, as they rise together from the water.

IN MEMORIAM

In general practice, the accumulation of years inevitably leads to a steadily growing mental catalogue of personalities whom one has met, sometimes come to know well, and for one reason or another have moved on again – to another county or country or, all too often, away from this mortal coil entirely.

Kenneth was one of these. He "adopted" me in my green years when I was newly arrived at my practice, nearly half a century ago. And while he certainly had the avuncular air about him – with which I felt comfortable enough – he was clearly a vulnerable and wounded man. Relapsing depressive disorder had been a part of his life since his own youth. He was anxious to discover just who had replaced my predecessor in the practice, and anxious to know how I would take to him. We quickly became comfortable with one another. For he was not a "demanding" patient in the sense that we GPs tended to use the word. Appointments never went over their time. He seemed happy enough to know that I would continue to see him once a month for an update, a chat about things in general, and his repeat prescription. At that time he was on a monoamine oxidase inhibitor, sticking to the prescribed regime obdurately in the manner that slightly obsessive people tend to do. "Ah, it's Kenneth next" I would murmur to myself with a sense of relief when I was tired or running a little late. For I knew that, if the occasion required it, he would not delay with me. "I can see you've had a busy afternoon, doctor."

He learned very quickly that I had a young family. "What they need, of course, doctor, is plenty of fresh vegetables". And he left a bag of the most delectable purple sprouting broccoli from his allotment, at the reception desk the next day for me. I don't think the children were quite into the brassicae in those days, but that night my wife and I feasted upon it.

"Do you enjoy gardening, doctor?" he enquired the next time he called. I told him I was something of a novice, but yes, I *did* enjoy it. But our garden, being in the city, could only cope with a modest display of annuals. I was a potato and tomato man myself, but space simply did not permit it. I don't think "grow bags" had arrived at that time. And that was the gist of our conversation.

"What about an allotment?" He asked next time. I told him that I would love one, but in those days there was something of an allotment craze, and the waiting lists could be years long. "Don't worry about *that*, doctor. I'm on the Committee!"

A month later he was helping me to dig the couch grass out of my newly acquired patch, leased to me at a rental of about £3.50 a year.

Life got busier with the children growing and the increasing professional demands. I had taken up postgraduate teaching by then, with its inevitable intrusion into my time away from the surgery. Kenneth said to me "You need to watch out, doctor" and went on to enlarge "I see your ground's not looking its best. Could be a problem there." I agreed, sheepishly. "Problem is, doctor, the *women*". I did not understand what he was on about. "It's *women* – on the *committee*! Cor, they want the whole site to look like it's been manicured!" He did what he could to help me. But things went from bad to worse, and one August we returned from a holiday to find that it had been "requisitioned" as Kenneth put it, by a fit retired couple with plenty of time on their hands. I never saw it looking so pristine. But the soul had gone out of it, I thought.

This unfortunate turn of events coincided with a deterioration in Kenneth's health. He developed an intestinal problem which worried me a bit and him a lot more. I told him I'd like him to see a specialist. I don't think I fully appreciated the anxiety this suggestion provoked in him. At his appointment he was told he would have to have a barium x-ray, for this was in the days before lower intestinal tract endoscopy was the almost routine matter that it is now. He was terrified at the prospect. Not the thought of the procedure itself, but by the horror of the notion that it might cause him to be incontinent when he got home, and soil the carpet. He was not to be reassured. He quickly relapsed into depression, so profound that I feared that he might go so far as to make an attempt on his life. The bowel problem was put on one side, and an urgent psychiatric referral set in motion.

"Do you think they'll give me the electric shock treatment, doctor?" He was utterly changed from the man who had helped me weed and sow on those sunny evenings the previous spring. "I do hope they will. It really brought me through the last time … "

All this took place at a time when electro-convulsive therapy had slipped from favour. Pressure groups claiming to champion the "victims" of psychiatrists were in the ascendance. Doctors had been sued.

His appointment came through very quickly, to our mutual relief. But when he saw me the next day he was in a state of near despair. "They say they don't do it now. They want me to start some different tablets".

The following morning, when I was away at a conference, one of my partners was called to the block of flats where Kenneth had lived to certify him dead. "He was very dead" she assured me, visibly shocked, that afternoon. "His brains were splattered all over the floor of the basement."

The Coroner said that because it could not be certain that he had intentionally thrown himself down the stairwell from his fifth floor flat, he would record a verdict of accidental death. His wife was grateful and relieved about that. But I did wonder, as I have often wondered since, if we really do have an accurate idea of the incidence of suicide, and whether the denial of what is pretty self-evident really serves to help people with mental illness. It is certainly clear that it provides a modicum of comfort for their grieving families.

From time to time I am called to that same block on visits to other patients. The heavy steel hand rail on the stair case at the ground floor still bears the concavity where Kenneth's head made its final and catastrophic impact with it, and cascaded its contents on to the floor below. And I think of his honest, gnarled hands as he helped me to lift the first crop of new potatoes from the good earth on a warm summer evening forty years ago. And I think of all the things he did for me, and of all the things I was never able to do for him.

THE GUNS

'I hate him. I hate him so much that I know that I must one day kill him,' murmured Francisco.

'That is a hard thing to say of your own father.' But the voice of the older man, half reclining on the ground beside him, registered little surprise. His sightless eyes seemed to gaze at the distant horizon. 'But I can understand why you should hate him. If, as you said, he killed your mother ... '

The young man nodded. 'He met another woman. Before he left he told me that if I breathed a word about what he did to my mother, he would kill me too ... '

'And he is coming back soon?'

'Yes. He will dock in a few days from now.'

* * *

It had been some weeks before that Francisco had wandered into the hills in his grief and fear, and discovered the old man, living as a hermit in the deserted army encampment. José was sick, very probably dying. He was almost blind and struggled to forage for what dried and tinned food remained in the store in the wreckage of the barracks. Francisco took pity on him and brought him what he could from the town in the valley to make him more comfortable, and a friendship was forged. Soon he won the old man's confidence. It was then that José showed Francisco the guns.

The boy gaped when he first saw them, resting on their massive cradles on the hilltop. They were huge and menacing. 'This pair of guns was made by a British company in the time of the civil war, to defend the port. They are designed to fire 380 millimetre shells, weighing almost a ton for a distance of forty kilometres.'

'In the time of the civil war, you say? But – they look almost new. How can that be?'

'I made it my business to maintain and care for them after the rest of the men left or died. To my mind they are beautiful. To me it is a duty, and one I am proud to honour.'

'How long is it since they … since they were fired?'

'They have *never* been fired. Never since their first trials almost eighty years ago. Their very presence kept the port safe. No ship would have dared to challenge them.'

* * *

'José, tell me: if you wanted to fire the guns, would you be able to? I mean, after so long … '

The old man laughed when Francisco returned two days later and slung the rucksack off his back. He put the question purposefully.

'Did I not tell you that they are in perfect condition? Of course, they *could* be fired. But unfortunately, now, it cannot be done.'

'Why not?'

'Because it takes two men to operate them. Two to load the shells and raise the gun barrels into position. And I am the only man left.'

'*Were* the only man left. I have joined you now. You could show me and together we … '

'Francisco, what are you saying? No-one has been near these guns for years, other than you. They have been forgotten. Have you any idea how loud they are when they are fired? The hills would be overrun within hours by curious and frightened people, and the police, no doubt, and it would be all up with me.'

But a gleam in the old man's sightless eyes told Francisco that his suggestion had sparked a dream. It was like a quiver of excitement and awakening of a dormant passion. He paused for a minute or so and then said, quietly:

'There are violent storms forecast for tomorrow evening. There is a good chance, surely, that when the guns fire it would be taken for thunder in the hills. Think about it, José: all the dedication and care you have shown in keeping them so well would have a real purpose in the end. And you know you cannot go on for very much longer. Do it for the guns and in honour of your dead comrades.'

And then he knew he had won the old man over. 'You are nearly blind, now, José. You cannot see the headland any more. It is exactly twenty kilometres from the gun emplacements. That is where we shall aim'. *And it is round that headland that my father is due to sail, at just that time* he thought to himself. His eyes closed in anticipation of a dramatic and deadly revenge.

* * *

Vincente held the young woman close to him as they gazed across the sea towards the mountains on the far side of the great bay. The weather had become hot and close, and now lightning danced among the distant peaks. An almost constant growl of thunder rolled across the low swell.

'It's so dramatic – frightening really'. She spoke softly. The man tightened his grip across her shoulders.

'You know, they say that once there were two mighty guns up in the hills to protect the port at the time of the fighting.'

'It's almost as if they had woken again'. Another thought crossed her mind. 'Will your boy be safe in this?' A violent squall was suddenly upon them. They retreated from the ship's railings under the cover of the deck canopy.

Vincente shook his head. 'The young pup will be skulking somewhere in the town. No doubt expecting me to dock in the old fishing boat. But no! Here I am, sailing round the headland in the greatest cruise liner on Earth, in the company of more than a thousand of the world's wealthiest citizens, one of whom I have married!'

They did not recognise the sound when first they heard it. But as the low whine grew louder, finally reaching a crescendo, fear gripped their hearts. Like the hissing of a thousand monstrous serpents, the voice of approaching death encompassed and enveloped everything. The great detonation, at last, was beyond their hearing.

AURORA

Aurora, as you know, was the Roman goddess of Dawn.
It was also the name of the princess in the story of
'The Sleeping Beauty'.

A man was waiting for me outside the stage door of the auditorium. Slight build, with a short beard, spectacles and receding hair.

'Excuse me – I wonder if I might have a quick word, Miss Appleby?' He was nervous and I thought, probably quite harmless.

I looked at my watch, then glanced back at him. Probably an admirer wanting to compliment me on the performance. If he was a nutter I could deal with him. But not out here in the dank evening in the late fall in New York. There was something earnest in his voice that provoked a feeling of, well, not quite pity, but a kind of sympathy.

'That's fine. But shall we go back into the foyer? They won't be closing the doors for a while.'

Over a coffee he introduced himself as Max Leveson.

He did indeed want to express his appreciation for the two Prokoviev sonatas I'd played that evening. But I knew there was something more pressing on his mind. He was not long in revealing it.

'Miss Appleby – I should tell you that I work at the Jet Propulsion Unit at Pasadena.' He paused as if in expectation of a response.

I had a feeling about where this was leading to but thought it best not to be drawn. I merely nodded and waited for him to continue.

'Your daughter, Merope. She's one of my postgraduates. Doing research for her Doctorate.'

I nodded. 'Yes. I believe she's doing quite well at the Institute. Is there a problem?'

'No. No problem at all. And she's doing … she's doing more than "quite well". In fact her work is outstanding. One wonders if she hasn't inherited something quite remarkable from your father, her grandfather. We are all familiar with his work at Cambridge, you know. We were wondering if … if she keeps in contact with him.'

'Actually, no. In fact she's not seen him since she was a very small child. For some reason he seemed to have a problem with her having "followed in his footsteps" so to speak. This was the reason we – she – chose to move on to Caltech when she graduated from Imperial. My husband – her father – seemed to think that he might even try to block her progress. I trusted his judgement on that, as I did on most things.'

He nodded as if not entirely surprised. 'A pity. Do you know, the work she is doing on life support systems is an exact parallel – or rather, I should say, a continuation of his own. I think it won't be long before she cracks the problem that always bedevilled him and kept the Nobel prize just out of his reach.'

'You mean – what she calls the "reversal"?'

'Yes. That is exactly what I mean.'

* * *

It was two years later that I met Professor Leveson again. Not in America, but at my father's home in Cambridgeshire. He had flown together with three colleagues to pay their respects. My father had died quite suddenly two weeks earlier. I was hosting a reception after his funeral at the house where the old scientist had lived for the greater part of his career.

Once again Leveson took the opportunity to have a few words with me on his own. I guess that I was rather dismissive of the ritual – but I suppose necessary – expression of condolences. I had few good memories of my father. In fact he had had little enough to do with me for most of my life. After the death of my mother when I was less than a year old I'd been adopted by a cousin of his and her husband who themselves had been childless. It was they who had inspired me and propelled me into my career as a pianist.

He seemed unfazed, even unsurprised by my lukewarm response. Again he spoke about my daughter: 'I'd like to congratulate you on your daughter's achievement. You know that her thesis has been published in 'Nature'. It's caused ripples right across the world.'

'She's really rather modest about it,' I replied. 'When she manages to get to London she's more interested in getting out and about – "getting back a life" as she calls it.'

He nodded. 'That's good. A diet of pure academia isn't a healthy one. But she must have had some feelings for Professor McKinnon. I know it wasn't easy for her to re-arrange her schedule to be here at this time.'

I hesitated. But knowing that the circumstances would be common knowledge soon enough, I went on: 'the fact is – completely to our surprise, that my father left his entire estate to Merrie. She is the executor of his will and the sole beneficiary.'

'You mean to say that you … you've been left *nothing*?' He was clearly astonished.

'That's how it is. But don't trouble yourself over it. It means little enough to me. Anyway, it seems only fair that she should have some acknowledgement from her grandfather after all this time.'

'And can I ask – how did she react?'

'She was surprisingly unmoved. Although I know that she is anxious to access his research files. The ones he appears to have kept in his private laboratory here at the house. That may not be entirely straightforward though.'

'How so?'

'I understand that he worked in the old vaults under the house. Though I've not seen them – I've never lived here as an adult – I am told that they are as secure as Fort Knox. Whatever he was doing there, he wasn't going to share it. Merrie is intrigued, as you can imagine. No doubt she'll make it her business to get in there. But I can hardly imagine that she'll learn anything new.'

'Well, I'm sure you'll keep an eye on her. Of course, as her mother I know you will.'

'Are you trying to tell me something, Professor?'

Now it was his turn to hesitate. 'Your daughter, Miss Appleby, has an exceptional future ahead of her. Within the department, we are fairly confident that she may soon become the youngest woman ever to be awarded a Nobel prize. But more than that …'

'Yes?'

'As you know, she has been a leader in the development of … the process of suspended animation. Her grandfather, of course, laid the foundations of the science some years ago. She is on the verge of perfecting it. If you like, she took over where he left off. For this reason she has been in training for a … a special mission …'

I suddenly felt cold. 'What mission?'

He looked straight in to my eyes.

'In about two years, Miss Appleby, your daughter, will join the crew of a space vehicle. To be more specific – the first manned expedition to the planet Mars.'

* * *

Merope sat opposite me, gazing into the fire. We had both been kept busy in the ten days since my father's funeral. I'd tried to draw her out on her role in the Mars expedition – the prospect of which frankly terrified me. She was reticent, I suppose because the whole venture was wrapped in security protocols. What she did reveal, in a light-hearted way, was that she would be away for five years. But on her return she would have aged only a year. 'You see, mother' she had said, 'in suspended animation the aging process virtually stops'. If she had hoped that this would make me feel better, she was mistaken.

The various guests and well-wishers had long departed. Now only the two of us remained.

'Something on your mind?' I asked her.

'Mmmm … I was thinking. What a lovely name …'

'What name?'

'"Aurora". My grandmother's name. How sad that you have no memories of her at all. Don't you even have a photo?'

'No – no photos. No letters. Really, nothing at all.'

'She was drowned, wasn't she? When you were still a baby?'

'That's how it seems to have been. They were swimming on a deserted beach on the east coast. It was quite notorious for undertow in certain tide and weather conditions. Her body was never found. I learned later on that my father came under suspicion. But only briefly. They never found any evidence of foul play.'

'But could he have had any reason …?'

'The only thing that ever occurred to me was that he looked on her as an impediment to his career. He was a driven and jealous man. She was pregnant with me before they married. And things were very different then. But I've no business speculating. There was never a shred of evidence …'

She became thoughtful again. 'I often wondered why you and Daddy were so anxious to get me away when I took the direction I did.'

She did not appear to expect a response. And I did not give one. By way of changing the subject I said:

'I agree. It is a lovely name. And my father's cousin, my adoptive mother, did tell me once that she was a beautiful young woman. When she last saw you – you'd have been about sixteen or so – not long before she died, she remarked upon how much like your grandmother you were.'

Merrie made no further comment. She was silent for a few minutes, and continued to gaze into the fire. I could see that she was preoccupied with something. I asked her: 'So – is everything all right?'

She looked up at me. 'Why, yes … well, it's just that I've … I've broken the codes – the sequences on the locks to grandfather's laboratory. There was nothing particularly difficult about it, in fact. I'm fairly certain that it is what he intended – that I should be the one to have access to whatever it was that he was doing there. I am going to go in tomorrow.'

'Well, take care, won't you.'

She shrugged her shoulders. 'I'm not expecting any surprises.'

Somehow, I felt, her voice lacked conviction.

* * *

As it happened, I had to spend the next two days in London with my agent. I arrived back at my father's house in the late evening. Merrie was in her room and did not appear for almost an hour. When she did, I could see that she was agitated.

I asked at once, 'have you been … down there?'

She nodded briskly. 'Yes. And I … I was not entirely surprised at what was there.'

'And what *was* there?'

'Well, not much. Other than three chests.'

'Chests?'

'Uh-huh. I think they are, well, I *know* they are … hibernation chambers. But the design is an old one – the sort that he and his team were building right at the start of the programme.'

'You say that you *know* that that is what they are. What makes you so certain?'

She looked directly at me. 'Two of them may be empty. Or at any rate, if they contain anything then it isn't anything alive. But the third …'

'Yes?'

'The monitors in the casing indicate some activity … all the parameters suggest that there is an … an *organism* inside the chamber that is in suspended animation …'

'You mean – a *living creature*?'

'That's what it seems. And if it is the case, then it seems very probable that, whatever it is, it has been that way for upwards of fifty years.'

'Is that very remarkable?'

'Barely credible would be more like it. That is more than *ten times* longer than any other living thing has been kept in that state.'

'But *why* so long?'

'Probably because Grandfather never discovered the reversal technique.'

'But *you* discovered it at Caltech a good two years ago. You could have told him …'

'Mother, he never *asked* me. He never made any contact with me or anyone else at the institute. But I am very sure that he knew we had cracked it. He must have had a *reason* for keeping quiet …'

'What are you going to do now, Merrie?'

She looked at her watch. 'It'll be mid-morning in California now. I'm going to call Max. I'm going to ask him to get a flight over here just as soon as he can, and bring some … equipment. Together we'll initiate a reversal. And I'd sooner do it with him alongside me than on my own.'

* * *

Max needed no second bidding. He was clearly excited when he joined us just two days later. He trundled a large aluminium case on wheels into the room and made some light comment about just being within the weight allowance. 'And don't worry, Alison,' he smiled at me, 'I've not broken any laws so far as the contents are concerned!'

The two of them made their way down to the laboratory the following morning. They remained there for the whole of the day. That evening Max came up alone. He took me aside.

'Alison … I wonder if … the fact is that Merope is tired … very tired. She doesn't want to join us this evening. In fact I think even now she's gone upstairs.'

Overhead I could hear footsteps. 'I must go to see …'

Max put a restraining hand on my shoulder. 'No Alison. Best not. This has all been a little overwhelming for her. It's not turned out quite as we … she had expected. Best leave her be …'

'But what … what's *happened*?'

'Nothing terrible. Just unexpected, is all. She just hasn't taken it all on board. Please – let's leave it until the morning. I promise that we'll be finished by this time tomorrow.'

In spite of an almost overwhelming anxiety I did not demur. Had I done so I think that Max might well have physically restrained me.

* * *

I had hoped to catch Merrie the following morning before she and Max resumed their work. But she must have got up in the small hours. By the time I came down to the kitchen they had already locked themselves away in the laboratory. I found myself losing count of the time. It seemed that a whole day had passed, and yet when I looked at the clock it was still only mid-morning. I forced myself to walk for an hour in the extensive grounds surrounding the house. When I returned, it was only to an eerie silence.

It was about mid-afternoon when I heard a stirring in the passageway outside the living room where I had tried unsuccessfully to distract myself with a book. There was a knock on the door. It was Max. His face was strained.

'Well, Alison … we … we've finished. It's …'

'Is everything OK? I mean, has it … has the reversal worked?'

'Oh yes. We had to take it very slowly. It's been so long, you see. But it has been a complete success. Would you like to come and see?'

'Yes … yes, but what *is* it you found …?'

'Just … come. But be prepared for a surprise … it may be quite a shock for you.'

I found myself gripping his hand as we approached to door to the stairway that led down to the laboratory.

The room itself was spacious and well lit. A fine mist partly obscured the objects in front of us. And the two people who stood up to receive us.

And I could not at first believe what I saw. There was Merope – and *Merope* … another woman who at first seemed to be the identical twin of my daughter. Only she was slighter in build. And her skin was like alabaster.

My daughter held the other's hand and, tentatively, they stepped toward me.

Merrie smiled at me. 'Have you guessed who this is, mother?'

I looked at the woman. 'Who … who …?'

And now the other woman smiled at me. And then she spoke, her voice barely above a whisper.

'They have told me that you are my daughter. I … I am Aurora!'

TWO GOOD TURNS

'Jake,' said Dr Anne Morrison as her colleague, clutching a newspaper, joined her in the common room at the end of surgery, 'if I were to make you some *real* coffee, do you think you could come and look over the chronic disease register with me? We've only until the end of the month to get the figures sent off.'

She did not expect an enthusiastic response. Jake Sevrey had little affinity for paperwork. 'But I've got to visit the Brody sisters,' he protested. 'They're expecting me this morning.'

'Those old gannets?' Anne countered, 'They're not going anywhere. Put them off until later. We don't do this job just for love, you know. No figures mean no pay cheques. And with Dr Monkham on leave there's only the two of us. So you it has to be.'

'Oh, if you insist … '

'I *do* insist. And put that newspaper away.' She was not proud of her tendency to, well, to be bossy at times, but Jake could be so laid back. He tossed it down on the coffee table. On the open page a photograph caught her eye.

'My god! Surely this couldn't be our Tim …'

'Who?'

'It *is*. There's his photo. Tim Redfern. Used to be a doctor here. Oh, this is terrible!' She read from the report that had caught her attention. '*The rebels herded the clinic staff into the hospital and … set it alight. There are believed to be no survivors … Dr Redfern, an expert in HIV/AIDS, had previously worked as a general practitioner in London, before leaving the country and going to work at the mission in Central Africa.*'

Jake came to where she was standing and read over her shoulder. Anne's hands began to shake. She turned and laid the newspaper, open, down on the table.

'That's … that's just terrible,' breathed Jake when he found his voice again. 'How long ago did he leave here?'

'Five … no, six years.'

'From what I've heard, he wasn't what you'd call the most popular doctor'.

'He was a bloody good doctor,' Anne retorted, 'better than many of his patients realised. But he was … something of a maverick. He could be quite blunt. Some patients thought him uncaring. And in the end he fell foul of the General Medical Council.'

'And that was why he left?'

Anne nodded. 'That, and other things.' Memories flooded back. She shook her head slowly. 'He was such an idealist. But he could be so cynical. I did admire him though. His insights into … people … were amazing at times. He could see right through the selfish ones, and those who had expectations right off the scale. They got short thrift from him. Of course, the ones who *really* appreciated him were the ones who were gay, because …

because Tim was gay himself. He understood where they were coming from. Several had contracted AIDS and Tim, dear Tim, got his expertise by caring from them. He was utterly dedicated …'

'Perhaps he felt that he wasn't practising real medicine?'

'Mmmm … maybe. Anne stared into the distance, suddenly surprised to find that she was close to tears. It wasn't just the appalling way that Tim had died. There was the stark realisation that there was now no chance of her ever seeing him again. She fought to distract herself. 'On his last day,' she continued, 'I was helping him to clear his room. There wasn't very much to clear. No pictures, no children's toys. It struck me for the first time how lonely he was. And he told me something strange … that he could think of only two occasions when he'd made a real difference in people's lives. And it was the second that had him up in front of the GMC.'

She felt her lower lip trembling as she spoke. She pulled a tissue from her bag. Jake must have noticed. Mustering some tact he said 'Hey, why not take it easy a minute? I'll get the coffee, OK?' She felt him put his hand on hers for a moment, very lightly.

'OK,' she whispered. 'Oh, this is just so … so *awful* …'

He left the room through the door leading to the surgery kitchen. Mercifully there were no others of the surgery staff about. No receptionists to fuss – they were at their weekly meeting with the practice manager. *Get a grip on yourself, woman,* she hissed through her teeth, *you know very well that Tim had nothing for you.*

Jake returned with the coffee. 'Get some of that down you. It's the real stuff.' He seemed to be trying to take some control over the situation. Not really like the Jake she knew, but it had the effect of softening her frightening sense of vulnerability.

She took a mouthful. 'Thanks. I needed that …'

She relaxed a little as he watched her 'So. Just twice he made a real difference. And the second time got him into trouble …?'

She nodded. 'Deep trouble.' She put her cup down and gazed through the window into the distance again. She began to feel of a need to talk, to reminisce over times past. And Tim. Had she ever admitted to herself how she *really* felt about him? Jake sipped his coffee and stayed silent.

'There was this patient … Tim had to call on him once. He told me that he had found the old man 'in a state'. His home help had gone off sick. He was completely out of essentials – bread, milk, his fags. He'd no idea how he was going to last out the weekend. I remember it, because that evening his daughter phoned to say that she thought her dad was confused and talking nonsense … that the doctor had come out and done his shopping for him. I suggested that it was someone sent by social services, and I said I'd check it out. In the event I didn't. I don't know why I didn't. It was all so long ago. When Tim told me about it – the first of his 'good deeds' as he put it – it emerged that the man hadn't, after all, been losing it. Tim really *had* gone out and done his shopping. And I realised there was a side to Tim that I'd never appreciated.' She glanced up at Jake. 'Perhaps you think that was odd. But in what he had done I saw such a depth of compassion …'

Jake seemed on the verge of saying something. Something flippant, knowing Jake. But when he did speak his voice was soft. 'I think I see what you mean.' But did he? Anne wondered, given what he must have heard about Tim Redfern from those who thought less well of him.

Anne took another tissue. 'The second occasion was something quite different. I could never understand why he would have done anything so … so incredibly stupid.' She saw the expression of intrigue cross Jake's face. She slipped the tissue up her sleeve, picked up her cup and took a leisurely sip of her coffee.

'It was a patient,' she went on, 'Phil Lawrence. He had an illness that was gradually destroying his nervous system. He was paralysed from the waist downwards. Actually he was dying, and he knew it. Tim was the doctor most concerned with his care. Phil was a bitter, angry man, but Tim was never much troubled by that.'

'Tim told me that one day he made the mistake of asking him if there was anything more he could do for him. Phil responded by flying in to one of his rages. He told him that he was useless, and that the same went for all doctors. But he calmed down. Then, Tim told me, he cocked an eyelid and said mischievously, 'There is one thing, doctor: I don't suppose you could get a tart for me?''

Jake stared over at Anne. She felt herself blush. She was not sure how to continue 'Tim said he was flummoxed. 'But the truth was,' he said to me, 'I knew I probably *could*.'

'I had an idea what Tim was on about. Our part of the city was – is – no middle class haven. It has its seamier side. There used to be shabby newsagent's shop along the road with cards in the window, advertising … things. Some of these were clearly offering sex, coded to imply a double meaning. One offered a 'home visiting' service.'

'He surely didn't …?'

She took another mouthful of coffee and then continued. 'Oh, but he *did*. When he told me I was shocked. He laughed at me. He said he could see little difference between getting fags for one poor old bloke who had few enough pleasures in life, and a woman for another. Stupidly I went on about exploitation … how immoral it was and how unethical he'd been. And he just laughed at me again, told me not to be such a prude, that the woman in question wasn't driven to it by drug addiction, hadn't been trafficked …' Anne winced inwardly, recalling how pained she'd been that he should have spoken to her so.

'But how did he *know*?'

'Oh, he knew all right. He told me … that she was a patient, *my* patient. I asked him who, but he wouldn't say. He said it was something to do with funding her taste for luxury holidays. So Phil got his 'tart'. And the story got out. It was splashed all over the papers. They roasted him, held him up as a disgrace to his profession. That's when the GMC stepped in. They agreed. He was suspended for a year, not struck off for good as many thought he would be. Anyway, he resigned from the practice pretty soon after that.'

'Probably the only decent thing to do,' observed Jake.

Anne felt herself flare but controlled herself 'The only thing he *could* do. But even if that hadn't happened,

I think he would have left us anyway. He'd said more than once that he was wasting his time. Too much picking up the pieces after his patients had wrecked their own lives and trying to make good the damage done by *doctors* who'd been too enthusiastic with tests and treatment that were frankly dangerous. And I think he had a point.'

'But wasn't his cynicism a bit over the top?'

'Maybe. But he worked wonders in that mission. He was probably just too good, as a person and a doctor. So he ended up vilified here … and now he's ended up murdered, horribly, over there.'

Jake nodded and for a moment became pensive.

Anne continued, 'He had the attribute of honesty, though. And he loathed hypocrisy.' She sighed. 'And, do you know, it may have been that that finally got him into the situation where … where this terrible thing happened.'

'Anne – I can see that you admired him. For being … being *different*. I guess we learn from people like Tim, their bucking against the trend. The problem with us medical people is that, well, can be a stuffy crowd. A loose cannon like he was can shock us into reality, and that's no bad thing. And something else …'

'Yes?'

'You were privileged, to have known him and worked with him. Remember him that way'.

Anne hesitated. 'Really, Jake, there's no need to try to be kind. What business would I have grieving for something I … I never could have had?' She felt her breath catch in a sob, quickly suppressed. 'No, don't get me wrong. What Tim gave me – I mean, the insights –

I'll always have.' She got up from her chair and sighed 'Oh, hell, we really ought to get on with those figures …
'

'Fine. Let's do that.' No more resistance now. 'I'll take the cups through and put them away. Save the staff …'

She looked straight at him. Did he really understand? Tim was dead, and now the realisation struck home: that a small part of her had died with him.

MR MOMIJI

Jon Lawson stared at his wife across the dinner table. He could hardly believe that she had just spoken the words she had without the slightest hint of artifice in her expression.

She was lying.

The implication brought him out in a cold sweat. What possible reason could she have for denying what he knew, for an absolute certainty, to be the truth?

She was lying.

He had always believed that dishonesty of any kind was contrary to Ginny's nature. He had thought her to be a principled woman, both at home and in her work as a teacher. But yesterday he had seen with his own eyes how she had cheerily waved off the man from their garden gate. A man he had never set eyes on before. They'd not noticed him as he turned the corner at the top of the road. On impulse he'd retraced his steps, not returning for an hour or so. Of course, she'd not been expecting him so soon. There'd been yet another failed interview. He'd caught an earlier train, anxious to be home, imaging no reception other than one of quiet comfort and sympathy, or so he'd thought.

He had tried to make his enquiry sound nonchalant. Anyone called while he'd been out? His implication being that someone might have called round, or telephoned, about a job possibility when she got back from the school. She'd shaken her head.

'No. Not a soul. It's really been very quiet.'

For the first time he could ever remember, she had told him a lie.

She must have seen something in his expression. 'Something bothering you, darling? You've gone quite pale.'

He drew breath, on the verge of challenging her, yet quite unable to for fear of what she might tell him. He could only shake his head and mutter 'I don't know how much longer I can take these … these rejections'.

He'd hoped against hope that she would have told him that she'd had an unexpected visitor. If not about a job, perhaps one of her many cousins from Australia, visiting as they did from time to time. She'd have been telling him enthusiastically about the news she'd had about her family. But no. She had kept this meeting from him, and he could think of only one reason why she should have done so. Ginny was attractive in both looks and personality …

'Don't take it so badly,' she murmured, the ever-familiar concern in her voice.

Jon shook his head and said nothing. His redundancy had come out of the blue some three months previously. Shock had given way to resentment, resentment to suspicion that someone had had it in for him. And fear that Ginny, such a rock in the past, was beginning to lose respect for him. He'd been rotten company over the weeks, he knew. Sometimes he wondered how she put up with his moods. Was her cheerfulness and optimism just a cover-up? Yes, now it seemed as if had been all along.

'Who the hell wants to take on a time-expired university lecturer? And a lecturer in *botany* of all things?' The bitterness in his voice was scarcely concealed.

She shook her head 'You need a break, dear. It's a fine morning. Take your sketch pad to the park. The maples are looking so lovely just now …'

Jon nodded. 'Might as well. It's not as though there was anything else lined up.' In truth he wanted to get away from her, to find the opportunity to gather his thoughts. To decide what he must do.

* * *

The specimen of the *acer palmatum* was a particularly fine one, and exquisitely shaded in the early autumn. The fragment of pastel that Jon held between his thumb and forefinger ran deftly over the heavy paper block, reproducing the delicate tracery of the leaves and transforming the ephemeral reality into something that would outlast the seasons for, well, some years to come at least. As an illustrator he was good, and he knew it. His preoccupation took him out of the real world, and away from his mood of pain and anger.

His reverie was broken by a childish cry. 'Hey, Mama It's Mr Momiji! Let's see what he's drawing today'

He recognised the girl, a slight, pretty thing of about seven, with shiny black hair down to her shoulders. He put the block down on his knees and looked up and smiled at her. 'Hi, Minami! No school today?'

She shook her head. 'No … half term this week.' Of course it was. Ginny had told him. That was why *she* wasn't at school.

Minami's mother came up. 'Aren't you being a bit of a cheeky girl? I'm sure this gentleman isn't really called 'Mr Momiji''

'It's what *I* call him. And the other kids from school as well. It was my idea! My own special name for him'

'Oh.' Her mother looked apologetically at Jon, 'I hope you don't think she was being rude. You see, it's the name we give to the maple tree in Japan.'

'Not at all. And I already knew what 'momiji' means. I take it as a compliment'. And his thoughts drifted back to another time, some years before. The year he and Ginny had got married in fact. They'd been on a tour on the Hakone National park, in the foothills of Mount Fuji, south of Tokyo, at just this time of year. Suddenly a murmur of excitement had run through the throng of Japanese tourists on the coach, almost like a repeated sigh: '*Momiji … momiji!*' They had entered a forest of maples, their changing leaves ablaze in the afternoon sunshine. For some minutes silence fell on the sightseers. They sat gazing through the windows, mesmerised and enchanted by the beauty of what they were seeing. It had been as if the hills had been engulfed by a sea of crimson fire, the scent of lush, damp vegetation wafting through the open windows in strange contrast.

'Now you're looking *sad*, Mr Momiji. You've drawn such a lovely picture of my fairy tree. How can you feel sad?' Minami peered down at the block, her nose threatening for a moment to smudge the carefully applied pastel. 'And I think I can see the fairies in there. Yes, I can. You are *so* clever!'

Her mother smiled. 'Come on now, Minami. We must leave your Mr Momiji to finish his drawing.' And turning back to look at Jon as he rose awkwardly from his seat she said, 'You are a very talented man, I think. And you have a lovely way with children.' She paused for a moment. Then, softly, almost quizzically: 'Momiji *sensei* … I think you could have anything you might ask for.'

He delayed longer than he had intended, strangely reluctant to return home. But he doubted that Ginny would be much worried about him. Not now. He became lost in his thoughts. He still had not the slighted idea what he should do. A car sounded its horn loudly when he stepped off the edge of a pavement and almost into its path. '*You looking to kill yourself, mate*?' shouted the driver out of the window. Momentarily Jon thought, *well, perhaps I am …*

He felt his mobile vibrate in his shirt pocket. He flipped it open. A text from Ginny … his heart went to his mouth. '*What's keeping you? Someone here I want you to meet. Need to talk urgently.*'

Was this it? Was this the end? He grasped his folding chair then slung it under his arm as if it were a gun, wishing for a moment that it was. He steeled himself as he rounded the corner and walked the last few yards to the house. At the open door stood Ginny. And with her a man, a man he recognised only too well.

To his amazement she broke into an excited smile as he walked up to them. The man beamed as he held out his hand in greeting.

Ginny hugged her husband tightly. 'I'm just so sorry we had to keep it from you until Michael could be sure. And I told you such a dreadful fib when you asked me this morning, if I'd seen anyone. What you'd have thought if you'd turned up while he was here …'

Jon looked down and said nothing. Of course Ginny had expected him to be pleased. But his sense of relief in the realisation that the situation was not as he had feared was countered by a hot surge of resentment. Finding his words at last he looked directly at their visitor. 'Mr Beaumont, while I appreciate your offer, I'm afraid I can't accept it …'

The smile evaporated from Ginny's face. 'But Jon … Michael's offer is really generous. I mean, his publishing company is getting a name. And it's not as though you were an established artist. And he's said he wants the complete set!'

Jon ignored her, his gaze fastened upon Michael Beaumont's bemused face. 'I can't say that I'm exactly thrilled that my wife should have asked you here to go through my … my *private* collection of illustrations without asking me. They're my property, my own creations, and I'm not ready to part with them yet, however generous the offer I'm made.'

'I guess we miscalculated there, Mr Lawson. But you know, you have a real talent. If you change your mind … '

Jon shook his head. 'I think not. I am a teacher, a scientist. I'm well aware that my drawings are good, but they were never made to make someone's living room look cute.'

The man nodded, his lips pursed. 'I respect that.' He looked at his watch. 'I won't take any more of your time … and I have another appointment back at the office.'

* * *

Ginny stared at her husband after their visitor had left them, her eyes moist. 'Don't be angry with me darling – I meant it for the best.'

Her husband nodded abruptly, a set expression on his face. 'I don't doubt it, Ginny. But losing my job, being out if work is *my* problem. I need to sort it out in *my* way. You don't need to treat me as if I were a child.'

'So, what are you going to *do*? Why don't you give yourself credit. You … you could have *anything* … !

Now it was Jon's turn to look bemused. What Ginny had said. Almost an echo …

* * *

It was some days later that he stood at the entrance of the regional television company. Assertiveness had not been an attribute of his, not until quite recently. But his sense of humiliation and the surge of uncharacteristic anger at the meeting with Michael Beaumont had sparked something. He hoped desperately that he could sustain his feeling of self confidence in the interview that was about to ensue. He had managed to get this far by, well, by being insistent, even pushy, over the telephone. The company director's secretary had at last given in and agreed to speak to her boss. Miraculously, she in turn, for whatever reason, had agreed to see him.

Jon waited for an anxious quarter of an hour in the plush foyer, his hands white knuckled in his lap. The summons came at last.

'Mrs Holloway will see you now, sir.' The secretary held open the door.

At the sight of the slender woman who rose from behind the broad oak desk, his courage almost failed him. How on earth could such a … *coincidence* have come about? He had not thought for a moment …

Her smile was warm and disarming. 'Come and sit down. And tell me what you have in mind that you think we can use!'

He held his breath for a few moments, then took courage in both hands almost blurting out, 'I've this proposal for a new series – an educational series directed at a young audience … to show them something of the beauty and fascination of everything that grows in their parks, in their neighbourhoods.'

The woman slightly forwards across the desk and placed the fingertips of both her hands together. Her gaze was penetrating, but Jon did not flinch. Then she nodded her head slowly and smiled again. 'Well, Momiji-sensei you certainly worked your magic on my little Minami.'

'And *you* said that I … *I could have anything* …'

'Well, then, let's talk this all through. And we'll see if I am as good a judge of these things as I believe I am!'

A DISPUTED INHERITANCE

'I always thought,' Irene Hardiman stared across at the woman who was sitting opposite her in an easy chair in her spacious drawing room, 'that you were too good for Les. He's a selfish man, and with a mean streak. Inherited all that from his father, no doubt. Maturity hasn't improved him. Rather the opposite.'

Hazel Hardiman looked down at her folded hands, then shrugged her shoulders. 'Oh, I don't know. He's a hard worker. Committed. He's very demanding of himself … and others, too.'

The older woman ignored the apology for her son. 'And in my view, he is a bully, too. Just like his father was.' Her fixed gaze seemed to be asking a question. Hazel did not immediately respond. 'Well?'

Now Hazel looked up at Irene. 'Well, what …?'

'You know what I'm asking you. Has he ever … ever *mistreated* you?' The younger woman dropped her eyes and said nothing. Irene nodded to herself. 'I thought as much' she said quietly.

'He gets angry sometimes, impatient …'

'Two weeks ago, when you called in, you had bruise on your cheekbone, and I wondered. That wasn't the first time he's hit you, was it?'

The moisture in her eyes, and her silence, were answer enough. Irene nodded again, and quietly, more to herself than to Hazel, said 'So it seems that he … my son … has become a … a *brute.*'

A single tear rolled down the younger woman's face and dropped on to her hand. Then in a low voice, almost a murmur as if to no-one in particular said, 'So, what do I do? I sacrificed my career, I have no ready means of supporting myself, no security for the future …'

'You don't have to just *accept* it, you know. If he … if he does it again, go to the police!'

'Oh … I couldn't! God knows what he might do.'

The older woman nodded. 'Well, if you won't do anything then perhaps I will. I won't have you go through what …'

'No, Irene! It would only make things worse. Much worse!' she looked at her watch. 'I have to go! He'll be getting in soon. He'll want to know where I've been.'

As she walked down the pathway from the house, Irene Hardiman gazed at the receding figure through the drawing room window. Deep in thought, she crossed slowly to the other side of the room and looked across the wide expanse of lawn to the row of low trees and the meandering river at the end of her garden. She shook her head and sighed. Then she walked over to a small table and picked up the telephone receiver. She tapped out a number, and half a minute later said, 'Good afternoon. I would like to make an appointment to see Doctor Aldridge, please.'

* * *

'So – what was it you went to see her about?' Les Hardiman's question was curt, as if he were irritated that his wife had paid his mother a visit at all.

'Oh, only to take round a book I thought she might like. The Ishiguro novel I'd just finished.'

'Waste of time, I should think. The old gannet's half blind now and getting worse. She say much to you?'

'No. Not really. I don't think she's been so well recently. She said something about her diabetes – blood sugars a bit all over the place. I did wonder if she'd been having problems with her insulin injections … you know, with her hands being so stiff with the arthritis now.'

The man nodded. 'That could be. I'll talk to her when I go up. If needs be I can give her the injections for a few days.'

'I do wish she'd get more nursing input,' Hazel said, frowning. 'She could easily get in a private nurse if they weren't able to send anyone from the surgery.'

'I'm quite capable of seeing to my mother's needs, thank you.' His rebuttal was sharp, and Hazel said nothing more for fear of angering him. And she knew he was right about the injections. Les himself was an insulin dependent diabetic and quite prided himself on his ability to self-monitor, sometimes, she suspected, to the irritation of the staff at their local surgery. He was – what did they call it? Yes, a *control* freak. He could be quite obsessive, and when he felt that he was being hindered or thwarted in any way he was liable to fly into a rage.

'Well, you know what's best for her, I'm sure.' Her tone was conciliatory. Yet her inability to stand up for herself, even the loss of the urge to do so filled her with shame. He had her just where he wanted her.

'I do. And best that you keep yourself away from her. Understand? She's poisonous. You've plenty to attend to in *this* house without poking your nose into her business.'

Hazel said nothing. Presently she took herself into the kitchen and busied herself with the evening meal.

* * *

It was two weeks later that Les Hardiman spoke about his mother again. 'She's getting chest pains and seems to have gone off her legs a bit. She'd better have the doctor. I've got a busy day on, so I'll leave that to you to arrange.' He hesitated, then, rather to Hazel's surprise he added, 'Best if you could be there when the doctor calls – you know, get any prescription made up.'

He left the house and Hazel made the telephone call to the surgery. The receptionist answered, brusque and officious 'I'll pass the details on to the doctors, and he may be in touch with you. They're very busy today, you know.'

To her surprise Doctor Aldridge himself called back within ten minutes. He was Irene's own doctor but owing to heavy commitments and his popularity with the patients he could be hard to get to see.

'Chest pains, you say?'

Hazel relayed what she had been told by her husband. 'It would've been better if he'd spoken to me himself,' the doctor commented, 'but it looks as though she ought to be checked in any event. It could well be her heart. I'll call up to her this afternoon. Will anyone be there to let me in?'

'That's kind of you doctor. I know you're under pressure. I'll be going up to her shortly and I'll wait with her until you arrive.'

'Good. You know, your husband's mother is surprisingly uncomplaining. Stubborn with it. It's that sort of person who can be a lot more ill that they would want you to believe. But we'll see.'

* * *

Doctor Aldridge clearly knew Irene Hardiman well. She was indeed inclined to be dismissive about her symptoms, but the doctor was not one to be easily misled. His questioning was at first general, then becoming more focussed. He undertook a cursory examination of her chest, but Hazel guessed that his mind was made up even before he put on his stethoscope.

'It may be nothing too serious. Possibly to do with your arthritis. Or acid from your stomach. But given your diabetes, you are at risk of heart problems, you know. We really ought to check that out. I'd like them to run a few tests at the hospital.'

'When? You know what I think of hospitals, doctor. They do their best, I daresay, but best to steer clear of them in my view.'

'I think you'd be taking a greater risk if you don't go. I doubt they'll want to admit you. But you'd be unwise to refuse their advice, though no-one can make you go in if you don't want to.'

The old woman grimaced. 'Well, I've always trusted your judgement in these things. So I suppose I must. '

Doctor Aldridge nodded curtly. 'I'll put my partner Doctor Harris in the picture so he can follow things up if needs be. I'm going on leave from tomorrow and won't be back for three weeks. And I'll be too far away to keep in touch myself.'

'New Zealand, is it? To see your sister?'

The doctor nodded again. 'Now, if I can have the use of your 'phone I'll make a call to the coronary care unit.'

With characteristic efficiency, the doctor arranged for an assessment in the cardiac unit in the local general hospital for the following morning. 'Can you or your husband get her up there?' he asked Hazel. 'She'd be more comfortable in a car than in an ambulance. And there'd be less hanging around.'

Hazel nodded. 'That won't be a problem. Les has a lot on, so it'll probably be me.' But when he arrived home late that evening her husband dismissed her offer offhandedly. 'No. I'll go up for her myself. I can rearrange my schedule. If they want to keep her in then I'll make sure she stays, you can be sure. I won't take any of her nonsense. Unlike you.'

'That's fine. But let me know if she needs anything if they want to keep her. Night things and that.'

* * *

But Irene Hardiman never made it to the hospital. An hour after he left the house the next morning to collect her, her son telephoned Hazel.

'It's mother. She's dead.'

'Oh, Les. I am so sorry.' The woman's voice caught.

'Must have been her heart. I've called the doctor. Doctor Harris isn't it? Aldridge has gone on leave, they told me.'

'Yes … yes. That's right. It's a pity it has to be a strange doctor … '

'Makes little odds in the circumstances. She's past caring anyway. Look, I must hang up. I think he's arrived.'

She put down the receiver, feeling shocked and numb. She knew her mother-in-law was frail, but never really considered that she might die so quickly. It dawned on her that she had lost one of the only friends she'd had or been allowed to have. Les had seemed remarkably unaffected. Surely, though, it would sink in soon enough and he might need her comfort.

But when he arrived home late in the morning he seemed as controlled as ever. He paid scant attention to Hazel. He went to his desk and pulled out various files, scrutinising and re-ordering the sheets of paper. She made him some coffee, and when she returned from the kitchen he was talking to the undertaker on the telephone. He sounded impatient as he often did.

'No. There isn't going to be a post-mortem. Her own doctor diagnosed angina yesterday and she was to be taken to the cardiac unit today. Doctor Harris agreed to issue a death certificate, and he's getting the cremation forms drawn up. How soon can you arrange it?'

Les, Hazel thought, seemed to relax once the negotiations with the funeral director had been concluded, seemingly to his satisfaction. He settled into a chair and looked at his watch. 'It's early, but I could do with a drink. Can you get me a whisky? A large one. Have one yourself.'

Hazel thought it best to acquiesce to his suggestion. It would be alright, just so long as he stuck to the one, or two at the most. But when she handed him the glass he sipped it slowly, then put it down on the table. He looked thoughtful, and she could see that he was preoccupied with something.

She took her opportunity. 'Dear Les,' she murmured, reaching over to take his hand, 'you must be devastated. You did so much for your mother. You must miss her dreadfully.'

Her anticipation that he might melt, even in to tears, was promptly dashed. He pulled his had away. 'Oh for God's sake, get real will you? She hung around for far too long as it was. When Dad died he left everything to her, and a successful business which she sold. I should have taken it over, but she was just too damned tight. She wanted me under her thumb, and of course I had to tow the line. The old bag was loaded, but she did nothing with it. But I can tell you now, *my* life is only just beginning. I've a lot of lost ground to make up, and with what I'm coming in to I'm going to do just that – big time.' As he said this a grin crossed his face, and he looked away from Hazel into the distance. She caught her breath, a hollow sensation in her stomach. *His* life. Not *theirs*. The realisation hit her that he was cutting her out of his future.

Slowly she pushed the glass away from her, then got up and quietly left the room.

* * *

The cremation and funeral service the following week were bleak affairs, and clearly arranged with brevity as the main objective. There was a minimum of prayers and no eulogy, hymns or music. Outside the chapel,

Hazel was taken aback at her husband's apparent relief, even ill-concealed elation.

'Now we can get on with the real business,' he remarked, looking at his watch. 'I must get to see the solicitor tomorrow. Go through the Will. See to probate.'

The reality of her own situation struck Hazel like a hammer blow. *He was going to leave her … with nothing.* She grasped his arm. 'Les, *please*, what am I going to *do*?'

'You do what the hell you like. What you do is no concern of mine.' He wrenched himself from her hold.

* * *

Back at their home she had taken herself to her room and tried to gather her thoughts together. Where on earth could she go to? Perhaps her sister might have her, for a week or so at least. But she really hadn't the space …

She became aware of her husband's voice downstairs. He was speaking loudly on the telephone. The familiar anger was there … now what?

'Look, Mr Bremerson, I still fail to see what this has to do with my … my wife. I am the sole beneficiary. And the executor. I went through everything with her, years ago.'

Hazel did not hear the solicitor's response. What on earth could be happening? Whatever it was, it had made Les angry. She gained the impression that Bremerson was digging his heels in and was resisting any attempt by Les to intimidate him.

'Very well then, if you must have it that way I'll bring her with me.' She heard the handset banged down into its cradle. Quietly she retreated back into her room and closed the door, a sense of deep foreboding rising within her. Then, in a moment of decisiveness she opened her handbag, took out a mobile phone, and punched out and sent a brief text message.

* * *

'No, I *don't* know why he wanted you along as well. I guess it's some protocol or other. But if you know what's best for you, you'll hold your tongue. Just answer any questions he may have but keep it brief. Any nonsense from you, woman, and you're going to regret it later, believe me.' Hazel and Les were sitting together in a small and rather sombre waiting room at the solicitor's office. The neglected plant on the windowsill and the winter gloom outside did little to raise her spirits. Thankfully, they were not kept waiting. A prim secretary ushered them in the Mr Bremerson's presence.

Introductions and the offer of condolence – scarcely acknowledged by Les – out of the way, the solicitor invited Les and Hazel to seat themselves opposite him at the table. For a moment he seemed to hesitate and peered across at them over rimless glasses. His gaze shifted from Hazel to her husband.

'Mr Hardiman – we are here, of course, to discuss your late mother's will. I gathered from our conversation over the telephone yesterday that you are … are not aware that not long ago she decided to revoke the will I drew up originally on her behalf – the will in which you were the sole beneficiary – and asked me to draft a new one. This I did. It has been witnessed and signed according to the requirements of the law. So we have a new and, in my opinion, perfectly valid will. But I fear that its contents may come as a shock to you.'

Hazel sensed even before she saw her husband's face change colour, his body stiffen. Her hands clenched the underside of her chair.

'What the hell are you trying to tell me?' Leslie's voice was low, but even.

'You mother, Irene Hardiman, has bequeathed everything – *everything* – to her sole daughter-in-law, your wife, Hazel. The estate, not including the house which I imagined would be worth a substantial amount given its size and position, is valued in the region of three million pounds.' Mr Bremerson paused, then continued quietly. 'I can see that this news has come as a complete surprise – to both of you.'

Leslie erupted. 'You're bloody right it has. To me at least.' He swung round and turned his wife. 'You and she were up to something, weren't you, you bitch!' He spat the words out. 'But you won't get away with it. Be very sure I'll see to that! I can have this new will invalidated. You … you coerced her … she wasn't mentally competent … she was demented!'

Hazel shrunk under the onslaught. 'Leslie!' she pleaded, 'I'd no idea … absolutely no idea. I never asked her, never wanted … '

'Mr Hardiman!' the solicitor seemed almost to have expected Leslie's outburst, 'Kindly moderate your language in this room! You are making allegations which are simply untrue. I can assure you that your wife had no knowledge of her mother-in-law's intention or action. Mrs Hardiman stipulated that Hazel was not to be told.'

'But the woman was off her head! She didn't know what she was thinking!'

'I think you will find that you are mistaken on that count as well … '

'Just how the hell can you be so sure of that?'

Ian Bremerson paused, as if about to play his final card. 'Mr Hardiman, at the time your mother made the decision to change her will, two weeks before she died, she arranged an appointment with her doctor. It was quite an in-depth consultation, I believe. She requested that he undertake a mental assessment in order to confirm that she was of sound mind. It would seem that she had anticipated that the validity of a new will might be challenged on the grounds that she was mentally incompetent at the time. I can inform you that he gave his absolute assurance that she knew just what she was doing and that she was doing it of her own free will. I had some discussion with him on the matter, with your mother's consent, at the time when I was drafting her new will. And both Doctor Aldridge and I were witness to her signature, as you can see.' He took the document from where it lay in front of him and passed it over to the man, now quite speechless, sitting opposite him.

Leslie Hardiman snatched the document from the solicitor's hand. He stood up, seemed almost to stagger for a moment. His expression was one of cold fury. But when he spoke his voice was measured and purposeful. 'Don't either of you think that I am going to take this lying down! The house, the money – they're mine by right. And I'll make damned sure I get them.' He swung round and made for the door slamming it behind him as he left the room.

* * *

Hazel stared across at the solicitor with an expression of utter astonishment. She shook her head slowly.

'My dear,' he said gently, 'I am only sorry that this has come as such a surprise to you. Your mother-in-law did tell me what was behind her decision. And it was not one made on the spur of the moment. It was very carefully considered. She knew exactly what she was doing. But I fear that your husband may try to make things very difficult for you, although I do not believe for one moment that there are any grounds for a legal challenge. You have properly inherited the entire estate.'

'Thank you, Mr Bremerson.' Her voice fell to a whisper. 'This is, as you say, a complete shock to me. I think I might … I might go away for a while, a few days, to gather my thoughts. My husband is clearly upset … well, that's understandable. I need time to think through this. Somewhere where I won't be … under pressure.'

'I think that would be very sensible. Do you know where you might go to?'

The woman nodded. 'Mmm … I have a sister, my twin sister Jenny. She lives in Scotland with her husband. When things got … difficult … after Irene died I got in touch with her. She said I could come and stay. Until things settled down.'

'Good. I think you should do that. And my advice is that you do not delay. But we ought to keep in touch. There are certain formalities we need to attend to. Here … ' The solicitor leaned over and passed a card to her.

'Thank you. I'll contact you as soon as I am settled.'

She left the office and walked the half mile to the railway station, where she collected a suitcase held in the left luggage facility. An hour later she boarded a train to Birmingham, there catching a connecting train to the north.

'It's about time, my dear girl, that you stood up for yourself a bit.' Hazel's sister looked directly into her eyes. A rugged, outdoor life made Jenny look older than Hazel, and they had developed differing tastes in clothing over the years. There was no doubting who was the stronger, both physically and mentally.

Hazel nodded, her eyes moist. 'I know you think I'm my own worst enemy. I took it all lying down, and I'm paying for it now. But I am scared of him, really really scared. Even before the business of the will … but now … I just don't know what he might have done if I'd gone home to him after we'd seen Mr Bremerson.' Her voice caught in a sob.

Jenny placed her hands on her sister's shoulders, and kept her gaze fixed on her eyes. 'Thank God,' she said, slowly, 'that you *didn't*. Because I have a terrible feeling that he might have done the same to you as I believe he did … to his mother.'

'Jenny! You're not saying,' Hazel gasped, 'that Les *killed* her?'

Her sister nodded slowly. 'Everything you have told me about what happened at the time she died points to that possibility … probability. And if I am right, then it's only logical to assume that you would be in the greatest danger if you were to go back to him.'

'But *how* did he kill her … ?'

'Any number of ways. Poison … or smothering. Something like that. These things can be difficult to detect, unless a doctor or the police had reason to be suspicious. But the scene had been well set to make it seem that it was her heart. And her usual doctor, who might have been the one person to suspect something, was on the other side of the world.'

'But it's too late now … I mean, she was *cremated* … '

Jenny nodded. 'Didn't you wonder why Les was in such a hurry?'

Hazel shook her head. 'No. I was too upset, confused. Do you really think … ? Oh, what a blind fool I've been. What should I do now? Please tell me what to do!'

Her sister shook her head. 'The only thing I'm telling you to do right now is to rest here with us and recover as best you can from all you've been through. As to how you go forward so far as you and Leslie are concerned, that has to be your own decision. You've been doing what other people tell you to do for far too long. If you don't buck up and stand on your own two feet you'll never get out of his grasp. Believe me, Hazel, if you don't stand up to him he will get what he wants and you will be left destitute.'

'I think you're being a bit harsh. You don't know what sort of a man he is … '

'Do I not? I'm convinced your husband is a murderer, a callous, brutal murderer of the worst kind. *He killed his own mother for what he could get out of her*! If you won't stand up to him for you own sake, do it for Irene's. Surely she's entitled to some sort of justice?'

'But Jenny – he'll *kill* me. You've said as much yourself!'

'Yes, he may try. He will see it as the only way to get hold of his mother's estate, and as a way of getting his revenge on you of course. That's why I'm glad you came straight here to me and Jake. You've got to consider your options, in a calm frame of mind and where you are safe. But what you do in the end can only be for you to determine. That way you will regain at least some self-respect.'

* * *

It was five days later that Hazel announced to Jenny and her husband that she was returning home. 'Not to Leslie. To Irene's … *my* home. I need to go over some things with Mr Bremerson.'

'That's the girl,' her sister smiled at her. 'Have you thought about what you'll do if Les contacts you, tries to see you?'

Hazel nodded. 'I'll try to be … will be … firm with him. I've had a couple of chats with Mr Bremerson. If needs be he'll get a court order … if Les gets difficult.'

'That's all right for the short term. But I doubt it'll make him give up.'

'Of course it won't. If there was only some way that we could *prove* he's killed Irene. Doctor Aldridge will be back any day now. I wonder if he might be able to help at all?'

'Oh, Hazel … don't hold out too much hope there. He may well have a view on it, but these doctors are very cagey about saying things they can't substantiate. Without a body … '

'Still, I need to face the fact that Les will almost certainly come looking for me when he hears I'm back.'

Jenny nodded. 'I think that's inevitable. Just promise me you won't be so stupid as to see him on your own.'

Hazel looked directly at her sister, but said nothing. She had suddenly realised that, whatever the risk to her, she needed time alone with her husband. That was the only way she might get the truth out of him.

'But it's been lovely having you, even if times aren't so good,' Jenny continued. 'Pity you've got to go back – the weather's been pretty bad down south, it seems. Don't go and catch a cold!'

* * *

'Thank you, Doctor, getting back to me so quickly,' Hazel was speaking on the telephone in the drawing room of Irene Hardiman's house.

'Well, I was keen to talk to you. I am so very sorry to hear of the loss of your mother-in-law. Dr Harris told me that, as we'd suspected, it was her heart.'

'Mmmm – that is what was entered on the death certificate. But surely, as there was no post-mortem the conclusion was, essentially, based on probabilities?'

'I'm not quite sure what you're trying to say to me, Mrs Hardiman. Of course one can never be entirely certain, sometimes even with a post-mortem. I'm sure that Dr Harris was right in his decision to issue the certificate as he did. It is certainly accepted practice to do that on circumstances and clinical grounds alone.'

'Of course. I understand that. I just wondered if, had you not been away, you'd have acted differently.'

'I couldn't possibly comment on that. But I … Look, are you going to be at the house for a while yet? I think I might get out the records, maybe talk to Doctor Harris, and then call round so that we can talk together in confidence, if that's OK with you.'

'Yes. I'd appreciate that.'

'Fine. Be about five o'clock. Maybe a little after. The traffic's been slow with this fog. And it seems to be closing in rather.'

* * *

Hazel put down the telephone and walked slowly over to the patio doors. She unlocked them and peered out into the gloom. She was deep in thought. She had been able to tell from Doctor Aldridge's voice – a slight hesitation, a momentary uncertainty – that he had been taken aback, and possibly disturbed, by what she had said. Might she be able to persuade him that there was a real possibility that Irene's death had not been … natural? But could that be proved now? Would he be willing to contradict what his colleague had concluded? That might cause all sorts of problems.

Yes, as he had said, a mist was closing in. At the far end of the lawn it rose more densely over the river, running high with the recent rain. She closed the doors again, turned away from the bleak outlook and sat down in an easy chair. Time lay heavily on her, but she felt unable to settle into anything. She had been deeply troubled when Jenny revealed her suspicions, and the awful realisation grew upon her that she could be *right*.

And Irene had left everything to her. 'Oh God,' she breathed, 'as things stand at the moment, were I to die, it would all go to … to *Les*!'

She desperately fought off the rising sense of terror within her. She'd been submissive, weak for too long. Had she stood up to him sooner, Irene might still be alive. For the first time that she could remember she felt an iron determination, even anger. He would *not* get away with it any more …

A noise outside the front of the house, a crunch of gravel, made her instantly alert. Was it Doctor Aldridge? She hadn't expected him so soon, but perhaps he had set out early in expectation of the weather closing in. A car door slammed shut, followed by the sound of approaching footsteps. Whoever it was hesitated at the front door. And then she heard a key turning in then lock.

Summonsing all the courage she could, she got up from her chair and walked out of the drawing room and into the hallway, just as the front door opened. She could see a figure framed in the entrance. He was wearing a long raincoat and a hat that she recognised immediately.

'Les! I wasn't expecting you.' She fought to keep her voice controlled.

'Hazel! I thought you'd gone away. I just came to … to … '

He sounded taken aback, as if she'd been the last person he'd expected to find there. Or was it feigned surprise? She *must* remain calm. 'I've not long been back. I thought I'd best come back here to start sorting … there's so much to do … '

Les took off his hat. 'You don't mind me coming in, do you? We need to talk … and I can help you with … with all you have to do.'

Don't be fooled by his conciliatory tone! she told herself. *Play along with him. If he thinks I suspect, then I'm done for!*

'What did you want to talk about, Les? Don't you think that any discussion we have would be best done together with Mr Bremerson? I can understand your being pretty cut up about this. But you really need to know that I had nothing to do with your mother's ... your mother's change of mind. I'd really no idea. You *know* it was a complete shock to me.'

He nodded. 'That's what you and Bremerson kept telling me. But don't you see the injustice of it all? After all I did for her? Look, perhaps I was being unfair to you after all. Can't we work something out between us so that we can *both* benefit? Don't fool yourself into thinking that I can't challenge this ... this new Will. So either you agree to negotiate, or I'll make sure you end up with nothing. *Nothing* – do you understand?'

Hazel stood her ground and stared at her husband. For a moment his eyes dropped. On impulse she grasped a sense of advantage. 'Don't be so sure of yourself. There's something else you need to know.'

'And what's that?'

'Doctor Aldridge ... when he came back from New Zealand and heard ... he's clearly not happy ... '

'Not happy with what? What's it to do with him?'

'The cause of death ... that there was no post-mortem.'

'Just what are you suggesting?'

Struggling to remain calm she replied, 'that her death might not ... might not have been due to natural causes.'

'You bitch! Are you suggesting that I *killed* her?'

Amazed at her own sustained composure, she held him with her gaze. 'Well, Leslie, *did you*?'

He was clearly unnerved. For some moments he hesitated, his expression confused. *By God*, thought Hazel, *you really did, didn't you*!

He took a few steps towards her, at the same time feeling in the pocket of his coat. At once she realised that he was intending to corner her. Still facing him, she backed into the still open door of the drawing room. He advanced on her, his right had grasping firmly whatever he had been searching for in his pocket. She continued cautiously to move backwards into the room, coming at last into contact with the patio doors. Reaching behind her she sought the handle.

Seeing that she could back away no further he hesitated. 'Look, Hazel … I really don't want to hurt you. Just agree to come to some arrangement with me. Even if we split everything in half we'd both be very rich people. I never thought of you as greedy.'

She stared into his face. *I'll never believe anything you say to me again. Whatever I agree or don't agree to now, you want me dead. I'm certain of it.*

Slowly she shook her head. She could tell that her defiance had thrown him off balance. He returned her gaze, and slowly withdrew his had from his coat pocket.

In it he held a hypodermic syringe.

He spoke, quite calmly. 'There is sufficient insulin in this to send you into a coma in a matter of seconds. That's exactly what it did to my mother. Her time was up, of course. It was really an act of mercy. But as for you … well, you've only yourself to blame. After all, you've stolen what didn't belong to you. For that the price you will pay is only fair.'

Panic welled up within her. But she did not take her eyes off him for a moment. She grasped handle of the patio door, pushed it down and with a deft movement of her hip thrust the door outwards. She turned and ran into the swirling mist and gathering darkness, her only thought to put as much distance as she could between herself and Leslie. Once she slipped and almost fell on the wet grass as it began to slope downwards. Then the realisation came that there was nothing ahead of her now but the river, deep, swollen and treacherous. She recognised the dark outline of a stunted willow tree and grasped one of its branches to steady herself. She suppressed her rapid breathing and listened for any sound of pursuit.

Inevitably it came. Leslie was not running but seemed to be covering the ground steadily as if he knew that there was no need to hurry, that there was no escape for Hazel. He reached the riverbank about twenty yards to her left. He paused and listened. Then he turned and walked slowly in her direction. At last she saw his silhouette looming out of the mist. She resisted an almost overwhelming urge to run back towards the house, recognising that she had somehow reached a moment of destiny. Her fear drained away from her.

* * *

The coroner brought the proceedings to an end and gave a verdict of accidental death by drowning. He expressed his deep regret to the family of the deceased. Jenny Lawrence, sitting in the public gallery, found herself weeping quietly. Seated on her left, Doctor Aldridge tried, somewhat self-consciously, to comfort her.

Jenny shook her head. 'No, really, I'm OK. It's more relief than anything else. That this whole dreadful saga has come to an end.' She turned to the woman on her right and took her hand. 'But it was so much worse for *you*. You've taken it so well. You've been incredibly brave.'

Doctor Aldridge suggested a cup of coffee. 'But let's get away from this place,' he said. 'There's a decent café in the next street.'

The two women agreed. Jenny found herself talking to the doctor as they made their way. 'I just can't help thinking how fortunate it was that you arrived at the house when you did, and that you found the door open.'

'I suppose it was. But I just had a bad feeling about things. I recognised the car in the drive. And then I ran through the house. But I guess I was too late, anyway, to have done anything …'

Too late? Oh no – your timing couldn't have been better. Leslie was just about to … but you distracted him at the last moment. Then I grabbed his wrist and held it, twisted it round with all my strength. And then I … and just pushed him away from me.

* * *

Three weeks after her husband's death she still had difficulty taking it all in. *I wonder* she continued to muse as she walked a few paces behind her sister and the doctor *what they would have thought if they'd found that syringe. It could be in the sea – anywhere by now. But that's all in the past. And it will stay there …*

Jenny turned back. 'Are you all right Hazel?'

Hazel caught up with them. 'Really, I'm fine. Just relieved it's all over and we can move on. To better things … much better things.'

THE TWISTED SERPENT

The old lady sat alone on the park bench. Her back straight, she seemed alert, waiting. A man approached, thick set, his head close shaven, a dog walking in front of him. Strapped around the dog's chest and forequarters was an elaborate harness, embossed with metal studs. The animal was heavy jawed. It was not on a leash.

The woman turned and fixed her gaze upon the dog. Its attention was caught. It stopped, hackles rising, and stared back at her, lips curling to reveal its teeth. It gave a low growl.

Without taking her eyes off the animal the woman reached with a gloved hand into a small shopping bag on wheels, and took out a pistol, a silencer fixed to its muzzle. In one smooth movement she took aim and shot the dog between its eyes. It slumped to the ground with no more than a faint whimper.

The man was dumb-struck. Wide eyed, he took a step towards the woman, raising his right hand in a fist. 'What the hell … why … you … ' he spluttered.

Now it was he whom she held in her gaze. Once again she raised the pistol and said, 'This is for *you* – for what you did to Mary.'

She fired twice in quick succession. Even as he fell forward across the corpse of the dog, the woman dropped the pistol back into her bag, and got up from the bench. For a few seconds she stooped over the man, appearing to take his pulse as if to satisfy herself that he was dead, then made off down the path and vanished behind a low building.

* * *

The incident, occurring quite early in the morning in February had been witnessed by only one person: a student who had been out jogging and had stopped, concealed from the man and his killer by a clump of bushes, when he was overcome by cramp. He insisted that his account, given to the police, was accurate. The victim of the shooting was reported to have been a drug dealer, one Kevin Murphy, with a reputation for extortion and violence.

I had read the newspaper report the day before I set off to drive from Taunton to South Wales where I was to board the ferry to Ireland. A painful task lay ahead of me: finally closing the small holiday home where Niamh, Rory and I had shared many happy times together. My sister Elena, who had been such a support to me through my grief, had persuaded me to go through with the sale of the house so that I might 'move on'. She was right: it served only as a reminder of a time that was irrevocably lost to me, and being there on my own did nothing other than threaten to draw me again the brink of despair. Her son, Danny, should have been travelling with me, but at the last minute he'd got a job interview and I wasn't going to allow him to miss that.

There was a briefer reference to the murder in the paper I picked up the following day at a motorway service area. I pondered over it while sipping coffee. The police had no lead whatever, it seemed. The trail was becoming cold.

The place was crowded. A young man approached my table with a tray. 'Is this seat taken?' he asked, indicating the chair opposite me. 'Would you mind if …'

'No. Not at all. Help yourself.' The boy was Irish, of course, a pale complexion and a shock of deep, almost copper red curls. *You are so like Rory!*

'Am I interrupting? … I can find somewhere else.'

'No, really, you're fine. I was just looking at something in the paper.'

The young man looked down at the open page. 'Oh, *that* – it was on the TV last night. Drug dealer, wasn't he? Good enough for him … '

I wasn't inclined to offer an opinion although, God knows, if anyone had a right to one it was I. I folded the newspaper and put my hand out. 'I'm Alan Bygrove. Go on … take a seat. Going far?'

'Unless I can get a lift, I'm not going anywhere. And I'm Ruaidhrí, by the way, Ruaidhrí Connery.'

I tried not to let my astonishment show. The Gaelic and English versions of the name are common enough and any difference in their pronunciation little more than a nuance.

He continued. 'So where are *you* heading?'

'I'm getting the ferry over to Rosslare tonight. Visiting relations.'

'Rosslare?' I'd caught his interest. 'Look – I don't suppose you could … I mean you couldn't take me as a passenger, could you? I really need to get over there. It's a family problem. I've got called over urgently and you'd be doing me such a favour …'

Ruaidhrí … *Rory*. In any other circumstances I'd have made some excuse. I'm not usually great with strangers, dreading inane conversation. And I really didn't want to talk about myself.

'I'd stay in the back of the car,' he went on. 'Probably just go to sleep. And I'd find my own corner on the boat, out of your way.'

I stared over at him. 'Well, I … '

'I'll make it good with you!'

I shook my head. 'No – that's not it at all. It's just that I don't usually … but in fact my ticket is for two people – driver and passenger. My nephew was meant to be crossing with me.'

'There you are then!'

'OK. I'll take you. But you won't find me good company. I've a lot on my mind at the moment.'

'I won't be any trouble to you. You'll probably need to wake me when we get to the ferry terminal.'

He was as good as his word. He got into the back of the car and in not very many minutes he had dropped off. I occupied myself with my own thoughts as I drove on through the night. The ferry was due to set sail at shortly after two in the morning and I'd reserved a cabin. I would leave Ruaidhrí to himself on the crossing.

Quite probably he'd disembark with the foot passengers and that would be the last I would see of him.

At the check-in at Pembroke Dock a uniformed woman took my papers and peered into the car. She noticed the empty front passenger seat.

'Doctor Bygrove? Just yourself is it? There's two of you down to travel.' She'd not seen the sleeping form curled on the back seat.

'My nephew was to come with me. But he got an interview for a job and … '

'Fine.' She handed my papers back through the window. I'd been about to explain about Ruaidhrí, but she waved me on.

As I drove up the ramp on to the car deck Ruaidhrí stirred. 'I'll let you fend for yourself now,' I said to him as he gathered himself together. 'Will you be OK on the other side?'

'Sure. I'll be getting a bus.' He didn't say where to.

We pulled ourselves out of the car, stretching after many hours on the road. Ruaidhrí stared around the car deck. His attention was caught by someone or something he had seen near to the front of the line of vehicles. Suddenly he moved himself behind me, then ducked back inside. He reached across the seat for his bag, dislodging it so that it dropped into the foot well, scattering its contents.

'Something up?' I asked him. 'Seen someone you know?'

'Someone I'd rather didn't see *me*.' He scrabbled on the floor of the car to retrieve his belongings.

I glanced over to where he had been looking. Four men stood talking then went together through one of the forward exits.

'Well, it's all clear now.'

Ruaidhrí emerged from the back of the car, clasping his rucksack to him and pulling fast one of the zips which had been half open.

'You'll be OK' I said, in a lame attempt to reassure him. 'Try to find somewhere you can lie down.'

'Don't worry. I'll manage.' Not waiting for me, he walked hurriedly to one of the exits at the rear of the car deck.

I locked the vehicle and went to collect my cabin key from the purser's desk.

It must have been over two hours into the crossing that I was woken by an urgent hammering on the cabin door. A man's voice called out, 'Doctor Bygrove? There's an emergency. Can you come please?'

I reached over, switched on the wall lamp, and made my way to the door. Opening it I saw a man in the ferry company uniform and recognised him as the purser who had given me the cabin key.

'Sorry to disturb you sir. Are you a medical doctor? A passenger's been hurt – badly hurt … '

I nodded. 'I'm medical. Not much experience with trauma cases, though. I'm a family doctor.'

'I'm sure that you can do a lot more for him than we can. We've a couple of crew who are first aiders. They've got the bleeding under control. But they think it's his spine, and that's way too specialised for them.'

I followed the purser to the bar. In the far corner a man was lying supine, with a crew member kneeling on each side of him. The room was otherwise deserted, apart from three men seated together near the doorway. They gave a furtive glance in our direction.

I recognised the injured man as one of the group on the car deck that had caused Ruaidhrí such unease. The three by the door were his companions. The next thing I realised was that he had been shot. In order to staunch the flow of blood the first aiders had cut away the man's T shirt. One of them lifted a thick wad of blood soaked gauze from his chest, and I recognised the ragged exit wound of a bullet a few inches below his right armpit.

He was still conscious.

'Damage bad?' his voice came as a hoarse whisper. 'You a doctor?'

I nodded. 'Look, we need to keep you as still as we can. We think your spine may be injured. Is there much pain?'

'It's my back. The bitch shot me in the back. Yeah – it hurts OK. But my legs – I can't feel them. I can't bloody move them … '

I feared the worst. 'Don't try. Just stay as still as you can. Breathing OK?'

He nodded slightly. 'Just bloody hurts.'

Without equipment a proper assessment was impossible. In the circumstances I could do little more than take his pulse. The man was in shock, probably from blood loss.

I turned to the purser. 'How long before we dock?'

The man looked at his watch. 'About an hour and a half.' He paused, then asked quietly, 'd'you think he'll make it, Doc?'

I shrugged my shoulders and said nothing. The injured man now lay with closed eyes, breathing shallowly.

'So – does anybody know what happened? … Who shot him? And do we know who this man is?'

'Seems it was a young woman. This one's name's Jimmy Murphy. He makes the crossing fairly regularly. A traveller, likely as not.'

I frowned. 'So what's the situation with the woman? Is she still about … with a gun?'

'Seems she got out on to the decks. The captain's said he's not risking any of the crew sending them out looking for her. The police will pick her up when we dock. We've already alerted them, and the emergency medics.'

At last the captain announced that we would shortly be docking. He warned the passengers that disembarkation would be slow. 'Unfortunately we had an incident out at sea.' He did not give any detail. 'The guards will be speaking to all passengers as you pass through the check points.'

The ferry made its entrance into the harbour and was made fast. Within minutes two paramedics in uniform, accompanied by a woman wearing a loose fitting green top and trousers, walked quickly into the bar, encumbered by heavy bags of equipment.

'You're the doctor?' asked the woman.

I nodded. 'Alan Bygrove. I've no great experience in trauma work, but in view of his injuries I felt it best that we just concentrate on keeping movement to a minimum.'

'I guess it was all you could do. I'm Deidre Johnson. I'm a trauma specialist, from Dublin. Can you give me some idea of what's happened?'

I explained that he had been shot through his spine, the bullet passing right through his chest. As I gave her the details, the two paramedics worked deftly to set up an intravenous line. The doctor in turn checked the man's blood pressure and sounded his lungs. She turned to me.

'He'll survive at any rate. But I'm not optimistic about the back. His spinal cord is severed. I doubt that anything can be done there.'

For the first time I noticed that two policemen had come in and were standing a few feet behind us. They saw that they had caught my attention.

'Is he conscious, Doc? Can we have a few words …?

'Not now!' Doctor Johnson snapped.

'He was with some other men,' I added. 'Probably best you go and talk to them. And there's a woman loose on the ship somewhere, with a gun.'

One of the officers nodded. 'We've got a dozen men searching out on the deck. Don't worry – they'll pick her up. His mates tried to give us the slip, but they didn't get far.' It was clear that the men were known to them.

The second guard remarked quietly, 'Well, Jimmy'll not be good for much now, I'm thinking, if 'good' is the right word for it at all.'

* * *

At the check points every vehicle was stopped and the occupants questioned. I'd been on the lookout for Ruaidhrí, but I didn't spot him. Without travel documents he would have some explaining to do to the police. I might have had some explaining to do as well had he left the boat with me and it became apparent that he was not my nephew at all. I suppose it was my reluctance to add a further complication to the distressing task ahead of me that caused me not to make any reference to him when the guards questioned me. They clearly knew that I was the doctor who had attended to the injured man on the crossing. They spoke to me with some deference, asking only for a telephone number in case I should be required to give any further information or statement.

I arrived late at the house. I had brought sufficient provisions with me to avoid having to visit the village shop and face the inevitable expressions of sympathy. Niamh and I had been well liked in the small community. The young couple who came later to see the house seemed charmed by it. When they drove off at last they assured me that they would be contacting me again.

The next morning I occupied myself with sorting documents in preparation for an appointment with a solicitor in the neighbouring town. Afterwards I went in to a newsagent to pick up a paper, curious to see what might have been reported about the shooting on the ferry crossing. It had made headline news, with a photograph of Jimmy Murphy featuring prominently. I went into a café and read the whole report while I drank coffee. No trace of Jimmy's assailant had been found in spite of a thorough search. Witnesses of the shooting told how the young woman had been sitting alone in the bar. Without warning she had shot Jimmy in the back, then quickly left through one of the exits to the deck. It was possible, of course, that she had given the police the slip while the boat was making fast.

These dramatic events and my own preoccupations had put my meeting with Ruaidhrí quite out of my head. It was not until a week later that I thought about him again, when yet another tragedy was reported in the papers after my return to England: a body of a young man had been washed up on the shore of Cardigan Bay in Wales. It had not taken long to identify the dead youth, and the report included his photograph. When I saw it I recognised him instantly.

It was Ruaidhrí.

But the name given was not that told to me by the boy who had pleaded with me to take him as a passenger on the ferry. I read the details, such as they were: *Michael Delaney had been working in London for the last nine months. He had arranged to take a week's holiday and it is thought that he intended returning home to County Carlow in the Irish Republic. How he came to have lost his life is as yet not known. The police are continuing with their enquiries. His widowed mother, his only close relative, has been informed.* A reference was made to the small market town where his mother lived.

It dawned on me, to my horror, that I was probably the only person who had known that Ruaidhrí – or, rather, Michael Delaney – had been a passenger on the ferry to Rosslare just over a week previously. And that I had effectively smuggled him on board. The terrible thought occurred to me that he might well have been lost at sea on that very crossing.

I realised that I ought to do something – to report my involvement with Michael Delaney to the police. But if I did it would surely get me into a situation which at this time I really didn't want to be in. Yet neither was I in the least comfortable with the thought that had I refused the young man's request he might still be alive.

By way of distracting myself – and postponing a difficult decision – I set about cleaning my car which was the worse for having been driven some hundreds of miles in mostly wet weather. Having washed the outside I took a hand brush to get the dried mud off the interior carpets.

It was under the front passenger seat that I found the ring. I thought at first it was a coin. But when I held it up in the daylight I saw that it was neither of these. It was heavy for its size, probably solid gold. It was in the form of a spiral, and at each end it had been fashioned into the shape of a snake's head. Small stones, possibly garnets, had been set into both heads to represent eyes. I had never seen it, or anything like it, before. How had it come to be there?

Then I remembered the boy who'd called himself Ruaidhrí. How, in his confusion, he had allowed his bag to fall on to the floor of the car, spilling its contents. This ring must surely have been in the bag, and had dropped from it and rolled under the seat. And Ruaidhrí, or rather Michael Delaney, was dead and so could never reclaim it.

I was in no doubt that it was valuable, if only for the weight of the gold from which it was made. As to what I should do with it, it occurred to me very quickly that there was only one course of action I could take.

* * *

Having parked my car a little distance from the centre of the small town of Clonegal I walked back to the post office. Rather to my surprise my enquiry about a Mrs Delaney produced a ready response with the remark that 'the poor soul has just recently lost her son – drowned at sea. And after what happened to her lovely daughter, it's surely a tragic family.' Without hesitation the woman behind the counter told me where I would find the house.

Ten minutes later I was knocking on the door. Slow footsteps approached from within, and a hesitant voice called out 'Who is it?'

'My name is Dr Alan Bygrove,' I called out. 'I wonder if I might have a word with you?'

I heard the sound of a chain being attached. I stepped back. The door opened a few centimetres and moments later I was being scrutinised by a woman with spectacles and untidy grey hair. I said nothing.

When she spoke there was an edge to her voice. 'I'm not one to speak to strangers. Bygrove, you say? If you're going to tell me you're owed money, there's nothing for you here!'

'No! I've not come here to ask you for anything. It's just that I have … I have something that I think belonged to Michael …'

'Something of Michael's, you say? How would you have come by anything of Michael's?'

'I … I gave him a lift in my car a short while back. I believe it dropped from his bag. I found it a few days later. It's really as straightforward as that. When I read in the papers what had happened, the report said that his mother lived in this town …'

She continued to stare at me. Then the door shut abruptly. I heard the sound of the chain being slipped from its fastening.

The woman who stood in the doorway was perhaps in her late forties, but her grey hair and unkempt appearance made her look older. 'You'd better come in. But don't try anything! What Michael might have done is nothing to do with me. What is it that you have, that you say belonged to him?'

'It might be best if I told you how I came to meet him …'

She nodded her assent. 'You'd best sit down … over there!' She pointed to a chair at the far side of the room. She then sat down herself, near to the door.

I explained how I had met her son and that he had asked me for a lift – to take him with me on the crossing to Rosslare. I said nothing about my own business in Ireland or about Michael Delaney having given me a false name.

'He was never checked in as a passenger on the ferry. I can explain why that was. More importantly, I can't deny the possibility – the probability – that he was lost overboard in the night. I am dreadfully sorry …'

She held me in her gaze. After a moment she spoke, quite slowly and in a quiet voice, scarcely audible: 'Yes. He had told me that he was going to make the crossing. If you hadn't taken him he'd have found someone who would. He said he was bringing something back to me. Something that had belonged to Mary, before … before …' Her voice faltered and caught.

'Mary?'

'My daughter – Michael's sister. She was two years younger than him. She was just a baby, but what that man did to her …'

'What man? What happened to her?'

She seemed not to hear me. A distant expression came over her face 'I'm thinking it's a ring that you've brought. Gold. Made like the old Celtic rings. *A twisted serpent.*'

I nodded. I slipped my hand in my pocket and took out the ring. I stood up, walked across to her and placed it in her open hand.

She looked down at it and nodded. *'Yes.'*

Something seemed to be piecing itself together in my mind. I found myself thinking again about the newspaper report. The shooting of Kevin Murphy in the park.

'This is for you, for what you did to Mary.'

'Mrs Delaney … What was it that your son did? I mean, what was his occupation?' I half anticipated her answer.

The woman nodded her head. 'He was in theatricals. When it came to dressing up … oh, he had a rare skill. He used to turn up here and fool the whole town. I wasn't easy with it. It was always women, girls.' Her face clouded. 'I pleaded with him, when he said he was going for Kevin Murphy, but he wouldn't heed me. When he said he was going to get the ring off him I knew he meant it.' Again, the words in the newspaper report flashed back to me – *'appearing to take his pulse as if to satisfy herself that he was dead'* 'He loved Mary … we all did.'

She stared at me again. 'Mary was easily led, got in with the wrong crowd. Kevin Murphy took a shine to her, gave her – things. In the end he took control of her and … and …'. Her gaze dropped and she said in little more than a whisper, *'she took her own life.'*

Rather lamely, I said. 'I am so very sorry. It's such a shocking and needless waste. But *both* your children. It's difficult to imagine …'

She stared down at the ring, lying in her open hand. 'No – I don't suppose anyone can possibly know … '. She looked up at me again. 'Do *you* have a family?'

I shook my head. I had, after all, come to talk about her and her family, not mine. But what she said next took me by surprise.

'I was reminded, when you came in, of something … someone. It was in the papers last year. I thought for a moment that there was something familiar – something about the name …'

Suddenly I wanted to be away from this place. I sensed an impending exposure which I desperately did not want. Perhaps it showed in my face.

'No. It was someone else, I'm sure,' she continued. 'Those drug gangs – destroying so many lives. I was thinking of two people, two quite innocent people. A mother and her son, I think. It was in Limerick. There was a shooting …'

I didn't know what to say. She must have sensed my agitation.

'*Bygrove* did you say your name was …?'

'Mrs Delaney, I think I …'

A faint smile of understanding crossed her face. 'I must be thinking of someone else entirely …' I was quite certain that she was not. 'But thank you for coming today. It's some comfort at least to have the ring back. It was my mother's. She gave it to Mary not long before she died. I think she'd wanted her to have it for her wedding ring one day.' She paused for some moments, then stared out of the window. 'Michael did what he did. I can understand why. He was convinced that there was no justice to be had. '*And they are rich enough to employ the best lawyers in the country. And they get off.*' Was what he used to say. And so he took what he saw as justice into his own hands.'

She looked back at me again. 'I wonder how many lives will be saved, now that one of them is dead, the other crippled? That's how Michael would have justified what he did. He thought that they – the big dealers – were the worst people ... '

This is for you, *for what you did to Mary* ... Once more the flashback struck like a blow.

'And of course,' she went on, 'the lives of that other innocent, the totally unconnected. That mother and son in Limerick ...' She stared hard at me.

'Yes. The mother and her son in Limerick. Caught ... caught up in the cross fire of a wretched gangland feud.'

'I ... we, may have been denied justice. But Michael gave us our vengeance, I'm thinking, for what little worth that might be. But it was never worth his life.'

* * *

'So you've laid some ghosts to rest then?' My sister dropped her arms from my shoulders and looked into my eyes. 'No – I'm sorry. That wasn't the most tactful ...'

I shook my head. 'I know what you're saying, Elena. The past is the past. There's no undoing of it. The people who did ... what they did ... aren't around anymore or at least they're no longer able to harm anyone. There are no more unanswered questions.'

'And the house is sold?'

I nodded. 'Just a few formalities. The young couple fell in love with it as soon as they walked through the door. How could they have done otherwise? It had Niamh's touch'.

Elena hugged me again. 'Good memories. Hold on to the good memories. And try not to be too sad.' She paused, looking once more directly into my eyes as if somehow she'd sensed the change in my train of thought. 'And I wonder what it is you are thinking about just now?'

'Not about what's happened. I was thinking about something I found. And I was trying to work out in my head how vengeance can equate with justice. If it ever can.'

'You know, I once had quite a debate with your Rory on that very subject.' She smiled. 'He was such a fine young man. He would have gone far …'

'Who knows? But Ruaidhrí … he was someone else again.' And I looked over her shoulder and through the window to her garden, where the vibrant yellow spikes of new crocuses contrasted with the subdued colours of the remnant of winter. How Niamh had loved them and their message of the supremacy of life over death.

My sister looked momentarily baffled. But she did not pursue my remark. 'Come on,' she said, linking my arm, 'things are coming to life in my little garden, as you can see. Come on and I'll show you.'

OBLIVION

Λήθη

I could not begin to imagine where he had been, but he was coming back.

The briefest flicker of an eyelid. A painful attempt to swallow. I dimmed the light, and passed a moistened cloth over his lips. He drew in a breath, then gave a faint cough. His eyes opened.

'Dave … is that you?' His voice was hoarse, barely audible over the hum of ventilation fans.

'Yes, Max.'

'How – how long have I been …' His voice started to fade under the effort of speaking.

'You have been asleep for sixty three days. Today is the second of February.'

The faintest smile. Then: 'I did it! I missed Christmas!'

'You did. Scrooge would have been proud of you!'

* * *

The implications of what my brother, Doctor Max Stilman, had achieved were astounding. This was

Nobel class science. Not that he would have been much bothered by that. Besides, with his reputation – notoriety even – he wouldn't be allowed within a hundred miles of a Nobel Prize committee. No – Max's interest was purely commercial. He used his genius for material gain and to wield power over others, as I had found to my cost.

It was in the previous autumn that he had taken me into his confidence. We were together in the small studio that he had built in a patch of woodland, half a mile from the house where he lived alone with his dog. It was a squat building, solid, with grilles over the windows and triple locks on the steel-reinforced door. Security mattered a lot to Max: he had plenty to hide.

'It was a chance discovery the detail of which I won't go in to. Believe me, though, this is something that people are going to *want*. And they will pay handsomely for it.

'But Max, how the hell will you get this past an ethics committee? I mean, you'll have to submit it to clinical trials …'

'Ethics committees be damned. They're hide bound by regulations. I'm surprised any useful research on drugs gets anywhere these days. And the people who will want this stuff aren't going to wait around for years while a crowd of idiots does this test and that on it. A good many of the punters won't have that sort of time anyway.'

'Max – your last attempt to short circuit the protocols got you struck off the medical register. And damned nearly got you a spell in prison. They'll throw the book at you if fall foul of them again.'

'Which is exactly why I have no intention of letting any of them get wind of this. This is *my* baby – I should say, *ours*. We're in this together – you can consider yourself my accomplice. And I think that you know better than to renege on the understanding we have together.'

I knew well what Max was referring to. He had always been the dominant one. The memory of my involvement in the genetic research he'd pioneered made me wince. Even years later, if he chose to make this public my own career would be in tatters. I might even attract a criminal charge.

I said nothing.

'I'm not asking much of you. Just that you keep an eye on things – on me – while I'm … away.'

'You really mean to try this stuff on *yourself*?'

'Uh-huh. In the best traditions of medical science. And it didn't kill Bella, so it very probably won't kill *me*.' He nudged an elderly yellow Labrador, stretched out on the floor with his foot. The dog gave a perfunctory wag of its tail.

'You've given it to your *dog*?'

'Sure I did. She slept like a baby for sixteen days. And was none the worse for it.'

A scrabbling noise in the roof distracted us. 'Bloody squirrels!' He jumped up, grabbed a heavy book from the desk and hurled it up to the ceiling. There was a loud thud as the book struck, followed by a frantic scuttling. 'I'll need to get those trees cut back from the house. That's how the buggers get in.'

* * *

That evening, back at the main house, he showed me what he called his 'hibernation chamber'. He had built it in the basement. There was nothing particularly high tech about it. He had rigged up a framework on to which he had fixed plasterboard, and had wrapped what looked very much like loft insulation around it. A small refrigeration unit sat squat upon the floor next to the chamber, connected to it by flexible ducting. This, he told me, was designed to keep the temperature in the chamber between 8 and 10 degrees Celsius.

'And this is where you come into it. The initial stages are quite critical. The subject, in this case, me, will need to be watched carefully. Respiration, cardiograph and encephalograph monitored meticulously. But when stable hibernation is established, you can bugger off to the sun for all I care.'

'Max, are you serious?' I stared wide eyed at him. 'If this goes wrong – if you … if you don't wake up, don't you see that I could be on a murder charge?'

'Quite right, little brother. And that is why I have every confidence that you will follow my instructions to the letter.'

As the weeks passed he fine-tuned the process. I assumed the role of his assistant. He told me no more than I needed to know, which was remarkably little. His discovery was not something that could be given a patent in the short term and he was taking no chances. Then one day, late in the year, when all the preliminaries had been attended to, I stood by him as he slipped into unconsciousness. I sat through the night, watching the tracings on the display units become ever more feeble until it seemed the body lying there before me was all but lifeless. I could detect no sign of breathing; his heart rate had dropped to less than five beats a minute.

For the next twenty-four hours I scarcely ate nor slept. I did not leave the room where the chamber stood. The only sound was the faint murmur of the pump of the refrigeration unit. Then stabilisation occurred exactly as Max had predicted. His ethics might leave much to be desired, I mused, but his science could not be faulted. He was indeed on the threshold of pulling off one of the greatest advances in the history of biological science. And perhaps one of the most terrifying.

I had little to occupy me for the bulk of the time he lay in suspended animation. I made more than one attempt to deduce the secret he had managed to unlock, but got nowhere. There was no question of looking through papers and records relating to his research, for the simple reason that there weren't any. All the data relating to his work was stored electronically, and even if I had dared to attempt to locate it there was little doubt that his elaborate security would have been impenetrable. But not, as it turned out, immune to the consequences of events that he hadn't predicted.

* * *

His recovery was swift, which may have been a reflection of his level of fitness before he submitted himself to his experiment. He had no recollection of anything that had happened during his sleep – scarcely surprising since his electroencephalogram had shown no activity. Neither had he had any sensation of the passage of time.

I wondered how best to choose the moment to tell him about the fire.

Three days after he woke, I found him sitting up in an armchair in his bedroom. He had been left considerably weakened, as he had predicted. But a high calorie intake and graded exercise were showing results. It would not be long before he could leave the house. And I guessed the first place he would make for would be the studio where he had housed his complex array of computing equipment.

I sensed that something was troubling him. Later that day he told me what it was. 'There seems to be a residual effect that I hadn't predicted.'

'What is it?'

'My memory. My short term memory's buggered up. I think it is starting to improve. But I'm not entirely sure. No matter. I'll spend a few days going through my files. Everything I need to know is there.'

'Max,' I interrupted, 'there is something I have to tell you. Something that happened while you were asleep …'

He sensed the unease in my voice. 'Something happened? What, exactly?'

'There was a fire. The studio … it burned down just over a week ago.'

'*Burned down*? What do you mean? How …'

'I was away from the house at the time – I had to collect something from the town. When I got back I saw the blaze. I called the fire brigade immediately, of course. But it was too late. The place is gutted, and everything in it was destroyed.'

He sat in stunned silence as the news sunk in, and then exploded. 'Bloody Hell! That is where I kept my data. All of it! How in God's name did it happen?'

'The fire service say it was most likely an electrical fire. Seems to have started in the loft space. Then I remember you told me that squirrels had been getting in. That seems to be what caused it – chewing through the insulation ...'

'Squirrels? What squirrels?'

Max appeared to have no recollection of our discussion the previous autumn when he had reveal his discovery to me, and how he had hurled a book up at the ceiling to scare off the intruders. 'Help me out of this ...' He struggled as he tried to lift himself out of the chair, 'we're going over there, now. There might just be something ...'

But there was nothing. I joined him in probing the charred remnants of the studio, he with a garden hoe and I with a long stake. Something bearing a resemblance to what might have been a computer terminal lay in a shallow depression among the ashes, but it was clear that it could hold not a shred of retrievable data.

* * *

Three days later he was quite recovered. I found him with a large scale map spread out on the table in front of him. On a computer monitor at one end of the table a section of what appeared to be the same map was displayed. He was concentrating and didn't appear to notice that I'd come in the room.

'Looking for something?'

He jumped, and turned sharply. 'You could say so.' He returned his attention to the map, pouring over it and making occasional marks with a pencil.

'So will you tell me what you're trying to find?'

He hesitated, as if uncertain whether or not to let me in to his confidence. Then he said, 'I must have made a backup and kept it somewhere away from the main computer. It's something I know I always did. But my memory is more or less a complete blank concerning the details. And nothing's returning in a hurry.'

'Nothing on the hard drives here in this house?'

He shook his head. 'No. I've checked, but I would have wanted to keep data copies well away from here in any event. Not least because I've long known that there are … others … who have a particular interest in what they think I may have been up to, may have discovered.'

'You mean, the police?'

'No. Other … researchers. And people who knew from my earlier work and my subsequent abandonment of mainstream research. It is quite possible that they have tried to put two and two together. Any conclusions they might have come to would have been likely to be wildly wrong, but that's not what matters. It is the fact that they are interested in what I do that matters.'

I began to understand what he was talking about. He had come into contact with some pretty ruthless people in his time – major players in the field of scientific and industrial espionage.

He scrolled down the map image displayed on the monitor, and then zoomed in on a particular section. He thumped his fist into his left palm. 'I think I've got it!'

I peered over his shoulder. I could see that the map was one of a sparsely inhabited high ground and moorland. At the intersection of two rough tracks was a symbol of a chest, under which was the inscription "Λήθη". I was pretty sure that the script was Greek, but had no idea what it meant. Judging by Max's excitement, it was no mystery to him. He jotted down some numbers from the top of the screen, and then quickly exited the programme and shut down the computer.

'So, will you tell me what this is all about?'

He gave me a penetrating stare, as if debating whether or not I could be trusted. 'You know what a geocache is?'

I'd certainly heard the word before, but had to admit that it didn't mean a lot to me. I shook my head.

'Something hidden – on or below the ground, and its location recorded on a map. Either for others to find or, as in this instance, only known to the person who placed it.'

'The symbol – the chest – there was an inscription under it. Is that significant?'

'But of course. And that is what indicates – to me – that it is what I am looking for. It is quite certain that I placed the cache myself, although I've no memory of it. Those characters are Greek – ancient Greek.'

'And it means?'

'"Lethe" – one of the five rivers of the Greek underworld. The river of forgetfulness. It also means "oblivion". Apt, don't you think?'

'So what are you proposing to do?'

'Find it, of course. It's a good distance from here and I may be gone a couple of days. But once I have it, then we can more or less continue from where we left off. And one thing you may as well know – prepare for, if you like – it's your turn next!'

For a moment the implication of what Max had just said to me did not sink in. Then I found myself wondering if he could possibly be serious. But he was not given to flippancy.

'Max – just what are you saying?'

'Oh, come on Dave – don't act so surprised. I'd the confidence to use myself as a guinea pig and survived. Now I need to observe a subject – a human subject – for myself. And far better that he should be someone who is in on the act – and you are the only person who is. What did you think I was to do – advertise in the local paper?'

'And someone who you've got … exactly where you want him. I know you – you're hardly going to make it easy for me to refuse.'

He gave me a penetrating stare. There was a coldness in his voice. 'How very perceptive you are.'

'Max – you've got to let me think about this. I never thought for a moment …'

'Well, think all you like now. I know that you will need time to make … arrangements. You will need to take a month … no, six weeks … away from your practice. Better tell them you're having a sabbatical, out of the country. Don't worry – they will be compensated for your absence. They can employ someone to cover for you, and more. I know your lot – they won't object when they sniff hard cash.'

Left to ponder over what Max had proposed, I found myself becoming more horror struck than apprehensive. I began to wonder whether he was entirely sane, whether more than just memory had been affected by his long sleep. And if the same were to happen to me, the effect upon my ability to continue with my own work safely, or even at all, might be profound. I felt that I had to resist him at any cost – even sabotage his plans by some means if there was no alternative.

* * *

Even now I wonder what it was that came over me to act as I did a few days after Max had told me his plan. I suppose I felt cornered, and in my gathering panic acted impulsively, even irrationally. I was becoming obsessed with the thought that he might decide that I was superfluous to his further plans. Or even that I might pose a potential security thread, that I might be bribed by a rival in the field. As an insurance against this he might let me remain in hibernation for months … perhaps for years.

Max had left the house on his mission to retrieve his backed-up data. He had given me no indication of where he was going to, although he did tell me that he would be staying at a small hotel in Telford, Shropshire for the two nights he was going to be away.

It seemed a reasonable assumption that on the second night, on his return journey, he would have what he was setting out to find in his possession. It should be possible for him to be intercepted there.

That was when I took the mobile telephone – bought specifically for the purpose of this call – and keyed in a number.

'Who is this?' The answering voice had a coldness about it.

'Who I am doesn't matter. What I have to say *does*.'

'So – what is it you have to say?'

'I believe you have an interest in the work of the scientist, Max Stilman.'

'Stilman? You know where he is?'

'I know where he will be – on the night of the 12th of April. And I believe that he will have something in his possession that would be of great interest to you.'

'Why are you telling me this? What do you want?'

'That can come later. Note down what I am about to say to you.'

I gave him the address of the hotel and a vehicle registration number. I ended the call, walked over to the hearth where I had set a fire half an hour before, and dropped the handset into the blaze.

* * *

On the morning of the 13th April Max was hit by a car being driven at speed out of the car park of the hotel where he had stayed. He was killed instantly.

'It seems it was his own car,' the police officer had informed me, his voice grave. 'We believe that someone had stolen it and he was trying to prevent it leaving the car park.'

I was stunned by the news. I realised at once that I had, by alerting a rival whom I knew to be totally ruthless, contributed to my brother's death.

'Do you know who it was? Have you found the man who …?'

The officer shook his head. 'We were on his tail within minutes, and followed him on to the motorway. He put on speed. Then it seems he lost control. The car flipped over and caught fire. The tank must have been full. Seems there's pretty well nothing left. The man driving was dead – burned beyond recognition.'

I was at the house when the police car had driven up shortly before midday. I had felt a sense of rising panic as the young policeman, accompanied by a woman officer, approached the door. Shocked though I was at the news, I felt almost relieved when I realised that they had not come to the house to make any enquiry about me.

'I … I'd better get over there …'

'We'd appreciate that. As next of kin, Doctor Stilman, we'd like you to confirm the identity … I'm sorry.'

I nodded. 'No … I know it's necessary. I'll set off as soon as I get a few overnight things ready.'

* * *

I would have preferred not to have had to book into the same hotel where my brother had stayed at on the previous night. But wanting to be away from the town centre, I'd no choice. The receptionist had looked askance at me when I checked in, but relaxed when I explained who I was, and murmured that she was sorry to hear of my loss. When I returned to the lounge to make arrangements for an evening meal, the hotel manager came over and introduced himself to me.

'I can't say how sorry we are at the hotel that this tragedy happened. We'll do everything we can to ensure that you are comfortable during your stay here, Dr Stilman.'

I thanked him. I expressed my regret that he and his staff should have had to cope with the distress and disruption that the morning's events had caused them.

He hesitated a moment. 'There's one thing … your brother left a bag, a small back pack on the reception desk when he rushed out … when he saw someone breaking in to his car. I was going to pass it on to the police, but it seems to be empty. Would you like to take it, doctor?'

'Well, yes … I might as well. Empty, you say?'

'Uh-huh. Just a gadget in one of the pockets. Looks like a rather stubby mobile phone. Bright yellow. I wondered if it was some sort of walkie-talkie. Apart from that, just an empty film case.'

* * *

Later that afternoon I sat alone in front of the blazing fire in the hotel lounge. Anticipating that I wasn't likely to be disturbed, I opened the back pack.

I recognised the yellow "walkie talkie" as the hand held GPS navigation unit that Max had used on his occasional forays over the moors. No doubt it was this that he had used to guide him to the location of his cached data backup.

I took the film case and shook it. It was light, and as the manager said, apparently empty. But I flipped off the plastic lid. Some tissue paper had been wedged into it. Pulling it out, I found what I had been looking for: a computer data key, not much larger than my thumbnail. On the label stating its capacity – which was certainly substantial – had been written in pencil a single word: Λήθη.

I knew then that I was holding in my hand a thing of such significance that it had the potential to change the course of history. I was almost overwhelmed by a sense of power and … terror. The implications of Max's discovery – the ways in which might be put to use for good or bad – were almost beyond imagining. The scale of the wealth that it might bring to whoever might wield it were mind-numbing. And its potential to corrupt, even destroy its owner, only too real.

I got up and crossed over to the fire. I held the tiny object between my thumb and forefinger directly over the flames. I closed my eyes.

A PAYMENT IN KIND

'Well, Joseph, I'd say you've made good progress. Real good. In fact I'd go so far as to say I can sign you off as one hundred per cent fit.' Doctor James Stuart Eldridge looked over his spectacles at the man sitting opposite him and smiled.

'Say – that's good news! The best I could have hoped for.' Captain Joseph Mason's face split into a grin. 'The men are as anxious to get away as I am. Best to make the Pacific crossing before the winter sets in if at all possible.'

Dr Eldridge nodded. 'I'll bring over the packages for you to deliver to Webb. I take it that your plans to travel east still stand?'

'Sure they do, Doc. I hope to be there before Thanksgiving. I'll deliver them to your boy personally. And I'll tell him that he should be proud – real proud – of his Pa. The best doctor in all Japan.'

Eldridge shook his head. 'Your recovery had as much to do with providence as anything *I* may have done. And your constitution. You're a strong man, Joseph. That counts for more in my view. Pneumonia spares some, and carries off others. But there – you came through it. So don't you go giving Webb any high falutin' nonsense about me. I'm his Pa is what's important. Tell him that his mother and I – and his sisters too – think of him every day. And we miss him. By God we miss him …'

A frown crossed Captain Mason's face. 'Is it really three years since you saw the lad?'

'It surely is. He writes, of course, but not all the letters get to us. And his mother and I write back. Frances writes most weeks, long letters. I guess it's harder on her. But the States is where he has to be if he wants medicine, the law or the military. The good Lord only knows when we may see him again …'

'But you tell me that you're founding a medical school yourself here in Japan – at Sapporo. Couldn't you have him there?'

'Wouldn't do. It's for Japanese nationals caring for their own people. Just because I've settled here doesn't mean that Webb would want to do the same. No – his mother and I have come to accept the situation. And one day, when the school is established, I may be able to hand it over and return to Philadelphia. I daresay it will come to that anyway – we've his two younger sisters to think about. No doubt they will want to marry one of their own.'

'Well, may the Lord guide you to the best decision. But you've become something of a legend here, let me tell you. There's a real thirst for everything western since Commodore Perry made his appearance – not least medical science. But, say, there's another matter …'

'Yes?'

'It's your fee … for treating me … for saving me …'

'Aw, don't trouble yourself just now …'

'But that's it. I *do* trouble myself. Fact is, there's a bit of a problem. With the delay in setting sail the crews' payment is overdue. If I don't settle some at least will jump ship …'

Eldridge held up his hands. 'Forget it. You're an honest man, Joseph. I know you'll settle up … maybe when I'm back home. And it's not as though I haven't a regular salary from the authorities here. It's a good living, you know …'

'That's mighty generous of you Doctor. But I was thinking – I have something on board ship that might just be of interest to you. Something that I have to admit I'd be quite glad to have off my hands. But a man with your wide interests and learning might just …'

'So what is it then?' Eldridge's curiosity was fired.

The captain smiled. 'What I'd suggest is that you come and see for yourself! It's not something that I can slip into my hip pocket. Perhaps you'd come down to the ship tomorrow morning with Webb's packages and I'll show you. There's just one thing …'

'What's that?'

'Better not bring Mrs Eldridge. Let it be a surprise to her!'

* * *

'Well!' breathed Dr Eldridge as he looked down into the hold of Joseph Mason's ship early on the following afternoon. 'She's a real beauty. The girls will love her, that's for sure. But you're right – their mother might not be quite so enthusiastic. But I'll get round that. I guess I'll accept your kind offer – and I'd add that I think it a most handsome recompense for my medical services. I'll present it to Frances as a fait accompli, so to speak. She and the girls are staying away overnight with friends in Yedo. You be sure that you're well on your way by this time tomorrow when she gets back to Yokohama. Then there'll be no question about you taking it back …'

The two men shook hands, promised to keep in touch and parted company at last. Dr Eldridge took charge of his acquisition and made his way carefully up the road away from the docks. He could see that he was attracting attention and did his best to ignore it, concentrating instead on the sometimes tricky task in hand. No doubt the excited onlookers had seen nothing like the spectacle before in their lives. Gossip was sure to spread far and wide, but with any luck would not reach his wife's ears before her return. He thought long about just how he would explain himself and what he had done, but by the time he went to bed that night he still hadn't worked out how she might be best won round.

* * *

Eldridge greeted his wife and daughters affectionately when they arrived in a carriage the following afternoon. Perceptive as she always was she looked askance at him.

'I declare you've been up to something while I've been away.' She looked about the room, as if half expecting to find something precious had been broken, or the result of another of her husband's occasional idiosyncrasic notions in the field home decorating. She could neither see nor sense any changes.

A loud noise from somewhere outside the house caused them to stare at one another. It had a brash, brassy, rather musical quality – the sort of sound that a pair of circus clowns might wrest from an old trombone that had fallen off the back of a wagon.

Frances's eyes narrowed as she fixed her gaze on her husband. 'Just *what* have you been doing while I've been away? What is it you've got out there? Don't you dare tell me you've bought that old church organ from Takeshi-san …'

'Now, my dear, just you calm down. It's nothing like that at all. In fact it's a very generous gift from Captain Mason, in appreciation for all I did for him. He nearly died, you know, but I got him through. I didn't want to take anything at all, but he absolutely insisted. He's a real good sort. He's going out of his way to take our packages personally to our Webb as well.'

'I could just about fancy that he'd set you up with a few cases of bourbon or rum, and that you'd been at it with your buddies behind the stables. But I don't smell it out of you and you're still on your feet. Well now – you'll just tell me right now what it's all about!'

The luckless doctor made a few more attempts to placate his wife but realised soon enough that his efforts were, if anything, making the situation worse. At last he said: 'well, dear, if you'll just come outside I'll show you. And bring Beatrix and Fanny as well. I know they'll be really thrilled.'

This last remark did appear to have some reassuring affect upon the indignant lady. Whatever outlandish prize her husband extracted from old Mason couldn't be too bad if he was so sure that his daughters would be enamoured of it.

Her appeasement, slight as it was, did not last for long.

She gasped at the sight that presented itself to her at the end of her garden – a garden emulating so beautifully the best of Japanese traditions in horticulture. A garden that was her greatest pride and joy.

'What in the name of the Lord is that … that *monster* doing among my azaleas?'

Flustered to the point of almost losing his power of speech, Dr Eldridge muttered a few words in Japanese: *'kore wa zo desu …'*

'I am neither blind nor a fool,' his wife retorted, 'of course I can see what it is. But what is it doing in *my* garden?'

The creature stared at Frances Eldridge, and as if to provide an answer to her question it waved its huge ears and let fall its trunk from its mouth to pull more hay from the broken bale scattered at its feet. Then, perhaps tiring of its staple diet, it reached over a low picket fence and grasped a fine specimen of *acer palmeris*, pulled it out by its roots and devoured it in a matter of seconds.

The doctor's wife shrieked. 'Did you see that, husband? It's going to destroy my life's work. Oh, what have you *done*?'

The reaction of the two little girls could hardly have been more different. They too shrieked, but with unconcealed excitement at what they clearly took to be a new pet, acquired by their adoring father for their benefit.

'Oh Papa! You've brought us a real, live elephant!' cried Beatrix, now aged nine and the elder of the two by three years. Little Fanny jumped up and down. She, effectively bilingual, cared for as she was for much of the time by her Japanese *ama*, called out over and over again: 'Zo! Zo desu!'

The elephant – whose one saving grace was that it was evidently not fully grown – was clearly alarmed at the family's various reactions. It took a step backwards, flattening a young conifer in doing so, and relieved itself voluminously on the grass.

It occurred to Dr Eldridge, who had always been an enthusiastic reader of the works of the contemporary novelist Charles Dickens, that he was witnessing a clear parallel between his incensed spouse's reaction and that of David Copperfield's aunt Betsey Trotwood when the patch of green adjacent to her house was invaded by donkeys. It also occurred to him that Frances was being at least a little unfair: elephants were hardly commonplace in that suburb of Yokohama while donkeys certainly were – he supposed – in mid-Victorian Dover, thereby constituting a far greater nuisance in terms of sheer numbers alone.

'Calm yourself, my dear,' he soothed. 'You must see that this little lady is scarcely more than an infant. Undoubtedly she can be trained. I understand that the species is most passive if treated well. I have every expectation that she will allow the children to ride on her, and … '

'Oh yes, *yes*, Papa!' cried the little girls ecstatically. 'Mama – don't you see how terribly clever our Papa is to have thought of getting an elephant for us? He is quite the *best* Papa that ever there was!'

But poor Mama was now rendered speechless, her hand clamped over her mouth at the spectacle of what the elephant had deposited upon the grass. She turned away and stammered, 'Please, just get it *away* from my beautiful garden. Put it in the paddock with the horses.' And her husband was glad to comply, seeing in the order a reprieve of sorts, a breathing space to give himself time to consider how best to win over his wife. The girls were proving to be sound allies who, in their utter delight at the new edition to their family of pets, were not going to accept lightly any insistence from their mother that – heaven forbid – the animal be got rid of.

'Come on young lady,' he coaxed as he led the passive beast to join the two ponies in their enclosure. By good fortune the ponies seemed quite undismayed by the presence of their new companion, who ambled over to claim a share of the fodder in a rack at the corner of the field.

A crowd of local residents had gathered at the perimeter fence, chattering and gesticulating to one another. They pointed to the elephant and called out to attract its attention. It ignored them completely, being entirely engrossed with consuming the generous, but rapidly dwindling stockpile of hay. Then they called out to the doctor: 'Eldridge *sensei*!' and demanded to know how he had come to acquire the amazing beast. The doctor was generally on good, if not familiar terms with his neighbours. Tradition and sometimes complex protocols governing social interaction in that time and place ensured that conversation never deviated from the polite and formal. When communicating with "foreigners" this formality was even more pronounced, and a subtle distance maintained. Having lived for more than ten years in the country, Eldridge's fluency in the language was beyond dispute. He had no hesitation in providing a full account about how he became the owner of the animal and reassured them that the enclosure was secure. As evening approached the onlookers dispersed.

The next few days passed without any incident of note so far as the elephant was concerned, although Eldridge observed that its appetite for good hay was prodigious. He feared that the two ponies might suffer were they to be denied their rightful share. He hailed a passing small-holder with a wagon full of cabbages and asked if he might buy a load or two. The farmer was delighted and, no doubt aware as to the reason why the foreign doctor was anxious to purchase cabbages in a quantity that would last a normal family for well in excess of a year, he quoted what Eldridge thought a considerably inflated price for them. After some haggling an agreement was reached which was still very much to the advantage of the farmer.

'Let's hope that Frank doesn't get wind of this,' murmured Eldridge to himself as the farmer departed with a broad grin on his face.

But of course she did. And she gave her unfortunate husband every bit as difficult a time as he had feared over it.

* * *

Eldridge recognised the robed official who called on him some two weeks after the initial procurement of cabbages – which, incidentally, had been followed by three further such purchases. The farmer was no doubt growing richer with each one, Eldridge poorer and his wife ever more outraged. But he did his best to engage as courteously as he might with whom he knew to be a man who held a prominent position at the Imperial Court. He had first met him when he and his colleagues in the Scientific Expedition to Japan more than ten years previously had been presented to the Emperor. The other members of the expedition had long since returned to the United States, leaving Eldridge to forge ahead with his own career as a physician and educator. He knew that he had come to be highly regarded by the Japanese government, and that the Emperor was aware of and gave his support – for the most part verbal – to Eldridge's work and ambitions. There had been rumour, nothing more, of a meritorious award that might one day be bestowed upon the doctor. Such an occurrence would certainly have far reaching implications for him in terms of his reputation and progress in Japanese society. But he knew better than to speak of it.

He bowed – appropriately low – to his distinguished guest. Customary small talk ensued and it was not until after tea had been served that he felt it permissible to enquire as to what lay behind the visit.

'Well, Minbukayo-san, I am wondering how I may be of service to you?' Eldridge enquired in Japanese.

The official bowed his head gravely before responding. 'It has come to our notice – to the attention of his Imperial Majesty, the Emperor, that you have on the grounds of this house an … an unusual creature.'

Eldridge was gripped by a sense of anxiety. He was not, of course, the owner of the property where he and his family lived. It was leased to him by the government. And while there were certain restrictions concerning how he might use and maintain the house and the land, he could not bring to mind any reference forbidding the housing of elephants. But no doubt there might be something in the small print that could catch him out. He thought it best to come clean.

'Indeed, that is so.' Thinking that it might be to his advantage to embellish the tale he went on: 'it was unfortunate, really – the captain of a United States merchant vessel was transporting the creature from Ceylon to California. By mischance the animal fell sick and it was feared that it might die. And I agreed to take it and do what I could for it'. Since Captain Mason and his crew were no longer in a position or corroborate or deny his account, Eldridge felt that he was on safe ground.

'A noble action, and one which my master, the Emperor, would approve. And is the animal now recovered?'

'Come with me, and see!'

* * *

Parting with his elephant was no small relief for Eldridge when, some days after the visit of the government official, a deputation from the recently established zoo in Yokohama came the take the animal away. The compensation given him was generous– certainly sufficient to cover the considerable expense he had been put to in foddering the creature. The Emperor himself had let it be known, indirectly, that the doctor had found still more favour in his eyes, for the collection and study of wildlife from all over the world was a matter of great interest to him. At that time there was only one other elephant in the whole of Japan – also in the zoological gardens in Yokohama – a male who was by all accounts pining and anxious for a mate.

In due course Eldridge was himself summonsed into the Imperial presence, to be honoured with the prestigious award of the Third Order of Merit for his services.

His dear wife Frances was immensely proud, of course, and quite forgave him for the disruption, not to say destruction, visited upon her routine and her beloved garden as a consequence of her husband's misplaced enthusiasm. But she determined to have words with Joseph Mason should they meet again.

Eldridge's two daughters never truly forgave him, however, and for a long time made his life suitably difficult to their great advantage.

Doctor James Stuart Eldridge, his wife Frances and his daughters Beatrix and Fanny were real people. Beatrix was my grandmother, and I can just remember visiting her at Christmas in London more than 60 years ago. Eldridge's son, Chauncey Weber, sadly died of rheumatic heart disease at the age of 15 while attending boarding school in Phildelphia. My great grandfather and his wife remained in Japan for the rest of their lives, and their remains are interred in the cemetery for foreign nationals in Yokohama.

These are facts. I am less certain as to the veracity of the story of the elephant, but it was told to me by my father at his knee when I was a small boy. He loved to regale me with accounts of his own boyhood in Japan. And he certainly had a talent for recounting tall stories while keeping his face as straight as a die.

Hanging in a handsome frame on the wall of my hallway is a rather magnificent document in rich Japanese calligraphy. When I showed it to the members of the Japanese Historical Society in Yokohama they assured me that it is indeed the certificate of the Third Order of Merit bestowed by the Emperor Meiji upon my great grandfather.

I am privileged to have in my possession this and much else pertaining to the life and work of my great grandfather, as a soldier who fought in the American Civil War and as a physician, researcher and teacher in Japan at the time of the Meiji Restoration.

NO FIXED ABODE

At first I thought Sam was sleeping when I found him lying under the hedge on that bright winter's morning. But he was quite dead. 'Poor old chap' I said to myself. For some reason my first instinct was to find an old blanket and cover him, though God knows, he was hardly in need of protection from the cold any more.

Over the past couple of years he'd been a "regular" in our street, appearing on my front doorstep and those of my neighbours where he could be fairly sure he'd get food or drink. I guess we are a pretty well disposed lot. No-one ever threatened him or sent him off. But then there was a decency, even a dignity about him. He communicated by look rather than voice, and in doing so he brought out the best in us.

I'm not sure how he came to be called "Sam". It may have been old Mrs Dobson, two doors up from me, who had so named him. She had a stone seat in her front garden, and Sam would make himself comfortable there on occasions, often dozing for much of a sunny afternoon under the shade of her cherry tree. She referred to him as 'just an old vagrant with a bit of a cheek'. But she let him be.

We thought it a nice touch when she had the small brass plate made and inscribed with "Sam's Place" and set on the back rest of that seat. And the engraving of the cat's head under the words wasn't a bad likeness of the old tabby. I miss him.

SHENANDOAH

*… Away, I'm bound away
'cross the wide Missouri.*

Today they told me that I have a grand-daughter. How that can be? But they have told me so much that makes no sense. I begin to wonder if, somewhere along the line, I have quite lost my wits.

Her name is Shenandoah.

When the expedition was launched, I had … well, I had a daughter. Just a kid – five years old. So how could I have a grand daughter? Are they playing some game with me? But surely they wouldn't be so cruel. Rather, they seem endlessly concerned for me. And they are keeping something back. I know it.

There's nothing wrong with my memory, I'm certain. I remember very clearly the day that the catastrophic power failure crippled the ship completely and for good. We knew what we had to do to survive. It would delay our return home, but not by so very much. I might miss Sarah's sixth birthday, perhaps her seventh. But when I eventually made it back she would still be my little girl and, one way or another, we would make up for lost time.

* * *

The desert had a strange loveliness about it. In the light of evening it became pink. The wind-sculpted sandstone reminded me of Petra – *Rose red city, half as old as Time*. And I think back on it as I try to make sense of the situation I find myself in now. Why won't they answer my questions? 'A stage at a time' is all they say. I think they are preparing me for a shock. A revelation of something dreadful that has happened. When I asked them if the other crew members survived it was their hesitation – and what they didn't say – that has made me certain that they did not. Some at least must have perished and been left behind. Maybe, in some way, they think I may be to blame for that. I was, after all, the life-support officer. An enquiry – I am sure there will be one – might indeed conclude that I was responsible through a failure of duty. But I don't remember …

I think again of the vast expanse of rust-red hills. Not so much so much John Burgon and his magical city, but Yeats and his vision of a 'terrible beauty'. That is the truth of it.

* * *

Oh! Shenandoah. I have become increasingly curious about the child, my flesh and blood indeed, whom I have never met. *I long to see you …*

They told me very gently today that my daughter, Sarah, is dead. For some reason I didn't erupt into hysterical weeping as you would have thought any normal mother would do. Later, on my own, I cried quietly and for a long time.

I looked up my grand-daughter's name. It seems it is an old native American name meaning 'daughter of the stars'. How beautiful and strange.

* * *

Today the doctor – I think she is a doctor – talked to me alone for more than an hour. I think that they are preparing me for something.

'How are you feeling since … the retrieval?' She hesitated as if the term were somehow unfamiliar to her.

'Why, I'm fine. Or I would be if everyone here wasn't so mysterious.'

She wasn't going to be drawn on that one. 'Your memory … how well can you recall the events leading up to … the power failure?'

'Fine. But it was chaotic, scary. For a while we didn't know if any of us would survive. No wonder things are a little cloudy now.'

'Hmmm – but you knew what you had to do. You'd been trained to react quickly in such a situation.'

'I don't know what you're getting at.'

'You need to accept from me that your memory of events is quite incomplete. Can you think of any reason why that might be so?'

I shook my head. 'You've lost me.'

She put her hand on mine and smiled. 'Don't worry. We expect a full recovery in time.'

* * *

My name is Anna Hamilton. I am – was – the chief life support scientist on the interplanetary ship *Endeavour*. I am about thirty three years old, although that is perhaps less certain than it was at the time of launching.

I'm thinking again about the grand-daughter I've never met. And that old song. The Wide Missouri had nothing … *nothing* … on the gulf that separated me from her when she was born. I am talking about the tens of millions of kilometres between Earth and the planet Mars. About Shenandoah they've told me scarcely anything. They've told me that she knows who I am and that I am coming home. They've promised that I will see her 'soon' but they were evasive when I asked if I might see a photograph of her. Is she ugly then, deformed even?

They are pressing me again about my recollection of what happened on Mars. 'Did they tell you,' asks the doctor, 'how long it would be before a rescue mission could be mounted?'

'Of course,' I reply. 'The second transit had been planned even before we set out. It wasn't intended to be a rescue mission. It was going to happen anyway. It was due to enter Mars orbit in about two more years. But *you* know that.'

A momentary change in her expression, the start of a frown, quickly concealed, tells me that she *doesn't* know. What's with the woman? What else doesn't she know?

'What made you decide to suspend?' I think this is a diversion tactic. 'Couldn't you have sat it out? I would have thought you'd have found plenty to occupy yourselves …'

I shake my head emphatically. 'No. We'd not sufficient food and supplies to last that long. Not enough air. Nothing like enough to last two years.'

'Then what about power to maintain the hyber-units?'

I shake my head again. 'No – that wasn't a problem. We had a fission-pile – a nuclear power plant. About the size of a small fridge. It could have kept us going for, well, for centuries.'

The colour drains from her face.

* * *

This time it is an eager young man who interviews me. Unlike the woman, he introduces himself.

'Hi Anna. I'm Dr Jackson. But call me Bud.'

I guess that he is a scientist or something. He doesn't quite come over as a medical doctor.

'Hi Bud. So what is it you want to ask me this time?' I think he senses the weariness in my voice. I am tired of these sessions.

'Not very much, you'll be pleased to hear. And then I may have something to tell *you*. Something we feel that you are … ready to hear.'

My ears prick up. Immediately, a question forms on my lips, but I supress it. These people always seem to react negatively to being pressured. Instead I say, 'OK. So fire away then.'

He looks at some papers that he has taken from a small case, and then looks up at me. 'My understanding is that you led a section at Pasadena, at the Jet Propulsion Unit.' The hint of hesitation before his reference to the JPU makes me wonder for a moment.

'Yes. But you must know that, of course. I and my colleagues developed the science of placing people in suspended animation. When it had been perfected it … it opened the door for long distance manned space exploration.'

Bud's eyes open wide. Now I cannot help myself. 'Bud – what *is* all this? You react as if I'm telling you something entirely new …'

He tenses, then relaxes again. He fixes his eyes on mine. 'The fact is, Anna, that there is a lot that *you* don't know.'

'Like what?'

He takes a breath. 'Just a few weeks after you and your colleagues … suspended, the west coast of America came under attack. It was unprovoked, unexpected and … devastating. Much of California was laid waste …'

I am speechless. He waits for me to absorb the impact of what he has said. Then, 'The response of the United States was immediate and proportionate. The rogue state that launched the attack was identified and … annihilated. Fortunately a global thermonuclear exchange was averted – just. But the repercussions were profound and worldwide. Recovery took … took a long time. It was inevitable that all further plans for space exploration lapsed.'

Bud will not be drawn on timescales. Soon he draws the interview to a close. I guess he has given me all the information I am going to get for now. He takes his leave. As he passes through the door a sheet of paper drops, unnoticed, from the bundle of documents he is clutching. I am about to alert him, but instead wait until the door is closed and go over to retrieve the page. I glance at it. 'Just some stupid memo,' I murmur to myself. This lot are certainly odd. Even the date is wrong. I mean, it is a century out.

* * *

I had such a strange dream last night. I was dreaming of my grandmother. Yes, my grandmother. She died when I was, oh, about 10 years old. I remember quite a lot about her. But in this dream I, well, I remembered pretty well *everything*. Her voice even. Normally old ladies have cracked, quite high pitched voices. But her's was a sort of contralto. Low and sensuous. Otherwise she was much as you would expect someone seriously old to be – deeply wrinkled skin and glasses with lenses so thick that it made her eyes sink back almost like pin-heads into her skull. And her hair was straight, short and the colour of steel.

She spoke to me. Her voice was earnest, as if she were desperately trying to get some message to me across the years. I've tried so hard to recall what it was she was saying. But I just can't.

* * *

They are looking furtively at me. Then they talk among one another again. Something of great moment is to happen today. I can guess what it is. But why are they so reluctant to come clean with me?

The doctor – the woman – has approached me. It seems to cost her such an effort. Her eyes glisten as if she is trying to fight back tears.

'Anna,' she says, 'the time has come.'

'The time for what?' But I know what. I think I am goading her.

'For you to meet your grand-daughter, for you to meet Shenandoah at last'.

I nod.

'She will be able to … to answer all the questions we have not answered.'

'The questions you were *afraid* to answer'.

She nods slowly, so slowly.

'My God', I say. 'There you are, so high and mighty … so *advanced*. And yet when it comes to the things that really matter you've all just funked it. You have to leave it all to … to a *child*'.

They can be in no doubt of the contempt, the utter contempt I feel for them now. You'd think they'd blush with shame. I gaze at them for many moments, but I see no shame. Just … well, just *sorrow*. And an icy hand grips my heart.

* * *

The room is spacious. Tables and comfortable chairs are scattered throughout its length. At first I think, apart from the furniture, it is empty. But no – at the far end there is a figure seated. Alone. Whoever it is sits quietly, gazing out of a small window.

I see that it is a woman. She would seem not to know that I am there. But I think she is only too aware of my presence. And indeed she turns towards me. I approach her and she looks straight into my eyes.

And I know that this is she.

And I seem to return to that strange dream. The wrinkled skin.The thick glasses.The steel grey hair. And then she speaks, her voice a low contralto.

She speaks her name.

Oh God …

THE CATS' MEAT MAN

I just can't believe, Jessica thought to herself, *that this is really happening to me.*

Jessica Mallow was a little over two hours into the flight from Perth to London. It was the first opportunity she had had to gather her thoughts since she'd got the news of her uncle's death three days before. His solicitor had telephoned her from Dorchester and told her that he had died in the nursing home where he had lived for the past six months. As his only surviving relative and the single beneficiary in his will, they had agreed that she should make the journey to the UK as soon as could be arranged in order to see to the various matters for which she, as executor, would be responsible. As it happened, it proved fairly straightforward to put off a couple of social arrangements. It suddenly occurred to her to ask how her uncle had died. Did she detect a slight hesitation in the solicitor's voice? And when he suggested that it was a matter best not divulged until they met, she did not pursue it. At least Uncle Jim has timed his departure conveniently: Jessica was a teacher, and the school holiday has just begun.

It was just about the only thing he *had* done that was in any way convenient for Jessica. She had not known him that well, but what she did know of him led her to conclude that he was stubborn, cantankerous and possessed of a sense of humour that could only be described as cynical, even cruel. As a child in England, on the rare occasions when he had come to see her mother, who was his sister, he and her father had argued bitterly. "Jim's barmy," her father would say, "plain barmy. And he hasn't a good word to say about anyone or anything. Except for those bloody cats of his."

Her mother was more charitable in her view, although Jessica knew that she was often perplexed by him. "I think you're being a bit hard on him, David. Spending so much time on his own has made him a bit, well, *odd*. But I wouldn't say it's anything more than oddness. He's eccentric – that's it, *eccentric*."

Eccentric Uncle Jim certainly was. And yes, any propensity for affection that lurked within his psyche was focussed entirely and solely upon his two Burmese cats which were admittedly beautiful, but spoiled rotten.

And then there was his Will. When last she had returned to England some five years previously he had asked her to pay him a visit, or rather, had summonsed her to his presence.

"So, girl, tell me – do you have any idea how much I'm worth?" He had glowered at her from beneath his shaggy eyebrows as he sat in a dilapidated armchair, one Burmese cat on his lap.

"I never gave it much thought, Uncle," she'd replied. But looking about her, she thought *not very much* given the mean state of the room where he had taken to living for most of the time. But Jim had something of a reputation of being a miser, at least so far as her father had been concerned.

He had picked up her furtive scan of the shabby living room. "Don't be deceived by appearances. I need little enough these days. I don't live like this for want of means, you know."

It had not occurred to Jessica that he had called her to discuss any sort of inheritance that might come in her direction. Since the death of her parents, within a year of each other, she had a fair idea that she was his only remaining flesh and blood. She had communicated with him rarely over the years that she had been in Australia, because, well because she really didn't like him. She'd guessed he must know this. So why on earth would he want to leave anything to *her*?

"No matter," he'd continued, "the fact is that everything I have is coming to *you* when I die. Who the hell else would I leave it to? There *is* no-one else." Observing to look of confusion on his niece's face he chuckled briefly, "I'm not the sort of fool who'd leave it all to a cats' home, you know. Too many damned cats …"

"Uncle, I've never thought, never expected …"

"Oh, I know that. I'm not a fool. I know *you*. The decision wasn't automatic, you know. I've been watching you." She had wondered how on earth she could have been watching her when she was on the other side of the world, but she didn't challenge him. "I don't have much of an opinion of people in general." For a moment he had seemed to struggle. "But you … I think you are … well, you have a level head on your shoulders at least.

Probably make less of a pig's ear of it than most." He had actually, with great effort, paid her a compliment. She was taken aback.

He reached over to a shelf, the cat jumping off his lap with a growl of objection, and grasped a parchment envelope. "But there are conditions," he'd continued. He fixed her with a hard gaze.

"Yes?"

"This is my Will. Essentially it leaves everything, virtually everything, to you. I won't tell you how much, but it's not to be sniffed at. One of the conditions is that you do not open it until after I am dead. If you do, it will become invalidated. The details are contained in it –what is to happen if you were to disobey me in this respect. The other is that certain things, very straightforward things, are to be done when I die. These instructions are to be carried out. If they are not, then again, it will be rendered invalid and the estate goes elsewhere."

For a few moments Jessica had remained speechless. She felt confused. He had seen, probably expected this, and waited in silence while she took it in. "Do you understand?" he'd said at last.

She nodded. "Yes. Oh, I'm sorry, Uncle, to sit here like an idiot. I'd really not expected … it's terribly good of you …"

He had shaken his head. "Well, best wait until I kick the bucket. You may be in for a bit of a … a surprise." Had there been a touch of malevolence in the faint smile that has crossed his face? It was that that had remained fixed in her memory of him, and troubled her from time to time over the years. She never saw him again.

Back home, Jessica had put the sealed envelope away in a secure box file where she kept other important documents: her birth certificate, marriage certificate and the paperwork relating to her divorce. She gave it little thought, and it never occurred to her to break her undertaking to Uncle Jim.

With the passing of years her memories of the old man dulled. She settled into the routine of her work and occupied herself with friends and her various interests. She engaged in a brief affair with a married man, which she herself ended when she sensed that she was being used and she could see no future in it for her. Contact with her uncle was occasional and brief, confined almost entirely to an exchange of cards at Christmas. He gave her no news of himself, although she wondered latterly if his health was failing. His few words seemed to be written by a trembling hand. The Christmas immediately before his death brought no card at all.

The telephone call from the solicitor, while not entirely a surprise, provoked a spasm of guilt. She had never really taken in that she was probably going to benefit, and quite substantially, when he died. Should she have done more for him in his last years? But he had never once asked her for anything, and had never said nor written anything that suggested that he had the least interest in her.

When the news of his death had sunk in, she recalled his insistence that she should not read his will before the event. She wondered, had she done so, how she might be found to have been in breach of his directive. And his making very clear the consequences of failing to carry out his instructions stipulated in the will itself had made her wonder just what it was that he had wanted done after his death. So when she retrieved the envelope and slipped the paper knife under the flap, she had felt a sense of trepidation.

Now, staring down at the shifting cloudscape below her she remembered the sense of horror and disgust that had nearly overwhelmed her when she had read and re-read her uncle's will. Yes, he had indeed left all his very considerable wealth to her. But the condition he had set had provoked a flood of nausea, which returned to her in waves when she thought about it. Could she go through with it? Would she be *allowed* to go through with it? Really, she wondered, would any amount of money in the world compensate for having to arrange something so utterly gross?

When she had convinced herself that she had not misunderstood anything – it was certainly clear enough – she had slipped the document back in its envelope. At this moment it was in a pocket in the large case that had been stowed in the hold of the aircraft. But she could recall the condition that Uncle Jim had set word for word:

On the matter of the disposal of my bodily remains I give the following instruction and make the leaving of my estate to my niece Jessica Mallow conditional upon this being carried out: that my body be dismembered, rendered and processed in such a way that it may be sealed and preserved in cans, and used to feed my two cats until all the processed remains have been so disposed in this way. There had been more, but even the briefest reflection on it turned her stomach.

Just what the hell did he imagine I was going to do? She pondered, *telephone the local Kittymeat factory and ask them to do a special job for me? There's surely got to be some law against such … such depravity.*

She shook her head. *No. I don't think I could go through with this. For any money.*

She spent the rest of the flight and the twelve hour stop over in Hong Kong restless and troubled. She pondered over what Uncle Jim's solicitor would have to say about it. Might he be able to find a way out of this? Could the will be deemed invalid on the grounds of … of insanity?

It was not until she booked into the hotel in London that she was at last able to rest. She slept for almost twelve hours.

On the afternoon of the day after her arrival she made her way to her uncle's solicitor's office in a suburb of west London. After a brief wait she was ushered in to his office by the receptionist. He greeted her with a smile and a handshake, enquired after her journey, and motioned her to a chair. He introduced himself as David Tilley.

"Well, firstly, Miss Mallow, may I offer you my condolences on the loss of your uncle. I imagine it was something of a shock to you."

She shrugged. "Well, I didn't know him that well. We were only in touch once or twice a year. And, please, call me Jessica. The 'Miss Mallow' thing … well …'

'Of course – Jessica. So – now I expect that you are anxious to discuss the content of your uncle's Will. My understanding is that he stipulated that you should not know the content of it until after his death?'

The young woman nodded.

'And – may I ask, have you read it?'

'I have. And I am – I am …'

David Tilley raised his right hand, in a gesture clearly intended to preclude any elaboration she may have intended. 'Forgive my interrupting,' he said, 'but I think it best that we leave the, er, *detail* of the directives contained in it. There is something I need to talk to you about first. You did ask me, when we spoke before you flew over here, about how your uncle died …'

'Yes. And you told me that you thought it best that …'

'Quite. Well, I can tell you now …' he looked down at his hands and seemed momentarily agitated, 'I am sorry to have to give you this news Miss Mallow – Jesicca – but your uncle died in a fire in his room at the nursing home where he was a resident.'

'Oh my God …'

'As you may know, the home is a converted manor house. It seems that he was trying to burn some of his papers in the hearth. He had fairly advanced Parkinsons disease, you know. It's not difficult to see how the … accident … may have happened'.

'The poor man. How *dreadful*'.

'Yes. Dreadful indeed. Fortunately the fire services attended very quickly. Although everything in his room was destroyed, there was little damage outside it. And thankfully, no-one else was injured.'

Jessica remained silent, absorbing the impact of what she had been told. After some moments, a question began to form on her lips. Once more the solicitor interrupted her. 'I understand that the heat was very, very intense. There was hardly anything left – nothing recognisable'.

The young woman looked across at him. And an understanding seemed to pass between them.

'Perhaps I need to reassure you,' David Tilley continued, 'that there is no reason than I can see why this regrettable event in any way affects his leaving of his estate to you. Some – other – things may be best put aside, if you follow me.'

'But I just wonder …'

'Yes, Jessica?'

'His cats … what happened …?'

'Oh, his Burmese cats. No, they weren't there. They were very old in any event. Just two weeks before he died the matron called in the vet. Because of his illness your uncle Jim wasn't able to care for them any more. Naturally he was very upset. But it was for the best.'

'Yes of course. For the best'. And she rose to take her leave.

THE BEACHCOMBER

Two police officers stood at the front door. Some questions about where I had lived before moving in to the flat. And then, with appropriate gravity, 'We have to inform you sir, that human remains have been found at that property.'

I was thrown by the announcement. In my initial confusion I found my mind racing back to happier times. When my son was preoccupied with the adventure of growing up, and his mother still my wife. He now irrevocably lost to me; she also lost to me, having sought solace, and finding disillusionment, with another man even while we still lived under the same roof.

I was shocked, and frightened. Were they accusing me? Would I be spending tonight and many more to come in a police cell on suspicion of murder?

'Are you able to account for them?'

Of course I could account for them. I knew at once the significance of their discovery, and wondered how I could have been so careless. Our leaving the house that had been home, a contented home to our small family, had been precipitate. It held too many memories, which could only sustain a grief that was almost impossible to bear. Even then Mary and I had started to bicker and on at least one occasion had had a furious row, over nothing very much in particular. I know now that this had more to do with our suppressed rage at our loss rather than anything seriously wrong between us. And a sense of shared guilt which I know now was groundless. Yet we were almost consumed by it.

Michael … Miko, you were my only son, my only child. And I adored you. What might you have become had had you not gone? Every parent sees their child as exceptional, but there surely was something quite unique about you. Not just the driving curiosity common to all young children, but the sheer joy you experienced in your discoveries. You were a hunter after things to fire your imagination, and your imagination fired further your desire to seek out yet more wonders in the world where you found yourself. You of the grimy knees, the scuffed shoes, unkempt hair and perpetual grin. Yet you were quite without guile. You were a respecter of wild things and their habitats, although there was little enough that they could keep secret from you. Fossil hunter and star gazer you were. And an avid beachcomber on our occasional holidays by the sea.

I hear his voice even as I think about him. 'Dad, Dad! What's this? It looks like a baby shark!' He had run to me clutching a dogfish, pretty much intact and only recently dead, judging by the absence of stink. He insisted on taking it home. 'I've seen fish pickled in jars in the museum. Couldn't we do that?' I warned him of what his mother might think, but he was not dissuaded. At a hardware store on the way home we bought a quantity of methylated spirit under the suspicious eye of the brown-coated shop keeper. An hour later the creature was consigned to an old sweet jar, suspended incongruously in purple preservative, and placed with pride on the mantelpiece in the boy's room.

He was drawn to the sea and the sea shore. Even the days in high summer were not long enough to satisfy his desire to seek out exotic treasures in the shingle and the flotsam cast up by the previous winter's gales. On two or three occasions we gathered driftwood and lit fires in a roughly constructed hearth of stones. Sausages cooked in a cheap frying pan, fresh bread and tomato sauce we feasted upon. I see Michael's ketchup smeared face split by his grin, and in my imagination I ruffle his hair again. No queen or king ever delighted in such banquets as we tasted then.

Back home he arranged his treasures haphazardly in seed boxes and placed them on roughly constructed shelves in the redundant hen-house. Outside he hung a sign 'Michael's Miniature Museum'. Friends and visiting family would be taken there for a tour of his exhibits. Not all shared his enthusiasm, but this invoked little more than pity in the boy. 'Dad, they just don't *see*' he once said to me in a tone of exasperation.

I saw his point – and theirs. Not many shared his enthusiasm for abandoned birds' nests, the bunch of porcupine quills given to him by a keeper at the zoo, and his prized dogfish. But his collection was essentially for his own enjoyment and it seemed that he thought little of other people's views on it. As the months went by it became clear that finding a space for everything was going to be a problem. And it was equally clear that any sort of a 'cull' was not an option for consideration. I noticed, however, that with the passage of time he did become more selective about what he picked up.

The last summer that I shared with him was what I guess was something of a pinnacle for the boy. We rented a cottage on a remote part of the Suffolk coast, close to one of its wide estuaries. Desolate and wind whipped, it clearly appealed to something deep within Michael's heart. I never saw him so happy. He did his homework too. 'Did you know, Dad, that a whole town was washed into the sea just here?' he told me as we walked at the foot of a low, sandy cliff. 'They say that on some nights you can still hear the church bells ringing deep under the water!' His mother put her foot down at his suggestion that we might camp out there so that we could experience the ghostly tolling for ourselves.

'You could get swept away by the tide in your sleep' she cautioned. He did not press the matter. For he had also learned that the coastal erosion was still very much ongoing. Yet he seemed content enough to occupy himself pretty much entirely with his searching among the sea wrack for whatever might lurk beneath the glistening fronds. This year, too, he became more inclined to wander off on his own, always promising his anxious mother that he would not go so far as to lose sight of us or we of him. The fact that he showed fewer of his discoveries to us caused us less concern. With hindsight it may well have been that we were remiss in showing less interest than we might have done. But this was all in the days before contamination with used syringes and other unsavoury human detritus had begun to blight our shorelines.

I did not discover the full extent of his collection until early in the next year, when I was able to steel myself to go through his things.

'Sir?' one of the officers jerked me out of my reverie. 'Are you O.K? It's not as if we'd suspected … the pathologist said that the bones are very, very old.'

I nodded. 'Yes, I know they are. Hundreds of years old.'

'Much older than the house even. Seems that they were put there. In a box, under the stairs. So you know about them?'

With relief I realised that the police officers were not, after all, making any sort of criminal enquiry. Perhaps they already had a pretty good idea of how the remains had come to be there and just wanted confirmation.

I nodded 'Five years ago … we, my son and his mother and I … we were staying near the east coast. It's a part that gets hammered by the gales in the winter. I'm told that the waves smash into the cliffs when the tides are high. They're soft, and several feet get cut away each year …'

I recalled the conversation I'd had with a local man, a retired coastguard from a nearby town. He told me how some years earlier the erosion reached the edge of the grounds of a long ruined monastery, encroaching at last upon the burial ground of the monks who had lived and worked there. It seemed that the sea was no respecter of the dead. In the wake of every onslaught was a scattering of bones across the shore. When he found them I think Michael must have realised what they were and could not resist taking such as he came across and adding them quietly to his other trophies.

But I did regret his not telling his mother and me what he had done. It was never in his nature to be secretive.

'We thought that might be the way of it, sir. Probably best if you have a quiet word with your lad some time. This has taken up some police time that could have been better used …'

'Of course. I'm sorry. I'll have a word with him … later today.'

They took their leave and left me to my thoughts, and the lonely evening that lay ahead of me. At last I put on my coat and set out on the familiar route to the cemetery. Ten minutes later I was standing by the grave. 'Well now, Miko … would you ever guess who came to see me today?'

BLIND ALI

'So, Jean – just stay calm and remember what I've told you. I'm on my way *now* and I'll be with you very shortly' The confidence in Maria's voice concealed her mounting anxiety. Outside a late autumn fog was gathering. And it was almost dark. Hardly ideal conditions to be setting out in a car.

The assignment itself didn't pose any anxieties for Maria. She was experienced and confident in her role, used to making quick decisions on her own. And she knew that this particular client was unlikely to pose any problems though getting to her in time might not be so straightforward. Things weren't made any easier by the fact that Jean Simmonds had delayed telephoning Maria. She hadn't wanted to appear to be making an unnecessary fuss, 'calling you out unnecessarily' as she put it. Maria hadn't liked to say that well-intentioned determination 'not to be a nuisance' could, just occasionally, lead to disaster.

She closed the door of her apartment behind her, heaved up her bag, and stepped out in to the gloom. A sulphurous taint in the air and occasional stuttering

detonation reminded her that it was nearly November –
it would soon be Bonfire night. Where did the people of
this supposedly deprived area of the east end of London
find so much money to just *burn*? She wrapped a scarf
around her nose and mouth. 'I think" she murmured
to herself, 'I *think* I'd be better off walking.' She did a
quick mental calculation. It shouldn't take more than
twenty minutes and she knew the roads well. At least
there were no other cases expected that night.

The streets, normally busy at that time of the evening,
were eerily quiet. From time to time, the headlights of a
car loomed out of the mist, the drivers keeping to a crawl.
It seemed to be getting worse, and once Maria missed a
turning and had to retrace her steps. She forced herself
to slow down a little, for a first time feeling a pang of
anxiety. What if she were not to get to Jean in time? And
there was no way that her husband was going to get
back any time soon. She'd told her that he was working
on a site in Birmingham all that week. The offer of work
was not to be turned down lightly in a construction
industry blighted by recession.

Her bag seemed to be getting heavier, and she swung
it round to her left hand. A few yards further on she
nearly collided with two young men coming from the
opposite direction. 'Watch it, darling!' one called out, 'In
a hurry, aren't you? You'll have someone over!'

Maria did not answer. At least they hadn't said
anything … well, *personal*. At any other time she
would have smiled and apologised, but just now her
overwhelming urge was to put some distance between
herself and the men. She hurried on.

The stagnant air was tainted with the stink of decay. A strange silence was falling – the street din and hubbub of traffic were subdued, distant. Even the noise of fireworks had reduced to just the occasional thud and crackle. The world seemed to be retreating before a sense of menace. She paused to peer at a sign under the dim glow of a street lamp. And then disaster struck: quite suddenly all the lights went out. 'Oh *no*!' she murmured, 'Not a power cut! Not now! *Please*, lights, come *on*!'

Twenty, thirty seconds went by … nothing happened. Maria found herself in total darkness. Tentatively she moved to one side, in the direction, she guessed, of the street sign. She misjudged, and her foot slipped off the curb of the pavement. In the distance she heard the crunch of a vehicle connecting with something solid, followed by a man's voice cursing. Painfully slowly, she made her way back across the pavement, coming into contact at last with a brick wall. She shivered, and hugged her bag to herself, seeking comfort and protection from it in her mounting desperation. A deathly silence had fallen, broken only by the drip of moisture falling from the leaves of a nearby tree.

Then another sound, a regular tapping noise, drawing near to her. It was as if someone, something, was seeking her out, bearing down on her 'My God …,' she murmured, 'what is *that*?' And now there were soft footsteps accompanying the staccato rapping, heading towards her. A sob broke from her lips.

'Who's there?' called out a man's voice.

'Don't touch me!' was the only response the terrified woman could summon up. She raised her bag higher against her body, clutching it to herself.

'I won't harm you! What's happened? Where is everyone? Why is it so quiet?' She gauged him to be just a foot or two in front of her. And suddenly she realised that the man was blind, guiding himself with his stick.

'There's a dense fog … and all the lights have gone out. I can't see anything!'

'All the same to me' said the man. 'Don't I know your voice? Aren't you the midwife?'

Maria, overcome with relief, recognised in turn who it was who had found her. 'You … you live in my block of flats, don't you?' It was the Asian man whose apartment was on the floor above hers. 'I'm Maria McPherson. And you, you're …' She stopped, realising that she didn't actually *know* his real name.

'Yes. I'm "Blind Ali". Not my real name, of course. But it's, well, convenient … and I daresay it has a certain appeal for some. And less of a mouthful.'

Maria knew too well that the man was the target of name calling on a regular basis. She knew how he must feel. Or did she? And to her shame, she realised that the words had been just about to come to her own lips. Did Blind … did this man *know*?

'I'm sorry, but I never heard your real name …'

'Chandra. Chandra Jayasuria. It's Sri Lankan'

'Oh, Chandra, you can't guess how glad I am that it's you. Are you able to find your way about in this?'

'But of course! I knew there was a fog, but not that there was a power cut too. And you … you're lost, aren't you?'

She nodded. 'Yes. And I'm desperately worried. I'm on my way to a woman who's in labour. God knows what must be happening to her. She'll be so frightened.'

'Does she live nearby?'

"I – I've no idea. I have no idea where *I* am, for a start. Do *you* know?'

"Of course. We are by the factory in Denman Road. Where were you trying to get to?'

She told him the address. 'OK. We'll be there in about twenty minutes ...'

She did not immediately grasp what it was he intended. 'But *how* ...?'

'Miss Maria ... all the streets within a couple of miles are imprinted *here*.' He raised his hand to his forehead. 'Just put your hand on my shoulder and we'll set off. No need to be afraid.'

Yet she *was* afraid. Not of the gentle man who had come to her rescue, but of the menacing silence about her. And desperately anxious for the young mother who was waiting for her. As if sensing her fear, her guide began talking quietly.

'You understand, I've been walking these streets every day for more than twenty years, since I first came to this country. Safer, I think, than where I lived in Sri Lanka.'

Maria's curiosity was roused. 'Because of the troubles there?'

'Goodness, no. We lived in a rural part of the island, nowhere near the fighting. My family ran a tea plantation. But even living in such a quiet spot carried its own risks'

Distracted from her anxiety Maria remarked 'I can't imagine anything much frightening about that.'

Chandra chuckled again. 'Well, you are right, of course. But alarming things *did* happen, even if not very often. I used to be sent out to work when I was a boy. Would you believe it, a herd of elephants once strayed on to the plantation and did terrible damage. Trampled everything and very nearly trampled *me*!'

'Chandra, you're kidding …'

'No. Really. But I think Pa and Ma were less upset of what could have become of their beloved son, than the devastation caused by those elephants!' He went on talking about his past, his coming to England to take up a place at University, and the difficulties he had experienced in adapting to his new circumstances. It was all small talk, calculated, Maria thought, to put her at her ease. He told her pretty much nothing about himself, and never once referred to his blindness. And then he asked 'So will you tell me, Miss Maria, how you came to be a midwife? I've always admired you. And I've always wondered how you came to have such a lovely Scottish accent.'

And so she told him about her own life and how she came to be where she now worked. She told him that she had been raised in Edinburgh, and how her choice of career had not met with approval from her adoptive parents. They were disappointed that she had not trained as a doctor. 'I am sorry to hear that, Miss Maria' observed Chandra. 'If you will forgive me for saying so, I should have been very proud were I to have had a daughter who did as you have done.' He paused as if considering something, then said, 'And I know too that you have to contend with … with insults as I do.'

How did he know?

'But enough for now. We are here at the front door of your patient.'

How did he know that I am black?

At that moment, the street lights came on. With a gasp of relief, Maria could see that the fog was thinning. She saw the lights flickering in the windows of the surrounding houses. Yes, this was Jean's house. 'Chandra – bless you for being such a wonderful guide to me. And for being so kind and reassuring. You must have thought me very silly.'

'Not at all, Miss Maria. It was my pleasure, and a privilege.'

He faced her and – later she wondered why he did it – he removed his heavy dark glasses. She stared at this face. It was horribly scarred. She realised at once that at some time in the past he had been burned dreadfully. She had to force herself not to recoil in shock, not doubting for a moment that he would sense her horror.

'Chandra – oh Chandra … what *happened* to you?'

A painful smile flickered across his lips. 'Fawkes wasn't the only guy they set light to, Maria. And your parents were not the only ones denied the pride of having a child become a doctor. That much we have in common.'

She shook her head. 'No …'

Maria took his hand and squeezed it.

'Now, you must go in' said the blind man. 'You are needed.' And again he hesitated before saying: 'They are just ignorant, you know. So perverse, isn't it, when we all should be grateful to people like you who come to live and work among us'.

So you must know – must have heard … they have a name for me *as well.*

She turned and walked towards the door. Another wave of anxiety gripped her. What might have become of her patient? Alone, progressing rapidly in labour, and in total darkness. The thought appalled her.

She knocked on the door. She listened intently for a response from within. She heard nothing. She knocked again, harder.

Fifteen, twenty seconds passed. Still silence. Her anxiety quickly turned to dread. She turned, hoping that Chandra might have waited. He could go to the nearest telephone … call the police, an ambulance. But there was no sign of him.

And then she saw a light come on through the frosted glass panels. 'Oh, thank God …' she murmured.

Slow footsteps approached the door from within. A hesitant voice called out 'Who's there?'

'It's Maria, Jean. I'm so sorry … I got delayed.'

The door opened. Jean, dishevelled and wearing a towelling dressing gown stood in front of her. Her hand rested on her swollen abdomen. For a moment she seemed to struggle to get her breath.

'I'm sorry … I was …'

'Jean, are you OK?" Maria interrupted, "has it been terrible …?'

'No, not really. The contractions are regular and getting stronger. But I did just as you told me. I took some paracetamol and went and lay down. And I dropped off to sleep!'

'You've slept all through …'?

'Yes. I was out for the count. Your knocking brought me to my senses. But come in out of the cold. It looks miserable out there. Did you have trouble getting here?'

'Just a bit. But my guardian angel came to my rescue. Now, let's get you sorted …'

THE CLEPSYDRA

You ask too many questions.

Alison glances over my shoulder and then shifts her gaze away from me as if her attention has been caught by something on the distant sea shore. She scowls. Close to us a wren bursts into song. Her scowl deepens.

You ask too few.

There's no need. I *accept*, you see. How can you find any meaning to your life when you believe in *nothing*?

Now *you're* the one asking questions. Only I think that you haven't the least interest in what my answer might be. Or perhaps you might be *afraid* of what my answer might be.

She looks back at me, peering at my face over her glasses. She seems to be searching for something. Some clue. But she won't find anything. She's not capable of it. And neither is she capable of acknowledging any challenge so far as her faith is concerned. It's not up for scrutiny.

Michael – questions are being asked …

Questions, questions. You really have a problem with questions …

No, seriously. It's that … that book you've written.

Which book? To date I've written seven – six published.

Her lips purse. And a hint of a flush intrudes upon the pallor of her unmade up cheekbones. My sister, scholarly and confident as she is, seems caught off balance. She looks down at her feet, then back at me.

You *know* which book.

Then refer to it by its title.

Of course I know which book she means. It appeared on the shelves, oh, three months ago, and it has caused quite a stir among literary circles and the wider public. I was never under any illusion that my sister would share my satisfaction, delight even, at its success. In fact she had been angry, and seemed convinced that I had timed its publication deliberately to coincide with what she thought, no doubt, was a pinnacle, if not *the* pinnacle of her career. And, you know, I don't think I can disagree with her entirely.

I won't – I won't utter any such *blasphemy*. I mean, it's foul …

I nod. Really, she is sometimes beyond my ability to understand. And then I smile.

You know, Alison, I really think that were it ever to be in your power, you would issue a *fatwa* against me. Your sort were burning people like me at the stake just a few hundred years ago. The way you go on, anybody would think you'd like to turn the clock back. This time, though, you may have to satisfy yourselves with a bonfire in the cathedral precincts.

Oh, don't be so childish …

A few drops of rain fall from the darkening sky, and a squally wind whips through the bare hedges.

Better come back into the vicarage.

She puts her hand up to her dog collar, as if seeking to adjust it in order not to appear in any way less than seemly in her domain. She leads the way to the back door of the house and into the spacious living room.

Is this one new? I ask. I am looking at a tall clock standing at the far end of the room.

Oh – Yes. David bought it for me. It's rather fine, don't you think?

'Rather fine' is an understatement. I know a lot about clocks and a little about antique clocks – even if nothing like as much as does my sister – and I would guess that this specimen is early nineteenth century. It wouldn't surprise me if doting, doddering husband David had parted with a good five grand or more to please the wife he adores. And as if in a rejoinder to a compliment it begins to strike the hour – four o'clock – a split second ahead of the five other similar clocks, great and small, in the room. The clanging, chiming and discordant ding-donging grates a little. We remain silent, unable to talk over the clamour, until the last reverberation is spent.

Well, I hope that you are well insured. And that you've got good locks. Matthew 6:19 and all that …

I can't resist the dig.

Alison's look would freeze hell. *Damn you* she almost spits at me.

I feign surprise. Such language, I say, from a woman who will soon be one of only the handful of women consecrated as bishops in the Church of England.

* * *

Later, in my own home in the less salubrious quarter of the city, I find myself speculating over the way in which our paths in life have diverged in the way they did. I have always been quite clear about it, although I suspect that Alison never really understood. She is some two years older than I, and as a child was rather bookish and solemn. Our mother had died when I was six. Father took over our care as best he could, with live in help. He was a churchgoer, although I had no reason to think that his faith had any depth to it. Surprisingly, it was at about that time that he gave his daughter and son a free choice as to whether we would like to join him at the Sunday services. Alison never hesitated in her reply. And neither did I. Father seemed quite unfazed by my response, although I can remember Alison looking quite aghast when she heard me. 'Father, you must *make* him' she had said. He just replied, firmly, '*No*' And that was the end of the matter. And if Alison did not understand me, she might have done well to speculate upon the fault she had found in me earlier that afternoon – it was all a matter of questions … questions. You see, even at that tender age I had the makings of a scientist. Also I was an atheist, even if I did not know it then, and it was only many years later that I started to read widely on the subject, and then to write about it.

For a moment my attention is caught by the object standing on its own in the centre of the low coffee table in the middle of the room. It is a water clock – a replica of an ancient Roman original. My 'time machine' I call it. It is the only timepiece in the room. And I find myself remembering a book I found in our school library at about the same time as the decision that sent Alison and me upon our separate ways: 'Man Must Measure' by Lancelot Hogben. Since then I have remained fascinated by mankind's attempts to measure all things, ever more accurately.

Alison has devoted almost her entire life, I think to myself, on matters lying out of the reach of science and measurement, obtaining her doctorate on a premise of no less than a colossal delusion. And I obtained mine working on the cold caesium atomic clock in Switzerland. Perhaps she thinks me just as deluded …

* * *

Alison does not contact me again in the few days remaining before her consecration, although I do receive a formal invitation to attend the ceremony. Even though I have not received a letter from her for many years I recognise her copper-plate hand-writing in the turquoise ink that always seemed strangely affected for a woman not given to idiosyncrasies. I place it on the mantle shelf, unopened.

On the day itself I remain at home. Maybe I am a little odd, but I find something quite sinister about men and women in robes, light and dark, en masse, much though I love places of worship for their beauty, their sublime music and their sense of intrigue. In due course I glance at my timepiece on its place on the table. It suggests – within its limited accuracy – that things must be well underway.

The telephone rings. It is David. I am surprised and think at first that that my water clock is being perverse, and badly out of synchronisation with Greenwich mean time. A quick glance at my wristwatch tells me that this is not so.

David is evidently flustered.

Where is she?

Who?

Alison, of course.

At the cathedral, surely, with all of you.

No … no. She never arrived. Has she been in touch with you?

No. I've heard nothing from her for days …

In the early evening, when the tide is receding, a man walking his dog finds a woman's body among the rocks at the bottom of the cliff.

They are not long in identifying her. It is Alison. She used often to walk on the high cliffs when meditating or in prayer, and it is soon assumed that this is what she was doing on the morning of her consecration.

Later two police officers call round with questions. I do not think I am of much help to them. Tell me, I say, do you think that she just went a little too close to the edge? Or did she …

No. There is nothing to suggest that it was anything but a tragic accident.

She left no note, and so we have nothing to substantiate any suggestion that she might have taken her own life. No doubt you will all be very relieved to hear that.

No doubt …

* * *

The next day the usual bundle of mail drops through the letter box. I am in the habit of receiving a certain amount of what can only be described at hate-mail, mostly from people who do not like what they are told I write. I can hardly imagine that they actually read it. They devise various fates for me at the hand of their gods. Most I recognise without even opening the envelopes, for they are betrayed by their semi-literacy or inability to spell my name. And these I consign to the fire.

The last in the bundle causes me suddenly to draw breath. The writing is copper-plate and the ink turquoise. I pick up the paper knife. Then I hesitate and place it back upon the table. I look at the writing, and then look again into the blazing hearth.

BILLY RICKY

In the borough cemetery in Writtle Road, Chelmsford, is a monument to the thirty nine people killed by the 367th *Vergeltungswaffe 2*, or V2 Rocket, to strike England. It detonated on Tuesday December 19th, 1944.

My uncle Tod was one of the forty seven people seriously wounded in the blast. He survived, although terribly injured, and so his name is not among those inscribed on the monument. He was blinded and lost both his legs.

After the War, and following many months of rehabilitation, he became a familiar sight on the pavements and parks of the city in his battered wheelchair, and always in the company of his black mongrel, Billy Ricky. He had many friends who would stop and pass the time of day with him or help him and his dog – who was by no means trained as a guide dog – to cross the busy main street. It was their kindness, and indeed the kindness of countless strangers, that kept him going. And they wondered how a man whose life had literally been blown apart could smile and tell a joke as he did. If he felt a single shred of self-pity, he never once showed it.

He always made me welcome in the little prefab that was his home. Life was not easy in those grey days of the aftermath of the Second World War, and luxuries were few and far between. But he always had some treat to share with me. I never met anyone so generous and unselfish. I envied him his attitude to life. He laughed off his disabilities, saying that he would rather concern himself with the good things that life had to offer, than to mope over his misfortune. And I wondered what on earth it could be that counted so much for him that he could be so dismissive of his terrible predicament. But as I said, he had a way of bringing out the best in people, and through his example he showed them that lives can be fulfilled and happy even in the face of extreme adversity. That is quite something, I suppose.

When he was failing at last and could no longer get out, I called in on him several times a week. I know he appreciated my visits. In turn I valued our friendship too – it was as if his good nature was catching. No-one taught me as much about the things that really matter in life as he did. It must have been almost the last time we shared an afternoon together that he took me by surprise by saying to me 'Born lucky, I was!'

'Lucky, Uncle? You can say that when … when …'

'When I've ended up a ruddy cripple?' he laughed. He could be blunt at times. But his smile seldom left his face. 'No. You see, if it wasn't for old Billy here, I'd have been dead.'

The dog, old and grey muzzled now, stirred at his feet at the sound of his name. His tailed thumped a couple of times on the floor.

'You see, he *knew* that rocket was coming. Those things broke the sound barrier. There was no warning. You didn't see anything, and the sound they made when they dropped on you was left miles behind them, up in the sky. But *he* knew. Billy was never given to making a fuss. Always easy going. But there we were, walking up Henry Road on the way to my shift at Hoffman's factory, when he just went berserk. Blimey – I thought he was having a fit, barking, growling, pulling … he pulled me right off the street and I fell in to the gutter, on top of him. And then the most god-almighty bang. That was the last I knew for a week, until I woke in hospital. But Billy was OK, weren't you, boy?' His old dog, drowsing on the hearth, gave another half hearted wag of his tail.

He became more serious. 'Yes lad, it could have been a whole lot worse. Not so much being killed, for my arms were still good, so I could haul myself along in the chair. And I can hear well enough even after that god-awful explosion.' That was a fair point. He spent many hours listening to the BBC 'Home Service'. That was how he kept himself as well informed as he was. He was proud of the fact that he lived in a town they call 'the birthplace of radio'.

The two friends died within a week of each other, not long afterwards. And so at last uncle Tod joined those others whom he would have considered the less fortunate ones in the Writtle Road cemetery. I found myself wondering if, had they ever been offered such a choice, they would have hesitated to change places with him. There can be few men or women who could have coped with the pain and devastation resulting from his injuries as he did, let alone be so convinced of the worth of his life.

As his nearest relative I was approached by the town council who wanted to have a memorial erected in his memory. They even suggested that his name should be added to the list of those killed by the V2 in the final months of the War. I thought carefully about this and concluded that my uncle would have wanted neither of these. Recognition was a thing that meant nothing to him. But to this day his grave is never without fresh flowers left by one of the many people who had befriended or admired him.

Billy Ricky I buried in my own back yard, and marked his resting place appropriately. With his name, of course, adding 'Through his Prescience a Life was Saved'.

For I have heard before that dogs are psychic, though I am sceptical of such notions.

But I am in no doubt at all that Uncle Tod would have been convinced of it.

PETRA

'This time, Bill, it's really serious.' Doctor Laura Tomkins looked up at the slight, frail man who stood at the doorway of her consulting room. How the years had caught up with him, she thought, since he'd announced his retirement. He'd more or less recovered from the stroke he'd suffered three months ago, but he was half the man he had been. She knew that he dreaded then prospect of leaving the practice. After all, it had been his life for more than forty years.

'Oh dear. What has happened *now*, Laura? Not another complaint, I hope?'

'Come in and – you'd better sit down.'

Bill Shotley closed the door behind him and made his way over to the chair facing Laura across the desk. He still had a slight limp. He'd got rid of his stick, rather sooner than he should have, she thought. It was an effort not to let pity show itself in her face. How he would have hated that. But the pressure of their work was unrelenting and gave no quarter to those who were not as strong in mind and body as they had been. The patients expected so much. Had they but shown a fraction of the care and concern to their doctor as he had given to them over the years ... but no. They expressed their dismay that he should be 'deserting' them, and their annoyance that his surgeries overran in a way that they never used to.

She let him make himself comfortable. Then she nodded. 'Yes. The PM told me this morning. She'd had a letter from Mrs Bullslip ...'

Bill knew Mrs Bullslip, of course. At the mention of her name his face fell. She was a summer visitor from London, taking up residence in her terraced cottage that overlooked the harbour. She wasn't a popular addition to the community, expecting pretty much everyone to be at her beck and call. And that included the two doctors at the village surgery, and all the staff. Her constant references to 'my Doctor Stanford' in Welbeck Street and the way he would treat this or prescribe that were a less than subtle reminder that she considered provincial GPs to be very much second rate.

'She was her usual blustery self when she came to see me last week, I remember. But I don't think I gave her any cause to ...'

'Bill – it's not *you* she's complained about. It's – it's Petra.'

'*Petra*? Don't tell me she ... she didn't have a go at Mrs Bullslip did she?'

'I'm afraid she did. I mean, we all know she's become, well, *disinhibited* these last few months. But on this occasion, the PM told me, that her language was pretty over the top.'

Bill Shotley nodded. 'Getting old, like me. You don't suppose she's going senile, do you?'

Laura shook her head. 'Whatever it is, Bill, it can't go on. You know it can't. I think we need to face the fact that we're going to have to let Petra go.'

'But Petra is … well, she's sort of a fixture here. Do you know, she's been here even longer than I have? I can't imagine what the place will be like without her …'

'Bill, I can't imagine what the place will be like without *you*. But I have to accept that nothing can be the same for always.'

'But what will she *do*? I mean, where will she go? She's been in Reception all these years …'

It was less than a week after their distressing conversation that a solution was found for the problem, pretty well by chance. Old Toby Grimshaw called in to Dr Shotley for his usual check-up and an exchange of news. He thumped a bottle of over-proof rum on the doctor's desk with a flourish. 'That's for you, Bill. Best medicine of the lot. But by God I'm going to miss you here. Still, you'll be dropping by of an evening, I don't doubt.'

'Try to keep me away, Toby.' The old doctor managed a smile. Toby had run the village's only pub, 'The Drunken Sailor' since he's sold his old fishing boat some five year earlier, and he was one of the very few whom Bill was glad to have as a friend as well as a patient.

Toby had the attribute of perceptiveness. 'Something up, Bill? I know it's a big change for you, but you always said you had so much to catch up with. Anyone with any sense can see that this is a job that no-one could keep up forever.

Bill observed ruefully to himself that a good proportion of his patients, then, weren't over-endowed with sense. But rather than engage in a discussion with the old seaman on the topic, he told him about his sadness over Petra.

'Is that all that's bugging you? Bill, give the old lady a chance. She deserves her retirement too, you know.' He paused. He became suddenly thoughtful, and then broke in to a smile. 'I'll tell you what … Petra can come and help me at the Sailor! Yes, let her come to me. If anyone can keep the punters on their best behaviour on a Saturday night, it'll be Petra. She's not one for any nonsense, that's for sure. And we've been pals for a good many years, as you know'

'That's true. But Toby, do you really mean it? It would be such a relief. And I'd get to see her even when I'm no longer at the surgery …'

'You surely will. It's a deal then. I don't suppose there'll be too much in the way of … formalities. She can start at the beginning of next week.'

Toby called back again the following Monday. He was expected. He went to reception desk and was about to speak to Ruby, who was on duty that morning. Bill Shotley, who had come to pick up his post, greeted his friend from behind the desk.

A voice boomed from behind Toby Grimshaw. 'I say, young woman, could you attend to me first? I have to catch the train to London, on urgent business'.

'Go ahead, lady,' said Toby, good naturedly. He stood aside.

Mrs Bullslip moved her bulk up to the desk. Behind Ruby something else caught her eye. It was Petra. 'Oh!' exclaimed the woman, 'I thought that you were going to …'

Petra eyed her and seemed to scowl. And suddenly she announced:

'*Move your fat arse, you old bat*!'

Mrs Bullslip turned puce, then purple. 'I've *never* been so *insulted*,' she spluttered.

'Good enough for you,' laughed Toby. Behind the desk, Ruby and Bill could scarcely contain themselves.

Toby called to Petra 'Come on then, old girl!'

And Petra needed no second bidding. She spread her wings and flew over to her new master and perched on his shoulder. She gave his ear lobe a gentle nibble. 'Pretty Petra! Pretty Petra!' she crooned.

Then, catching sight of her old enemy for what no doubt was the last time, she squawked loudly:

'Go piss yourself!'

For a large woman, thought Bill Shotley, her speed of exit from the premises was impressive. Probably done just what the old parrot had told her to!

PRIDE AND PALIMPSESTS

Like ninety nine percent of the general population, I'd no idea what the word meant. If I'd been wise to it, I wouldn't have come within a whisker of losing my inheritance as I did over the space of a few days last year – a few days the memory of which makes me shudder. I am my aunt Dorothea's only living relative, but her opinion of me was mixed at best and I knew she'd toyed with other ideas about what to do with her considerable fortune when the time came to pass it on, rather than leaving it all to me. She has a passion for cats, and there are more than enough good causes devoted to the wellbeing of the feline race.

Always trying to find ways to secure my niche in my aunt's good books – and indeed to reverse the phase of her ill-favour that I was enduring at the time – I thought I would treat her. I'd answered an advertisement in the county magazine: "Pet Portraiture and Palimpsests". Her birthday was fast approaching, and I was certain that a painting of her adored white Persian cat would go down a treat. I didn't bother to seek out my shorter Collins dictionary to find out what was a pali-whatsit. More fool me.

I should have suspected something wasn't entirely right when Tom arrived in a white van at my aunt's house one morning, by arrangement, when my aunt had gone up to London for the day. I mean, he was a caricature, complete with beret, Breton shirt and goatee beard. But I despatched him to the garden where I knew that Scheherezade had adopted a classic pose – as was her custom – in the sun. I sat and read the paper in the living room and let him get on with it. He was a fast worker, popping his head through the open window after not much more than an hour and calling out 'All done!'

He didn't hang around (I'd paid him cash in advance). I'd assumed that the finished work would be delivered in due course. That was another lesson I should have learned – don't take things for granted if you don't want to be taken for an idiot.

Aunt Dorothea returned late in the afternoon. She gave me a penetrating look as she came into the kitchen where I was making myself a cup of tea. She took what I suppose was a look of self-satisfaction on my face as an attempt to conceal a guilty secret.

'And just what have *you* been up to while I've been out?' she fired at me even before she took off her coat. 'Nothing good, I'm sure. Don't think you can fool your old aunt. I can see mischief written all over you. I wasn't born yesterday, you know.'

'Of course you weren't, Aunt. Even I can see that…'

'Don't you try to be funny with me! You think I'm a soft touch, that's your problem. And something else – it's about time you faced up to your responsibilities. A proper job might be a good start. I suppose you're still spending all your time banging drums?'

My aunt was less than complementary about the band I'd set up with some friends. It's not as though we did it for nothing. We did get paid, well, for some of our gigs anyway. But she, being an opera lover as well as a lover of cats, had no time at all for my kind of music. More's the pity.

'So you needn't think,' aunt Dorothea continued, 'that you'll get a penny of money out of me so long as you go on acting the wastrel.'

The band and the stark contrast in our musical tastes was what had got me well and truly into her bad books at the time. Some years before, when I was still at school, she had paid for singing lessons for me. But the glorious tenor voice she had hoped to nurture never materialised. And when the singing tutor finally pronounced me a lost cause my aunt was convinced that it was entirely my fault for 'not putting your heart into it'. I had sought desperately to find a way to reverse the rapid decline of my favour in her eyes, and to me the idea of the cat painting was a stroke of genius.

Aunt Dorothea composed herself and duly made her way out to the garden where her adored Scheherezade was presumably still sleeping.

Her shriek would have woken the Gods. 'Oh, you wicked, wicked boy! What have you *done*?'

She ran in, clutching the cat in her arms. To my horror I realised that Tom had painted her OK. I mean, *literally* painted her. She had been transformed – or should I say she had been 'transmogrified'? What had been one of the best cats of her breed in the whole of Britain had sort of metamorphosed – into a tabby, a very fine tabby indeed. The marking was classic. Only her eyes were the wrong colour, of course.

Fortunately, like most cats Scheherezade was fastidious, and lost no time getting to work on the overpainting with her tongue. I think that Tom, joker as he must have been, used paint flavoured to appeal to feline taste buds. Probably fish paste. But it took her two weeks to wash away with her pretty pink tongue the last trace of the results of his undoubted skill. I though it rather a pity, but was careful to avoid sharing my opinion with aunt Dorothea.

I did see Tom just once more, a couple of weeks later, driving too fast for me to hail him down as I should dearly have liked to have done. The familiar logo was on the side of his van. But as it receded in the distance I caught what was emblazoned on the back. I felt well and truly mocked:

Revamp your cat – just visit Tom
At tabbymakeovers.com!

APOCALYPSE

It was a good cover, mused Bryony as the train gradually put on speed and dropped down into the mouth of the tunnel. How little her innocuous-looking travelling companions knew of the momentous role she was about to play.

For a few moments her mind played with the encrypted message that had propelled her into this venture. *The attacking unit rendered the plant permanently ineffective. However, they found evidence that a quantity of fissile material had been removed prior to the operation. The likelihood is that there was sufficient to construct a device …*

'Excuse me', the girl seated opposite her leaned forwards and broke her reverie, 'but aren't you Professor Walters from Pasadena?'

'I am. But I hardly expected to be recognised here, in Europe. Can I ask how you came to know who I was?'

'But you're famous! I mean, the work you're doing. It's groundbreaking!'

'But how did you come to know …?

'The recent review in *The Scientific American* – on your paper on interplanetary travel. I'm doing an 'A' level in physics. And I read it of course.'

Bryony was really too preoccupied with more immediately pressing concerns to engage in polite conversation with an admirer. Little she knew about the other – secret – side of her life as a specialist agent with Interpol. And God, what a creature she looked. If she came to me for an interview for a place in *my* department she'd get short thrift. Why on earth would she be interested in what a top scientist had to say. Surely some pop idol would have more appeal to *her*. Some of the other passengers looked up from their books and newspapers and whatever else occupied them. A smartly dressed elderly woman murmured, 'space travel … I always wondered how all that expense could be justified with all the poverty in the world …'

Bryony did not rise to the remark. She had had to justify what she did so many times in the past that now she wearied of it. Another passenger, a tall,white haired man commented, 'You may be right. But there's something more noble about space exploration that the obscenity that's just about to start in Paris.'

'The G8?' put in another, a younger, smartly dressed woman. 'Face facts – this is the 21st century. Don't believe all you hear from the anti-capitalists …'

A heated conversation ensued. Bryony kept quiet and looked away. In the corner of the compartment was the one other passenger who showed no sign of interest in the argument being flung backwards and forwards. A tall, gaunt young man, shabbily dressed. Bryony noticed the aluminium case that he had pushed under the seat, now part concealed by his incongruously polished shoes. Odd, too, that he should be holding a copy of the Financial Times. He came over more as an impecunious artisan than anyone with an interest in investments and economics.

As the exchange grew even more heated she found her thoughts drifting again. … *which would have a yield of up to 10 kilotons. Serious consideration must be given to the possibility that such a weapon might have got into the hands of an extremist group. It is essential that all Western governments be vigilant …'*

'Anyway' an elegant, expensively dressed young man with a French accent put in, 'I do wonder if you've all chosen to visit my capital city at the right time. The security is going to be very tight. It might not be easy to get around.'

You are certainly right there, mused Bryony, *but you can have no idea just how tight it will be. And what it is that we are out to prevent. And that should that security fail you, me and tens – no, hundreds – of thousands of other people will be dead by this time tomorrow.'*

For the first time the tall, unkempt youth looked up and gazed quizzically at the Frenchman.

The train slowed down, coming eventually to a halt. Bryony wondered what was going on. She guessed that they must be just about half way through the Channel Tunnel.

… *we believe that the device is intended to be triggered by a sophisticated timing mechanism, giving whoever places and conceals it time to get well away before it detonates …*

Minutes passed. The train remained completely stationary. At last an announcement echoed through its length:

'Ladies and gentlemen – we are very sorry to inform you that there has been a major security alert and we have been told not to proceed. It may be that we cannot continue with our journey until tomorrow morning. We deeply regret the inconvenience that this will cause'.

Bryony saw the look of horror on the shabby young man's face. His legs flexed as if trying to push the metal case away from him under the seat.

A hand of ice gripped her heart.

CASSANDRA

Robert lost no time with small-talk. I'd scarcely got over the shock of seeing him when he asked me, in a voice that had changed every bit as much as his appearance, if I believed in ghosts.

'Of course not. C'mon – aren't we both rational people?'

He looked over to the window and studied the tangle of bushes and the mass of straggling grass and weeds outside, dripping and shaking like a wet dog, after the recent squally shower. He turned his head towards me again and seemed for a moment to struggle to focus.

'If there are no … ghosts, then it means that Cassandra's still … alive. But you're right. When we're dead, we're dead. So it can only be that she didn't die as we were all so convinced she had.' His voice caught, and he started to cough. For a moment he seemed to lose his breath.

'Here – let me …' I said. I took the plastic cup from the table in front of him and held it to his lips, uncertain if it was the right thing to do. But he seemed to expect it. He took a few sips and relaxed. He closed his eyes and let his head rest back. He let out a sigh.

'Has something happened?'

'Sure something's happened. Cindy – look at me!'

For a moment I felt frightened. I wasn't sure of what. There was a sort of *power* in this travesty of his former self. Or was it his barely suppressed anger that scared me?

'I'm sorry, Robert. I can't begin to think …'

'Cassandra did it.'

'*What?*'

'She made it happen. I think she meant that I should die. Die! I only wish I could. The most I can do is insist that they don't treat the next infection I get. Do you know, they got a psychiatrist up to check whether I was in my right mind. Everyone seems to accept that Cassandra killed herself after she found out that I'd left her for you. But here I am trying to convince them that she *didn't*. For a while I was afraid that she'd wait for the chance to finish me off for good. But I'm not so sure now. If I was dead I couldn't suffer any more. As it is I'm in this living hell with no hope of getting out of it. How she must love that!'

I'd often wondered if it had been their differences that had drawn Robert and Cassandra together, like two opposite poles of a magnet. I knew them both for a long while before our relationship began. There were so many things that they just didn't have in common. Others that they did. Cassandra had an unconventional spirituality about her. I guess she was some sort of a pagan. I'd heard it said that they actually met at Stonehenge when he was leading one of the archaeological digs in the 1990s. She'd turned up with a crowd of New Agers, celebrating the summer solstice, and got into conversation with him. I think what won him was her impressive ability to twist an argument around. Robert was a sceptic if ever there was one. But she went on about 'other realities'. It's very probable that she was on drugs, and may well have tried to persuade him to try for himself their 'truth revealing' properties, as she put it. But it wasn't in his nature to do that. The one thing I am sure of was that he was bewitched by her. But not by anything in any way supernatural – she was simply, he told his friends, the most beautiful woman he had ever seen. His impressive intellect was no defence against Cassandra's looks and her charm.

It wasn't difficult to see that such a relationship wasn't going to last. At least, not so far as Robert was concerned. When I joined his team from Cambridge, and we started spending time together, a different side to Cassandra began to show itself. A festering resentment erupted on two or three occasions into fierce rage. She'd tell him that he was messing her around and that he'd no idea what a dangerous game he was playing. She claimed that she could put a curse on him. He didn't seem too impressed by this, and when she made a physical attack on him when she found me in his arms one afternoon, he just took her by the wrists and restrained her. It was shortly after this that he ditched her and moved in with me.

Two weeks after that Cassandra disappeared. What I mean is, her clothes were discovered on the bank of a swiftly flowing, deep tidal estuary, together with a suicide note. No body was ever found. But it was enough to lead the coroner to conclude that she had taken her own life in a disturbed state of mind. The impact of the events took its toll on whatever Robert and I had between us, and we parted within weeks. I took a job on a survey of megalithic tombs in the north of Scotland.

And then, fourteen months after she'd gone, I got a text message from him, telling me that he needed urgently to speak with me and would I come as soon as I could. And I found him in a care home, paralysed from the neck down with no hope of recovery.

'She came back,' he told me. 'She tricked me into meeting her. It was because of her that I had the fall and broke my neck. And she looked down at me before she left me, no doubt expecting that I would die where I lay. And she said, "it's Cindy next". That's why I had to see you'.

'You mean, you want to *warn* me?'

'That's about the way of it. The woman isn't sane. She's convinced that she's in touch with some sort of supernatural higher order. But it was just the effects of the psilocybin or some muck she was on. There's nothing in that at all, of course, but there's plenty of ways in the real world that she can spread her venom.'

When Cassandra first made contact with Robert it was by telephone. His first reaction was that it was a hoax. But as they spoke that seemed less and less likely. She said things that only she could have said. She was very calm and even reconciliatory. When he said that he, and everybody else, had thought that she was dead, she said, simply, "Well, I'm not". She offered no explanation and for some reason Robert's instinct was that it was better not to ask.

And then she asked him to meet her. 'Just to tidy some loose ends', she had said. 'It will help us both to move on, don't you think?'

'I should have had more sense,' Robert continued. 'She said she was staying in a commune. But when I got there it was clear that there was no-one else about. In fact it was no more than a squat, in a pretty much derelict building, I think one of those old Victorian schools. She said something about the "family", as she put it, having gone out to get provisions. She was unusually charming, but kept her distance from me for the whole of our conversation, as if she didn't want me to touch her. At the end of it I made to leave, and as I stood up I heard the front door open, and voices. "Leave by the fire-escape", she said, "they're suspicious of visitors". We were on the third floor. It was then that I felt a bit panicky and got out in rather too much of a hurry. The moment my full weight was on the rusting cast iron staircase, it collapsed and sheared away from the building.'

'And who found you when you fell?'

'The commune guys, of course. There was a hell of a crash and they came running out to see what was going on. If they hadn't, then I wouldn't be here now'.

'And Cassandra?'

'There was no sign of her. The other squatters denied all knowledge of her. They said there wasn't any such person staying there. They were covering up, of course. They must have got her out to avoid any trouble.'

'And you think she might come looking for *me*?'

'I *know* she will. She said as much, didn't she? But she didn't know that I'd survive and warn you.'

'And have you told the police?'

'Sure. But they didn't take me seriously. So far as they're concerned the woman's dead. When I pressed them they got rather … hostile. Asked me if I wasn't wasting police time. I didn't pursue it.'

As I made my way back through the endless grey corridors of the care home I reflected on what Robert had told me. One thing I was sure of – he had told me the truth, even if the police had thought differently. I'd need to keep on the alert, but felt that Cassandra, crazy though she might be, offered little threat even if she managed to track me down at all.

It was that same evening that I got a call from one of the others on the team who had worked with us at Stonehenge, and kept in touch with me from time to time. We exchanged small-talk and bits and pieces of news. I said nothing about my meeting with Robert. And it was at the end of the conversation that she said to me: 'Oh, Cindy – do you remember that strange woman Robert got involved with at the dig? That hippie girl?'

'Why, yes …'

'You remember that she drowned herself after she and Robert split. Well, they've found the body at last. It was in the paper this morning. In a sea cave. Not very nice, I think. After more than a year she was pretty badly decomposed.'

As I put the hand set down, the mobile in my bag shrilled out at me. And I felt a hand of ice grip my heart.

HIS LITTLE SINGING THRUSH

Two strong hands grasped my shoulders from behind. I felt myself being pushed over the low parapet. Horror struck, I gazed into the blackness.

I knew it was my uncle Tod before I heard his voice. It wasn't just the power of his grip. It was the familiar smell of his hands. Sort of metallic and gunpowdery.

'You little bugger!' he spat down my neck. 'Just you let me catch you here once more and I'll throw you down – no kidding!'

I believed him. I'd have been about eight years old then. I don't remember what had drawn me to the well at the end of his and aunt Mavis's garden. I suppose that like most youngsters I was fascinated by anything deep and dark, more so if you couldn't see the bottom.

Later that day, when he returned, mellow, after two hours at Butcher's Arms, he spoke to me again. He wasn't angry like he had been. But he was certainly out to frighten me.

'I meant what I said about the well. There's no water to be had from it now. Not since they drilled the bores for the new estate. But d'you know what *is* down there, boy?' He brought his faced close up to me. The was a dampness on his brow, and beer on his breath.

I shook my head.

'Snakes, lad! Poisonous snakes! Just one bite would kill you. They'd be all over you. You wouldn't stand a chance …'

I took him at his word. Even when I left childhood behind I avoided going anywhere near the old well. But it wasn't too long after he caught me there that he left. He had a scrap yard that for some reason a couple of property developers had their eyes on. Tod Drummond, barely literate as he was, was cunning. He played the two off against one another, and by all accounts made a killing when he sold it. Aunt Mavis wasn't sure just how much he'd made as it was a cash deal, and he didn't hang around to tell her. She put it about that he'd gone off with what she called a "fancy woman". She was pretty upset for the first few weeks after he left, but then settled into a kind of routine. If you could call it that. She kept herself to one small room and kept it clean and tidy enough. But she let the rest of the house go. As the years went by it shed slates, gutters and plasterwork like a moulting animal. The garden became neglected and overgrown.

For a long time I made only occasional visits to my aunt. I was her only living relative, and I felt a sense of responsibility for her. I felt sorry for her, too. She'd had a hard life with uncle Tod. She'd been much under his thumb, and he had a nasty side to his character, which usually showed he was drunk. He'd come home from the pub and knock her about. Yet he could be affectionate too. In those days she'd been in the habit of singing about the house and in her little kitchen garden.

"My little singing thrush" Uncle Tod called her when he heard her.

I didn't like to see her home in the state it was and I offered to help her with repairs, but she always refused me. 'One day it'll be yours, Davy. You can do what you like with it then.'

When I started with the light engineering company in Sefton, just five miles away from where aunt Mavis lived, I started calling in on her more frequently. She always made me welcome and appreciated my doing the occasional bit of shopping for her. As she grew older she became less able to get out and about. She had arthritis and was inclined to be unsteady on her feet. She refused any other help and I guess I and my wife, Sally, were pretty much the only people she saw. I wonder now if this had something to do with uncle Tod. She seldom talked about him, but on the rare occasions that I referred to him, she was defensive. No doubt there was gossip in the neighbourhood, and she wouldn't have anything said against him.

Late one afternoon, as I let myself in through her back door with a bag of shopping, I heard her singing softly to herself. Her voice wasn't what it had been, but I recognised the tune.

'Hark the mavis' evening sang
Singing Clouden's woods amang …'

'That was a favourite of Uncle Tod's, wasn't it aunt?'

She was pensive for a moment. 'It was …' She was Scots, of course. 'Burns. Set to music by one of your English composers'. She stayed lost in thought. Then – 'he was a good man … once. Gentle, even, would you believe it? Then the drink got to him …'

'Perhaps it was as well he left.'

'Perhaps. But he took everything, Davey. Left me with nothing. He had money. But I never found … he never left me with a penny.' She looked away from me. 'All went on women and drink, I dare say.'

'You know I'd always help you out, aunt Mavis. I don't know how you manage at all on your pension.' She shook her head emphatically. But she never kicked up a fuss when I arranged for a few bags of coal to be delivered to stock up the bunker outside the back door.

Not long after that conversation things began to get busy at work. I sensed that there were some changes afoot and Jim Denton, the owner of the business seemed anxious to get a number of orders processed quickly. One afternoon he called me into his office. His jacket was slung across the back of his chair and his tie was loose about his neck. His hair was more than usually unkempt.

'David – thanks for dropping in. Take a seat.' He waved me to the chair opposite his at the desk. 'Thing is, there are going to be some changes around here and you need to know.'

'What changes, Jim?'

'To get straight to the point, I'm selling the business. Langton's have made me an offer, and it's too good to refuse. Mary isn't as well as she was, as you know. I'd like to have more time with her. And this is my chance to get out and retire reasonably comfortably.'

'That's great Jim! I'm pleased for you. Mary will be thrilled, I'm sure.'

Jim nodded. But he wouldn't look me in the eye. He must have known that his decision would have consequences for me that wouldn't be so good. Langton's was a much larger affair than Jim's, and a competitor. The chances were that they would simply close the smaller factory. And even if they didn't, I very much doubted that they would be inclined to keep me on as manager.

'I know this has come as a shock. I'm trying to get an assurance out of Langton's that they'll keep this set up running and hold on to the men.'

'D'you hold out much hope? I mean …'

He didn't let me finish. 'They *know* that this company is efficient and cost effective, OK. And innovative, too, thanks mostly to the work *you've* done. You've got a great future, David. If they decided there wasn't a place here for you, you'd have no trouble finding something.'

If his optimism was genuine, I didn't share it. Yes, I could probably get a job. But it could be a hundred, two hundred miles away. Sally would be devastated, and the kids would be upset too, having to leave their friends and moving to another school. And then there was aunt Mavis.

I stared at the distance out of the window. No doubt Jim knew more or less exactly the impact his news had had on me. 'Davey,' he said, 'you know that I would far rather that *you* took over the business, for all sorts of reasons. If you were in a position to match Langton's offer I'd …'

'Not a snowball's chance, Jim. You know that. I've a fair idea what the business is worth – what Langton's are offering for it. If I went to the bank and asked for a loan that size, they'd laugh at me.'

Jim took of his glasses and polished them absent-mindedly. I could see that he felt awkward. He'd been a good boss to me, and a good employer to the men on the floor. And I couldn't blame him for making the decision he had. In his shoes I'd have done the same.

'You'll make out, David. Any job you apply for, I'll give you a bloody fine reference. This business owes a lot to you, and so do I'.

'Thanks for that, Jim. There's no need to worry about me.'

* * *

Sally took the news badly, as I knew she would, when I broke it to her that evening. She tried to make light of it, bless her, but I could see that she was trying to sort out the implications of it all in her mind.

'I … I'd always thought that you'd take over the firm entirely one day. Jim had such a good opinion of you.'

'I think he's more worried about his wife that he let on. I can see why a clean break is so attractive. Particularly if Langton's are making the sort of offer I think they are.'

'Will you start looking for another job?'

'Uh-huh. It might be sensible to put out a few feelers.'

'Will we have to move? I mean, the kids are settled, and then there's your aunt. She's got no-one else, and she's really become quite dependent on us. And, Davey …'

'Yes?'

'It's just that I'm … I'm not too happy about her'

'Aunt Mavis?'

'Yes. I called in on her today, and I talked to her again about seeing the doctor. And she agreed …'

'*She's agreed to see a doctor*? That's not the aunt Mavis I know … something must be up with her. Did she tell you what was bothering her?'

Sally shook her head. 'No. But I didn't like her colour. Sort of yellowish. Davey – I think she's got jaundice. That could mean something bad, couldn't it?'

* * *

The doctor at the GP surgery was inclined to be reassuring. But I could see that he wasn't entirely happy. His decision to order a raft of tests 'just to make sure' suggested to me that he wasn't sure at all. I played down my misgivings to Sally, but aunt Mavis herself had an air of quiet resignation as I helped her into the car and took her home.

'Whatever his tests show, I want him to be absolutely straight with me. If it's bad I want to know. There's one or two things I need to sort out before I …'

'Don't worry, aunt,' I reassured her. 'These days they tend to be honest and up front, even if the news is bad. But I'm sure it won't be. Like he said – there's lots of causes of jaundice. Often people get better with rest and a change of diet …'

'Not so often when it's in people as old as I am. But we'll know soon enough, I suppose.'

She was right on both counts. Within two weeks she was told – as gently as these things can be done – that she had an inoperable cancer. There was certainly some effective treatment she could have that might give her a year or two. But she was quite adamant that she wasn't having any of it.

In fact I think she did not very much want to go on living. Perhaps because of this her health began to deteriorate quickly, and within a month she was admitted to the hospice in Sefton, just a short walk from where I worked. And it was from there, late one afternoon, that the sister on the ward where she'd been admitted telephoned me.

'Is that David Mason? I'm calling about your aunt, Mrs Drummond. She's taken a turn for the worse. She's quite agitated and she's asking for you. Can you come in and see her?'

'Of course. I could be with you in, er, twenty minutes or so. Is she very bad?'

'She's not good. She's got herself in a state. Just come as soon as you can without breaking any speed limits.'

Half an hour later I was at my aunt's bed side. For a moment it seemed she didn't know me. I think her sight was failing. But when she heard my voice she seemed to become calmer.

'Davey! Oh, I'm glad you've come to see me. There's something …'

'It's OK aunt. It's me. You're going to be fine.'

She shook her head. Her eyes closed. 'It's the end for me, Davey. But there's something … something I have to tell you.'

'What's that, aunt? Take your time. There's no need to upset yourself …'

'It's about the old fox, Davey …'

For a moment I'd no idea what she was talking about. 'The old fox? What old fox?'

'I killed him, Davey. I shot him with the rabbit gun. He was … blind drunk. He came for me with a knife. I shot him.' Her voice grew weaker, and she seemed to drift.

'Aunt Mavis … you don't mean … you can't …'

Her voice fell to a hoarse whisper. 'The old fox. Tod … the old fox …'

Her breathing became laboured, noisy. She lapsed into unconsciousness.

The sister looked in around the drawn curtains. She stepped over to my aunt and checked her pulse. She turned to me. 'Best let her rest now. She's comfortable – not in any pain.'

I nodded. I knew what she was telling me. Less than an hour later my aunt was dead. And on her death bed she had confessed to me that she had killed her husband.

* * *

The police officer who interviewed me was hardly overwhelmed by my account. In fact I felt rather foolish reporting it at all.

'So what you're telling me, sir, is that your elderly aunt told you, just before she died, that she shot her husband … about 15 years ago? Had you any reason to suppose she *did* kill him?'

'Nothing she ever told me before had made me suspect it. But with hindsight … I don't know. It was strange that he should just have *gone* as she always claimed, without ever any contact at all.'

I had given all the details as I knew them, and they were sparse enough. Little wonder the police were sceptical. They recorded the interview with me and said that they would make some enquiries and be in touch. I found myself doubting that they would even bother. In the mean time I had other business to attend to. I'd had a telephone call from a solicitor's office. My aunt had made a will, I was told, and would I come in to discuss it. She had left a small estate, and I was the sole beneficiary.

'It's all quite straightforward,' Mr Donaldson, the junior partner, told me. 'There is her property, of course, which she owned. And a small sum of money in a savings account. And there is a letter addressed to you which I understands contains instructions about her funeral.'

I was under no illusions as to the value of her estate. The house was small, in disrepair and worth little enough in the economic climate at the time. Sally had murmured to me that it might make the difference so far as an offer to buy Jim Denton's business. I'd shaken my head. 'There's no question of that, really.' And she'd not asked again.

Later that evening, I opened the envelope and scanned through the short letter. Its significance took time to sink in. 'Oh, God,' I murmured. Sally looked up from her book sharply.

'Something wrong?'

'No … well, yes. If aunt Mavis *did* kill him, then I think I know where she dumped his body.'

* * *

The two police officers leaned cautiously over the crumbling brickwork of the parapet and gazed into the well. We'd had to fight our way through the brambles to reach it. I hadn't been near the place since my encounter there with uncle Tod, so many years before. Yet an irrational dread reared up inside me.

'You OK sir?' one of the officers asked me, looking up. 'I can't think there's anything too bad down there. It's pretty much full of trash.'

I'd not expected to see the collection of old cardboard boxes, empty pain cans and assorted garden rubbish that nearly filled the well. It came to within a just a few feet of the parapet itself.

'Any idea who threw it all in there?'

I shook my head. 'I've not come here here since I was a boy. My uncle made it clear that I wasn't to go near it. Said it … it wasn't safe.'

He nodded. 'He was right there.'

'Well, whether you think his body is down there or not, if I'm going to have my aunt's wishes honoured I'll have to get it cleared.'

'I take your point sir. It would be sort of … disrespectful to throw her ashes in among all that garbage.'

There was the sound of a vehicle pulling up out in the road. The officers seemed to have expected it. 'That'll be forensics,' one of them muttered. Two white garbed men came round the side of the house carrying heavy cases.

'OK, sir. Best leave this to us now. If there are any … if there *is* anything under that lot, these guys will find out pretty soon.'

* * *

I'd never have the stomach to do the job that the police did over the next few days. I didn't ask what sort of state whatever was left of uncle Tod was in, and they didn't tell me. I think that aunt Mavis must have got his body into his old sleeping bag before she wheeled it down to the well in a barrow, because they asked me if I could identify a piece of material they showed me. Lying across the body they'd found the corroded remains of a .410 shotgun, and a kitchen knife with a long, stainless steel blade.

Things moved on quickly from there. Following an inquest, the Coroner recorded a verdict of the unlawful killing of my uncle Tod, and while it was never fully established that my aunt was the one who had shot him, the police told me later that, so far as they were concerned, they weren't looking for anyone else.

I felt duty bound to carry out aunt Mavis's wishes so far as her ashes were concerned, rather than have them interred in her husband's grave. The well, even after it had been cleared, was not deep, and there was no water at the bottom. I couldn't bring myself to just empty the little casket down it, and instead hired an extending ladder so that I could place the box with at least a measure of respect against the wall at its floor.

I can't deny that it was a scary experience. I've never liked the sense of being enclosed, especially in the dark. I'd taken a flashlight with me, and after I had placed the casket, it was in its light that I saw the two loose bricks in the wall of the shaft, just a foot or two from the bottom. As I reached to prize them out, a gust of wind blew through the tangled brambles that partly surrounded the well's mouth. The tremulous hiss brought back, momentarily, a terrifying memory.

'Uncle Tod's snakes … ' I muttered as the loose bricks fell to reveal what was hidden behind them.

* * *

'No. We're still negotiating,' Jim Denton told me in his office a few days after I had finally had the well filled in. I had asked him if the deal with Langton's had been completed. 'They're stalling, I think. In the end I'm afraid they'll drive a hard bargain. But whatever it is, I'll have to go through with it. Mary's no better, you know.'

'Jim – if I were able to offer you what Langton's had originally proposed, would you be prepared to consider it?'

He stared at me. 'Davey – there's nothing I should like more. But you told me you just weren't in the running. What's changed?'

'My late lamented aunt was rather better off than I'd thought.'

My left hand dropped to my pocket. My fingers clasped the small canvas bag that lay in it, and felt the stones, hard and smooth, inside it. Yes, my aunt had been better off than I thought. Or than she herself ever knew. Uncle Tod's legacy of gemstones was too well hidden, too well guarded, even if the snakes were no more than his fabrication.

Together Jim and I stood up and shook hands.

'Consider it a done deal, Davey! Congratulations!'

GOING IN CIRCLES

I realised that something had got Tommy really fired up from the moment he answered the intercom at the front door. It was something in his voice, though his greeting was as terse as ever.

'Mike – good you could make it. Join me in the study. And put the kettle on as you come down.'

The door release hummed. I let myself in. Minutes later I was standing behind him, a steaming cup in each hand, while he stared into the monitor on his desk. He spun his chair round to face me.

'So. Here you are. I thought you might be interested – well, I know you will be.'

'What have you got there Tommy?' I nodded towards the screen.

'Proof. Evidence. It's … it's mind blowing. But I knew. I've known for a long time.'

'Proof of what?'

'That they really are out there …'

'You're surely not still chasing aliens. I thought you'd left that one behind. I thought you were smarter …'

He slapped his hand down on the arm of the chair. 'Just get this, Mike. This is no wild theory. I've worked it out from pure observation. The maths is complex. It took me years to get on to the right track. But I'm there now. I'm at a stage where I can make predictions that are borne out by real events. Look at this …'

He turned back to the computer monitor and tapped at the keyboard. An image filled the screen. Strange, geometric and – yes – beautiful. I knew that I was looking at a photograph of a crop circle.

'But that's all been debunked! Guys going out into the fields at night with ropes and planks after a few drinks.'

'Mike, do you honestly think a crowd of drunks could have made that?' There was excitement in his voice.

'OK. So maybe they did this first and then laughed all the way to the pub.'

'Not this one …'

'So how do you know?'

'This circle appeared at the foot of Milk Hill in Wiltshire on the 7th July. Those are the map coordinates at the bottom of the screen.'

'So?'

'Mike – I predicted it. I knew – to the hour – when it would appear. And where. I'd known for quite some time.'

'You got some eccentric friends who do crazy things in their spare time then?'

'Stop being so bloody obtuse. Who – what – made this are no country yokels. They aren't even remotely human.'

'Not human. So what are they?'

Tommy's brow furrowed. He shook his head. 'That's what I don't know. The only thing I know for certain at the moment is that they make crop circles – or most of them – and other phenomena as well. They're immensely powerful – and much, much more advanced than we are.'

'So what's behind them – I mean, why do they make these things?'

'Looks as though they are … communicating. But that's just a guess. It's all part of a much larger pattern. Certainly it's not just confined to the Earth. It's possible, of course, that they make them as a sort of challenge, a test if you like.'

'Test?'

'Uh-huh. I mean, I hardly think that they aren't aware that there is intelligent life of this planet. Maybe they were just waiting for someone to suss it all out, and then …'. Tommy hesitated. I wondered if he felt he'd said too much. But I was really playing him along. I mean, the whole idea was so far-fetched. He had to be kidding.

'Are you thinking that they might do something when they realise that we earthlings are on to their game? Taking a bit of a risk there, aren't you?'

A smile played across Tommy's lips. 'I think you'll agree that I have little enough to lose. These guys can do anything, even …'

I shook my head forcefully. 'Your problems are one thing – but what about the rest of us? I mean, this could be one mighty can of worms …'

'Mike – don't try to kid me that if you had the chance that I think I have now – if what had happened to me had happened to you – that you would have hesitated for a moment …'

And he was right. They'd done their best for Tommy after the accident. But it would have taken a miracle to make him what he had been. Were it not for his intellect and his creativity I'm pretty sure he would have given up. Even so, he was tormented by frustration and resentment which could make him very difficult to live with. In the end, even his long suffering wife had found it impossible.

'I'm going for it Mike. And I'm not waiting. If I don't do it in the next few weeks, then it will have to wait until next year. And that's too long.'

'So what is it you're proposing?'

'You'll know in good time. I've worked out where and when the next series of circles will appear. And I am going to be there for one of them. Right in the middle. I'm going to meet them, Tommy.'

* * *

I couldn't take him seriously. In fact I worried if his frustration had sent unhinged him. It was just too far-fetched. Yet, as the weeks went by I found myself drawn to the web sites that monitored the appearance of the crop circles. Four, in fact, materialised in Wiltshire as the crops grew to maturity. One was clearly a fake, but the others I could not be so sure of, they were so strange and unworldly.

On another visit to Tommy he'd remarked on these. 'Oh, yes – I knew they were coming. But they weren't … weren't in the right place. Too far off the beaten track. But it isn't long now …' He wouldn't say any more. I guess he thought that I might interfere with whatever it was he was planning. But I don't think I would have done. Because I never really believed him, until it happened.

* * *

Within a few seconds of switching on my mobile phone that morning in late August the familiar jingle announced a text message. It had in fact been sent a couple of hours before I'd woken. It was from Tommy. Just two letters and two five-digit series of numbers, and the words "come now". It took me only a few seconds to recognise it as map reference. As a keen walker, I had a good supply of large-scale maps in the house, and it was only a matter of minutes before I was poring over a sheet spread out on the dining table. I pinpointed the spot quickly enough: in the low-lying fields south of the Vale of Pewsey in the north of Wiltshire. The heart of crop circle country.

A couple of attempts to raise Tommy on his mobile proved fruitless. It was switched off. Not even taking voicemails. That was unlike Tommy. For the first time I felt a sense of misgiving. I pulled on a jacket, grabbed some walking boots from the under stairs cupboard and went out to the car.

It was still quite early and there was no traffic to speak of. A diffuse early-autumn mist lying low over the ripening fields gave an atmosphere of soothing tranquillity. A copper sun hung above the horizon. As it brightened I pulled the visor down over the windscreen. Soon I was closing in on the field that Tommy had identified as the place where the event – and whatever lay behind it – was to happen.

Driving, now more slowly, over the brow of a hill, I was briefly dazzled by the glare of the sun as the tendrils of mist dispersed. I pulled over to the side of the road and stopped the car. And as my sight returned, I saw it in the valley below me.

I was at once reminded of one of those NASA photos of a spiral galaxy, seen obliquely as so many are. The thing was pristine, exquisitely sculpted. No, I thought to myself, this is far beyond the ability of human beings to have created. Could Tommy have been right? But Tommy, where was he? For a moment I wondered if he would come riding up the lane, calling out 'I told you so!' But there wasn't a sign of him. Then, as the after-image of the sun faded from my vision I saw something at the very hub of the circle. Something dark and crumpled.

I jumped out of the car and without even slamming the door shut I started running. I came up to a gap in the low hedge from where a trail of flattened barley that I knew had to be Tommy's track headed out into the field. In spite of the uneven ground I kept up my speed.

And at last I came to the eye of the circle and found what I had dreaded finding after that first glimpse from the hillside.

Tommy had adapted his powered wheel chair into what he called an "all terrain" model. He'd been quite proud of it, with its low centre of gravity and bulky tyres. This spot, with its proximity to the road, would not have presented any real challenge. But now it was almost beyond recognition. The tyres themselves had burned away, their remnants still smoking. The metal frame was twisted, scorched and broken.

As for Tommy himself – nothing. For a while I shouted his name, but silence was the only answer returned to me on that still morning.

In time the realisation came to me that he really had gone. But where to I don't expect I'll ever know. I miss him more than I could have anticipated. But there is a part of me that hopes, even believes, that he did find what he was searching for.

Tommy – if you are out there – somewhere – I hope that it is all that you wished it would be.

MYTH AND MISDEMEANOUR

Jane found her sister in the gardens. She was sitting on an upturned box, sketching a cluster of delphiniums with the stub of blue pastel.

'Hello Andie. Busy I see. Those are nice!'

The seated woman turned and looked up at her. Jane was struck by how her sister seemed to have aged. Her shock of curly red hair was as it had always been, but her face was more creased than since she was first sent here. Perhaps it was just exposure to the elements – she knew that Andie spent as much time as she could, or was allowed to, in the gardens – or perhaps it was the smoking. Jane, being a doctor, disapproved. And she knew that Andie played upon her disapproval, making a point of lighting up in her presence, which she did now.

'Andie – you know you shouldn't …' Jane shook her head.

'Come to nag me again, have you, big sister? I've told you – it's my body, my life. Stop talking to me like you own me.'

'I don't, of course, thank God.'

The younger woman sighed and turned back to her drawing. 'Look, I don't need lecturing. You've no right to come here annoying me.'

Jane sighed. 'No. Sorry, I didn't mean to. Look – something's happened …'

Her attention caught, Andie put down the fragment of pastel and turned again to look up at her sister. 'What?'

'It's Mother – Ma. She's not well. I was wondering if … if we could arrange for you to get over to see her. I don't think that they'd refuse you.'

'So it's something bad?' Jane hadn't expected that she'd be much impressed. The woman seemed to ponder for a moment. 'Why'd she want to see me anyway? She hasn't bothered herself with me for years now.'

'Andie – mother is … she's dying. Couldn't you at least try to make it up? What good can it possibly do, the two of you carrying on as if the other no longer existed?' She looked pleadingly at her sister.

'Is there any point? And does she *want* to see me?'

'I think she does. Anyway, it has to be worth trying. If there could be a … a reconciliation even at this late stage, you would, both of you would find some solace. I know you and she have had your difficulties, but she's not entirely bad.

'Much she's done to show it …'

The problem, Jane knew, had its roots in the fact that Andie and her mother – Ma as she called her – were more alike than they could realise or acknowledge. Things hadn't always been bad between them. When she was a little girl mother had adored her. She'd named her Andromeda – the daughter of the queen Cassiopeia in Greek mythology, and Ma's own name, although she was always known as Cassie. Mother was a romantic. She used to take them out on clear nights to show them their namesakes in the sky: the constellations of the seated lady, and her daughter awaiting her nemesis in the form of a sea monster sent to devour her. But as Andie grew up she became fiercely independent, constantly challenging her mother. And when she succeeded so spectacularly at art school her mother became envious and bitter. Fierce arguments gave way to physical violence and at last to separation and estrangement almost ten years ago.

'Andie – she's not the woman she was. The fire's gone out of her. And I think it would help her to make her peace with you before …'

'Before she dies? I … I'll think about it …'

Jane noticed that her sister's eyes were moist as they stared into the distance. *I do believe*, she thought to herself, *that I'm going to win on this one.*

A little later she made her way through the security doors, escorted by a uniformed officer. 'I wonder,' she asked, 'if I might make an appointment to see the Prison Governor before I leave?'

* * *

'No! I swore I'd never let her come here again. And I'm not changing on that!'

The frail old woman rapped her stick on the ground. She was seated on a low chair in the porch of her cottage, a shabby coat flung loosely around her shoulders.

'Leave her where she is!' she continued. 'It's the best

place for her. She was always one for trouble. She got what she deserved!'

'Mother – she'll very soon be eligible for parole. I was hoping that because … because you're not well now, they may even release her early on compassionate grounds.'

'Not on my account, they won't. She can just do her time and take herself off wherever she wants to when they let her go. Just so long as it's not within a hundred miles of *me*.'

'I wonder how you can be so unforgiving. And don't pretend that you haven't sympathy with the cause that got her in to all that trouble in the first place. Had you and she been on better terms you would have been camping there with her.'

'I was never one for violent protest. Chain myself to trees in front of the bulldozers, yes, but not arson! That security guard was lucky to escape alive! How could she have been so stupid?'

'As I said, she's learned her lesson. Don't imagine for a moment that being locked up has been easy for her. If they hadn't moved her to an open prison, where she can at least get out and draw, I do wonder if she'd have survived it.' The younger woman paused. 'Please, mother, for both your sakes … I've spoken to the governor. And she's agreed'

'You had no business doing that! I never want to see her again – can't you grasp that?'

'Mother … *please* …'

The old woman shook her head vigorously. '*No*. I won't have her here. Can't you get that into your head once and for all?'

No, thought Jane to herself, *you really aren't going to change the way you feel towards Andie. What am I going to tell her?*

* * *

Jane held open the car door for her sister having arranged her meagre belongings on the back seat. Once in the driver's seat she paused and looked ahead through the drizzle in the prison courtyard.

'Something up, sis?' asked Andie. 'You look a hundred miles away.'

'I'm afraid it is: mother … mother died last night. Peacefully. In her sleep.' She turned to face the woman seated next to her and saw that she was affected by what she had said.

'Dead? Was she *that* ill? Oh …' her voice caught. 'After we spoke … last time. I know I was negative about it all. But I thought, even dreamed about how things were once between us. I'd hoped we might share some memories. In the end I realised I really wanted to see her, to talk to her again … I wanted to say I was sorry …'

Jane put her arm around her weeping sister's shoulders. 'I know it's a dreadful shock. But there's something you need to know: her last hours were happy. Because she knew that you were coming to see her … to put the past behind you'.

'Really?'

'Yes. Really. Now, let's get away from this place. We'll go straight to her cottage. They haven't moved her yet.'

* * *

Andie leaned over the inert form lying on the bed and kissed per pale brow. 'She looks so peaceful. These years haven't been easy for her. Since Pa left. And I know she must have been dreadfully upset over all I did.'

'But deep down she always admired you.'

'Do you think she forgave me?'

'I *know* she did'.

Does she suspect? Jane wondered. What could she do other than tell her these … these lies? During her last hours, when she fell into delirium, their mother never ceased her venomous outpourings against her younger daughter. She had threatened to lay about her with her stick if she set her foot in the doorway. There was nothing for her there, she'd insisted. For all she cared, Andie could go destitute into the world.

Andie nodded. 'That is … that is such a huge relief for me.' The two women stood looking down at the lifeless form. 'So what will you do with the cottage? It must be worth a bit now.'

'I guess it must be. But I need to tell you something: mother had made me the sole beneficiary in her will, as I'm sure you know. That was after things got so bad between you. But when she knew at last that there was to be a reconciliation she asked me … made me promise … that I would see to it that I would pass the house on to *you*. And of course I agreed. I was delighted in fact. You know I've no use for it. I'm secure in the practice. But you – you could start up again here. It has a fine studio, where you could work.'

'I'd never have dreamed … But that was so, so kind of Ma. I've been such a bitch over the years. I really don't deserve this.'

'But you *do*, you know.'

* * *

Late that night, Jane stared up into the sky. There she was, among the most prominent of the constellations, the striking "W" of Cassiopeia.

'So that's what I have done, Mother. I think I was right. Oh, I know it was a lie that I told to Andie. But what you said was so unjust. You see, I began to question whether you were in your right mind. You were so consumed by your bitterness. So I hope you understand that the motive behind what I said to her was entirely for the best. Only you and I know what passed between us on that last night. Andie will never know the truth. The memory she will hold of you can only be the better for that. And she can rebuild her life again.'

AURORA #2

'Thank you for coming. Won't you please sit down?' Professor Fenton indicated one of the two armchairs separated by a low, glass topped table. I accepted his invitation with a word of thanks.

I noticed at once the object resting centrally on the glass surface, fashioned of metal and crystal, and strangely beautiful. The professor saw that my attention had been caught by it.

'Yes, it is a fine model, isn't it? And do you know what it is?'

'Of course.' I answered softly. 'It is a ship. I should say *the* ship. The *Europa*.'

'You are right. And it is on the matter of the Europa than I asked you to see me here today.'

I looked towards him, noticing his studied gaze. I was convinced he could sense the lump forming in my throat, and the wave of emotion rising in me.

'I believe that you … you knew one of the members of her crew?'

'Yes. We were … close, at one time. She was lost, with all the others, of course.'

The professor nodded slowly. Something in his eyes told me that he knew more about the tragedy than I realised. And that he had more than an inkling of just how close the two of us had been.

'I am referring, of course, to Doctor Merriman.' He paused as my gaze dropped to the table and the model that rested upon it. I nodded in acknowledgement.

'What I am about to tell you,' he continued, 'is in confidence. Can I trust you to tell no-one – *no-one* else?'

For a moment I was confused. 'Why, I guess so. Is there something that the general public wasn't told?'

'No. The press release at the time was that Europa had been lost in the Callistan Archipelago … that she had in all probability struck a rock. Communication ceased abruptly, and it could only be concluded that, whatever had happened it was catastrophic and without warning.'

'Yes. That's what everyone understood.'

'What I have to tell you is that there had been a … development.' The professor paused for a moment. 'The Europa has been found. She was damaged, but not destroyed.'

I stared at the scientist, wide eyed. 'But why … why is it that you should involve *me*? I had nothing to do with the expedition. Because of all the security I knew very little about it.'

'Firstly then, I need to tell you that Doctor Merriman is still alive.'

'*Alive*? How can that possibly be? I mean, it's …'

He interrupted me. 'You must accept what I say. I will explain the detail later. But she is alive, and she will very shortly be returned to the biomedical facility here, at Imperial College. For now I need to know a little more about you and your relationship with her. In time you will realise how important this is. I know this will be hard for you but we … we need your help.'

* * *

I was an undergraduate at the Royal College of Music when I first met her at one of our more modest concerts. She had walked up from Imperial College and I learned that she was doing post-doctorate research. She was also a keen – and quite accomplished – amateur musician. And since I was no scientist, it was music that was the subject of much of our conversation. When I did express an interest in her work she wasn't forthcoming. As the weeks went by and we became more absorbed with each other the subject just didn't arise any more. That was, until she told me that her work was going to take her away – a long way – from London, and for a long time. That was when she told me that she had accepted an offer to become a crew member on the Europa. I learned later that there wasn't actually anyone else who was remotely qualified for the particular role that she would undertake. She had been appointed chief life support officer to the expedition.

'So. I'll wait. I'm really not interested in anyone else. You know how I feel about you. I'll finish my degree and then get on with studying composition as a postgraduate.'

It was then that I proposed to her. And, very gently, she refused me.

'Davey – you don't know what it is I'm about to embark upon. It's a research expedition, of course, and

I've not told you much about it because I'm not allowed to. We will be away for a very long time. And then there is the matter of my age.'

She was twelve years older than I. Since I was only twenty-one it was not something easily dismissed. Yet I thought that it would have made little difference to me, or to the way I felt about her, now or in the future. She had misgivings, though. 'Honestly', she continued, 'if you meet someone else while I'm away, I'll understand. And I'll be happy for you.'

It was only after we parted, some two months later, that I learned the truth about where she had gone, and for just how long she would be away.

* * *

'I understand,' there was a slight hesitation in the professor's voice, 'that you – you made a gift to her just a few days before she embarked.' We were walking along the bank of the Serpentine in the late afternoon sunshine.

I nodded. 'Yes, that's true. It was a piece of music I'd written for solo flute.'

'Did it have … a particular significance?'

'Uh-huh. I believe that it was the best piece I ever composed. I've written some passable stuff since. But nothing came near to that. I wrote it for her, and gave it her name.'

'I believe you never published it?'

'No. I made the recording myself. Apart from me, she is the only person who had ever heard it.'

'David – I want you to play it for her again. Will you do that?'

'Professor – I don't understand. What is all this about?'

He turned to me and stared directly into my eyes. 'David – Doctor Merriman has been asleep for … for fifteen years. Since we retrieved the Europa and found her and the three other surviving crew members we have been unable to rouse her. We believe that your music was the last thing she heard before she – before she suspended. And we think that hearing it again might just be the trigger to … to bring her back.'

* * *

She was as lovely in my eyes as she had always been. The dusting of hoar frost had finally evapourated from her alabaster skin. My eyes misted over, but I needed no music score. I raised the Muramatsu to my lips. And I played … *Aurora*.

* * *

The planet Jupiter has an average distance from the Earth of about 700 million kilometres. Transit time in a modern space craft, such as the Europa, is some three years. It was the science of suspended animation, pioneered by Doctor Aurora Merriman and her team that had made it possible for the stupendous journey to be embarked upon, since for its duration they would effectively hibernate, hovering between life and death, their bodies at just a degree or so above freezing point. The deadly collision with one the colossal rocks in orbit around Callisto – the outermost of the four great moons of Jupiter – occurred before the sleeping crew had been revived. And those that did not perish slept on.

* * *

Shock and grief as the full realisation of what had happened came close to overwhelming her. Trained counsellors broke slowly to her the sequence of events. When they had gone I held her close to me as she wept for her lost companions. From time to time I took the flute from the table at her side and played for her. In that she seemed to find peace and healing.

'Remind me, Davey, how old are you now?' she asked one morning. It was a topic we'd avoided until now. But she was making progress and seemed to be adapting to her situation.

'I'm thirty-seven.'

'Well, it's time I knew something about *your* life – what you've been doing over the past fifteen years. I know that your reputation as a composer is an international one – and that's really no surprise. But you never told me if you found the love of your life, like I told you to …'

I did not answer her directly. Instead I walked over to the window and gazed down at the streets of South Kensington. And then I asked her in turn: 'Tell me, Aurora, how old are *you* – now?'

For a moment she seemed uncertain. 'Why – I … I'm … I must be nearly fifty.'

She looked away from me.

'No – not nearly fifty.'

'Don't be silly. Of course I am.'

'Aurora – come over here to the mirror, and look at yourself.' And she did. And I guess she must have known anyway, but I told her, told her what Professor Fenton had said to me when I first gazed down upon her in the incubator, and wondered at what I saw:

'*You must understand, David, that in suspended animation metabolism virtually ceases. And that includes the aging process. Aurora is the same age now as she was when the Europa was launched.*'

She nodded, and then whispered, 'Of course. You're right.'

'So I am thirty seven. And you are – still – only thirty three.'

As she turned to me the tears filled her eyes. 'Oh, Davey – what have I lost, what have I *missed*?'

I held her to me. 'Not me, at any rate. To answer your question, I did find the love of my life. I found her here, all those years ago. There's never been anyone else.'

And then, for the second time in fifteen years, I asked Aurora to marry me.

LELLA

I hear the gate latch rattle. And through the mist I see him. Josh. He opens the gate and just ... just stands there, staring at me. He smiles. He's got a bit of a cheek, really. I mean, he's left it a bit long. Just how long? Not sure, really.

I must have started, for Lella grunts – did you know that an ordinary moggie could grunt? – and slides off my lap. And then she spots him, and he calls to her. And I call out: Hey, Josh, who is it you've come to see? Me or my cat?

I didn't know Josh had a way with cats. Lella is shy, if not downright bad mannered when it comes to strange men trying to attract her attention. But off she trots, and in a moment is sidling around his ankles. He bends down and strokes her head.

'Hi missy!' he calls down to her. 'You're looking very handsome today. Did God tell you you're a Good Cat?'

Judging by Lella's reaction, God evidently has. I wish that I were so favoured. Then maybe I wouldn't be in the state I am now.

Josh looks up, looks towards me. But not at me. He is looking behind me, and it occurs to me that he is looking at the cherry tree again, heavy with blossoms. His face breaks into a smile, so enchanting that I feel my heart warm. Oh God, I do believe I am going to forgive him and let him put me through all that pain again. And now he is looking straight at me. His lips move, but whatever it is he is saying to me I am not hearing it. Something good, oh, let it be something good! I think he is asking me to look at the blossoms. But I can't … bloody … turn round. Lella must have heard my efforts for she is weaving her way back to me over the grass. For a few moments I am distracted, watching her lithe grace with deepening envy. And when I look up again, Josh is gone.

Bloody typical.

I smooth my lap ready for Lella to take up position again. But something has caught her attention. She's looking behind me now. Of course, she's admiring the cherry tree. Perhaps she's thinking in anticipation of the time a few months from now when it will be laden with fruit. Not that any self respecting cat would have the slightest interest in cherries. It's the blackbirds that take her fancy. But fat chance she'd have of doing a blackbird – or any other bird for that matter – a mischief, being the size she is.

Lella glides off behind me, out of my line of sight. Then I hear a rasping sound. If she's having a go at the wicker garden chair again I'll throw something at her. I really ought get someone to put that chair out of her reach where she can't get at it. But there are memories, thoughts of happier times …

I heave myself round. Where has all my strength gone? Or have the wheels on this bloody thing seized up?

Oh, thank goodness. It's not the wicker chair that Lella is working on with her damned claws.

It's that tree stump.

The sun disappears behind a cloud and a penetrating cold wraps itself around me.

MIXED MESSAGES

Being 'duty' doctor the day after a bank holiday weekend is a challenge. Massed ranks outside the surgery door half an hour before opening time. My co-duty doctor and I give each other a knowing look. 'Right – let's get stuck in'. One of our nurses has called in sick, so the nurse practitioner who would have made up the trio for the 'emergencies' has had to take over her clinic, leaving my colleague and me one third more patients to get through in the morning.

I am a fast worker when the occasion demands it. A forty year old woman with shingles followed by a mother with her little boy with a sore throat and cough take no more than six minutes each. A man who fears he may have skin cancer but hasn't, a few minutes more. No small part of the skill needed for this job is in not making them think that my brevity means that they have been short changed, and always to treat them with courtesy and sensitivity.

The next patient is desperately ill, evident to me as he stands in the doorway of the consulting room. He is grey and sweating, his right hand clenched over his chest. 'It's this pain – like a vice!' A few more quick questions, a glass of water and a tablet. I reach for the phone. 'Penny – I have Mr C here. Sudden onset of severe chest pain. Can we get him to the treatment room?' 'I'm on my way,' says our very able nurse, not wasting time with further questions apart from 'Have you given aspirin?' 'Yes, just now.'

In the treatment room she helps him on to the couch and, so casually yet so deftly you would scarcely notice it, places a box on the instrument table next to him, just out of his line of vision. Mr C doesn't know it, but this is the defibrillator that the same nurse checked on her arrival that this morning and which will kick his quivering heart back into life should the need arise.

The receptionist is already ringing for an ambulance and goes on to alert A&E where he will probably arrive in the next ten minutes, school traffic allowing. I quickly dictate a letter into the computer with voice recognition software and print out a potted history to assist them in the casualty department.

And all that took – eleven minutes.

A pause. We should be having coffee now, but fat chance of that on this post-holiday Tuesday.

'Henry,' says my colleague, 'I can deal with three of these visit requests. The usual – old folk feeling "a bit poorly" and I'd like you to come and check me out' sort of thing. But there's a new baby check. Can you do that?' 'Uh – on a busy day like this? It'll wait until tomorrow, won't it?' 'Oh, come on. We've broken the back of it now, and I'll deal with the others'. 'Oh, OK then ...'

I set off on my bike. Ours is an inner city practice, all 13,000 of our patients living within an area of a square mile. Quite honestly, the bike is quicker. I make my way through road works and badly parked cars. Then it starts to rain. Ahead of me I make out a sign outside a small non-conformist church. It announces: 'All sinners welcome here'. 'That'll be me,' I think, and hastily prop the bike in the porch and duck inside. There is no-one else there. I sit in one of the pews, brush the raindrops off my jacket and get my breath. I feel that perhaps I should be saying a prayer but the problem for me is that I've forgotten how to. The shower soon passes and I set off again. Funny – the sign is different now. This time it says to me '*Only* sinners welcome here.' I think 'funny thing – Christianity.'

The family with the new baby live in a modest terraced house, late Victorian I'd say. Rather shabby. Someone has done a repair job on the front path with cement. Some words had been scrawled into it before it had set – 'Jesus is Saviour and Lord'. Or maybe it was 'Lord and Saviour'. I don't know, but I guess there is a protocol about these things. And for some bizarre reason I found myself thinking back to another occasion when I had seen a notice near to the gate of someone's house when out on visits. This one had been cut into slate and was altogether more classy, and almost on pavement level. 'No Dog Shit, Please' it said. I wondered if either of these inscriptions would survive the passing of their respective homes to new owner. I conclude that the latter had the better chance, and I feel momentarily sad about that.

I am expected. An angel opens the door to me. She looks to be about five. 'I hear that you have a new baby!' I say. 'I'm the doctor and I've come to see if everything is OK!'

She grins at me. Her daddy is coming down stairs, a slight young man with spectacles. The angel takes his hand and they lead me to the front bedroom where the mother lies cradling her new baby. Two more angels, the younger sisters of the one who greeted me at the door, stand close by her bedside. They are clearly ecstatic with their new treasure. I think how beautiful the new mother looks, for a woman essentially so plain. No doubt hers is an occasional beauty…

I note a religious text on the wall, and two books on the bedside table, one a bible, the other of prayers. I am on my guard and I hope it doesn't show. In the past I have been guilty of more than one faux pas in the presence of committed Christians. One occasion I remember with particular embarrassment: it was not long before Christmas and I had asked a child if she was looking forward to Santa calling. She looked bemused and her mother looked icy. 'We don't have Father Christmas in this family,' she said. They never came to see me again, whether by intent or circumstance I don't know.

The infant is undressed. It is a little girl, their fourth, and exquisitely beautiful. Without meaning to I cast a glance at the father. One man among five women. Could be have been disappointed? Had he hoped – prayed for – a son? I suppose I will never know.

I ask if I may wash my hands and I am shown to the spotless, if chaotic, bathroom. As I undertake the ritual and routine of the examination of the new baby I 'talk through' what I am doing and why to the parents and audience of little ones, as has long been my habit. I enter all the details on a blue form, virtually the same form upon which I was trained in such examinations almost 40 years ago. How quickly time has fled by! And I speculate on the near certainty that after another such lapse of years I will be dead.

Funny – in all the years of doing 'new baby checks, I can't remember a single instance when I have picked up something that needed immediate attention. Well, nothing that the midwives hadn't picked up already. But I love seeing families with new babies. Is this what I am here for, though? Am I to be allowed the luxury of doing things just because I love them, when the demand on our time is as it is? I put aside this pointless train of thought and my mind goes back to the father with no son. Perhaps, when I am long gone and forgotten, he will be blessed with a grandson, as I have been, and know the ecstasy of the kick of a football with a laughing toddler in the park. And my darling granddaughter will fuss over me as I grow more feeble and she more lovely with the passing of the years. Yes, the imperfect among us cling on to our stereotypes with a grip that I do not believe will ever be broken – however hard they may try – by the proponents of political correctness.

Fifteen minutes after my arrival at the house I am setting off again. I spot Mrs Dobson in her front garden, and I pull my bike in and lean it against her fence. For a few minutes we talk together. She asks if I am having a busy day and I laugh and say that I should hate not to be busy. I look down at the stone around which she is carefully clearing weeds. I see for the umpteenth time the inscription on it that she has never seen – Mrs Dobson has been blind since birth. She knows the words by touch as well as I do by sight. She has told me that the stone was there when she first moved into the house with her late husband some fifty years ago. 'No doubt it is a memorial to someone – or something – dearly loved. So I shall tend it for as long as I am here.' I recite quietly to myself and I am glad that Mrs Dobson does not see my eyes mist over:

> *There is no darkness*
> *In the whole world*
> *That can put out the light*
> *Of one small candle.*

Old dog I may be, but I still learn new tricks every day, and still make the occasional addition to the repertoire of knowledge and skills demanded of my profession. Yet all that seems less important than it once was, retirement not being so very far away now, and feeling as I do a sense of saturation with it. But I learn much more these days about *people* and what makes them tick. And most of all, I learn about myself.

MRS MEE

Old Mrs Mee wrote down her next appointment with the doctor in her calendar. Then, just below the time, she added 'Problem – my dizziness'.

She liked to think of herself as a 'good' patient. One who wouldn't trouble the doctor unnecessarily, or take up too much of her time. She was a very busy lady, was Doctor Mabley, and Mrs Mee knew that she had a young family to get home to. That was why, she reasoned, that on each wall of the waiting room there was a sign that said: 'One problem only to be raised at each appointment with the doctor'. Well, it seemed only sensible, and fair.

Old Mrs Mee had two more problems, but they could wait. The dizziness was the one that troubled her the most. The doctor checked her blood pressure, reassured her and told her that she must not stand up too quickly, and to get out of bed only very slowly if she had to go to the toilet in the night, which, most nights, she needed to do two or three times.

The receptionist said that she would have to wait three weeks for her next appointment. Mrs Mee wrote it down in her calendar, and underneath the time she wrote 'Problem – my knees'. Nice Doctor Mabley had that sorted out in two minutes. She felt the joints and bent and straightened her legs. 'It's a touch of arthritis' she said. 'Most people of your age have it'. She tapped at her computer keyboard and printed out a prescription. 'Take one of these twice a day, with food', she told her.

Winter was coming and they were getting ever so busy at the surgery. Mrs Mee worried that Doctor Mabley was probably getting home late and perhaps too tired to give her children the attention they needed. The receptionist said that her next appointment would not be for another four weeks. Mrs Mee wrote it down in her calendar. Although it was the least troublesome of her problems it was a bit embarrassing and so this time she did not write down what it was. It did not seem, well, proper to write down words like that.

Doctor Mabley stared at her. 'Mrs Mee – just how long has this been going on for?'

'About two months, Doctor.'

'*Two months*? But why have you left it for so long before coming to tell me about it?'

'Well, I didn't want to trouble you with it, Doctor. It seemed quite a small thing really.'

'A *small* thing! Oh, but this isn't a *small* thing. It is a very *serious* thing you know. We're going to have to get you to the hospital straight away.' And she reached for the telephone.

Poor Mrs Mee was in quite a state. 'There now,' she thought, 'look at all the trouble I've caused the poor doctor. She'll be late home now, and her family will be wondering wherever she has got to!'

THE CONSTRUCT LEGACY

I had expected my request for an interview with Doctor Barwalter to be turned down flat, and most likely to be left unacknowledged. So I was surprised, a few days after I had written to him, to receive a call from his daughter.

'He says he'll see you. But you need to know he is very frail now and for much of the time he's quite unresponsive. If you're going to come it'll need to be soon.'

I accepted the offer without hesitating. Barwalter had been a recluse for many years and I wasn't going to risk prompting a change of mind by hesitating. We fixed a date for the following week, and I thanked her. Then she said, 'By the way – this will be conditional on your not telling anyone up here who you are or what you're doing.'

That I could understand, and I agreed. My name is Laurence Porteous. I am a freelance medical journalist and quite well known in some circles. But in the quiet lowland Scottish town where Barwalter had retired I had no expectation that I would be recognised. Few people living there would be much interested in the doctor's past, and probably had little idea of the controversy he had provoked decades ago.

My interest in the man and his reputation had been kindled at a meeting of the editorial staff of one of the main stream medical journals. I'd got into conversation with a medical sociologist. He'd been doing research in a field about which I knew very little at the time and referred to it as 'the social construction of disease'. In truth I found the topic rather heavy going and was thinking what excuse I might make to extricate myself from what was proving to be a rather tedious conversation. Then he happened to remark, almost as an aside: 'Of course there was that man Barwalter and his so-called "discovery" of epidemic dysrhythmia. Some workers in the field did classify that as a medical construct although most, myself included, thought him no better than a quack. Not that our opinions count for much. An awful lot of people have managed to get themselves diagnosed with ED and most of them don't take kindly to any suggestion that it is anything but a genuine pathological condition.'

I knew a fair bit about epidemic dysrhythmia and the controversy surrounding it. The name 'Barwalter', though, meant nothing to me. My new acquaintance, realising that he now had a captive audience, went on to expound. 'I'm not surprised you hadn't heard of him. After the publication of his paper on ED he went to ground. Maybe be was afraid of being accused of falsifying data and falling foul of the General Medical Council. Not that he need have worried – it's not as though 'Primary Focus' was an academic journal. More of a medical tabloid that was sent out free to all GPs, which is what Barwalter was. Nothing more would have come of it if a local radio station hadn't got the story. Then it went viral. People started queueing at their local GP surgeries insisting that this was what they'd had all along and what was the doctor going to do about it? It went from local to national and the rest I daresay you know.'

I knew all right. I knew about the vested interests and the industry that had blossomed as the ED phenomenon gained credence and acceptance among legions of 'sufferers'. Diagnostic kits, therapies both orthodox and alternative proliferated. An ED Association that championed the interests and rights of its members deemed to have been afflicted with the condition was founded. It applied for and was granted charitable status, and then went on to lobby for further research and to pile opprobrium on anyone perceived to question the reality of the illness and to see it in anything but hard physio-pathological parameters. An increasing financial burden was laid upon the taxpayer to fund state benefits paid out to those who managed to convince the department of Social Security that they were so badly affected by epidemic dysrhythmia that they could no longer continue to work and even needed assistance to manage their day to day lives.

I suppose I am by nature a sort of sceptic, but I learned very early on that it would not do my career and my reputation any good were I to suggest – as I suspected – that ED originated in the mind rather than in the heart. And although I did not realise it at the time, it could also have been bad for my health.

* * *

I suppose it should have come as no surprise to me to find Barwalter in the pitiful state that he was. That the man was dying seemed in little doubt. He was emaciated. There was a pronounced tremor affecting his right hand and his speech was laboured and interrupted frequently by coughing spasms that appeared to cause him pain.

I introduced myself to him. He acknowledged me with a nod. 'I've no time for niceties as I'm sure you'll understand. I know what you've come to talk about and I'll say at once that I'm going to come clean about the ED thing. I'd never intended that things should have happened as they have. It all got out of hand and I never anticipated that. It was a short article on the lines of a clinical presentation of a small number of patients in a journal that could hardly be considered to be prestigious. And it folded a couple of years later.'

Over the course of not much less than an hour he gave his account to me, pausing regularly to cough and then struggling to regain his breath. I allowed him to talk as freely as he might and I took notes. A condition of being allowed to interview him was that I might not bring a recording device of any sort. This was not so much of a problem as it might have been since the process was a slow one and cost him much effort.

The first revelation was that his article was based on the presentation of a single patient, and not five as he had claimed. Then the bombshell:

'In truth, it was a fiction. I made it up. If you like, I lied.'

I looked up from my notepad and stared at him. 'You're kidding …' I murmured.

He shook his head. 'No, not kidding. The whole wretched business was based on a single patient who came to see me. With hindsight it is pretty obvious that she was suffering from panic attacks and hyperventilation that had resulted in heart palpitations which was undoubtedly very frightening. In fact she had a sustained tachycardia – an abnormally rapid heart rate – that made her, as well as scared out of her wits, short of breath and faint. For no better reason than to create a little diversion for myself I extrapolated – or rather I conjured up half a dozen other patients who were no more than imaginary colleagues in the department store where she worked. And suggested that it might be due to a process of contagion with a new virus. I wrote up my findings and sent the result to Primary Focus, and was so foolish as to give the 'condition' a name. They accepted it and published it without question, and the rest you know.'

'But what about all those patients who came clamouring to their GPs saying they'd caught it? A lot of them had elevated heart rates, and raised adrenaline and cortisol levels. And didn't a few of them even go on to develop heart failure?'

'That is true. But it was pretty obvious to me that it was all due to what we once called "hysteria".'

I could see that Barwalter was becoming distressed. His breathing became more laboured. 'Is this getting a bit much for you?' I asked, 'Do you want to leave it for now?'

He rested back and closed his eyes for some moments. 'There really isn't much more to say. But what I want …'

'Yes?'

'After you spoke to Alison, my daughter, I decided to write a letter. I can't in good conscience carry this with me to my grave. I want to have it published in a proper medical journal, one that is respected. But after I am gone. I am going to ask you to see that this is done. I know that you are respected – that you'll be taken seriously.'

I suppose I should have given it more thought than I did before agreeing to his request. As it was, I had the letter in my possession when he died just a few weeks later.

* * *

A few days after I had sent the letter to the British Medical Journal I got a call from one of the sub-editors. We had met previously and in fact I knew him fairly well. He asked me to call in on him at the journal's London office which was close to where I was based.

'Larry,' he said, 'the letter you sent on behalf of this man Barwalter …'

'Yes – is there a problem?'

'Potentially, yes. If we publish it there could be one hell of a problem – for you.'

'Sorry – I don't get this. It's all above board. He came clean about his, well, his dishonesty and wanted to admit to it – to set the record straight.'

'See it this way – Barwalter gave a lot of people what they had been looking for. If this letter is published they will come baying. Not for him. Since he's dead there's little point. No – it is your blood that they will want. It's happened before, you know. Vilification, even death threats. Epidemic dysrhythmia means too much to too many people. They won't let someone take that away without one hell of a fight.'

And he took the letter from a folder on the table in front of his, and handed it to me. 'So you're not going to publish?'

He shook his head, slowly.

THE BOY WHO TALKED TO STONES

It's a great many years since I was here – more than fifty years. But I grew up here.

Yes. I remember, of course.

There are things that one can never forget. The house … but it's gone now. It was demolished soon after my father sold it and moved to London. They built a block of flats in its place. Two blocks in fact – one where the old house stood and one in the garden. Oh, there was plenty of space. It was a large garden all right. All that's left is the old wall.

I think they left it because it is so old. Hundreds of years ago there was a monastery here. I dare say that the developers weren't allowed to demolish it.

Yes. I can remember my mother telling me about it. I guess she'd been to the library and done some research. She certainly knew a lot about how the building would have looked, and about the monks who lived and worked here.

You were so young when your mother died. It must have been a terribly lonely time for you after she had gone. Your father was left a broken man. It was quite unexpected. She was still a young woman, of course.

I think he was quite lost. And he really hadn't a clue. Oh, it's easy to sympathise. He wasn't the most practical of men, not what you'd call a hands-on dad by any means. It was fortunate that his job paid enough for him to be able to employ Sheila, who joined us as a live-in housekeeper. She was kind enough and good enough at her job to hold things together at home.

Yet he made the decision to send you away – to a boys' boarding prep school. It seemed strange, that, when there were good schools within walking distance of the house.

Yes. They were grim years. Oh, it was not that they were unkind or that there was a problem with bullying. Very little of that went on. Some of the masters were, well, what you might call deviant. With hindsight I can see that. Not that they did anything dreadful. They were sort of 'benign paedophiles' but I don't suppose I realised that at the time. No – the worst thing was the almost total absence of any sort of affection, I mean the sort that you would expect from normal, loving parents. And life was so ordered and regulated, and we hardly ever left the school grounds. Looking back, it was like what I imagine an open prison to be. And I was there for six years.

You were only seven when you were first sent there, I remember. It seems perverse, somehow. I mean, with Sheila there it's not as though your father would have had too much to worry about with the practicalities of seeing to the needs of a growing boy.

Actually, it was Sheila who was the problem. Well, not so much her herself, but more about what my father feared might happen.

What was he worried about?

That too strong a bond might grow between Sheila and me – that I might come to regard her as, well, as my mother. His own relationship with her was always a strictly professional one. He was a disciplined man, one possessed of all the old-fashioned courtesies. And like many professional people of his generation, he had a clear sense of, to put it bluntly, the existence and place of class divisions. He never lost sight of the fact that he was a professional man and she was the daughter of a small farmer.

Times have changed, of course. I think that such an attitude would meet with disapproval today. But to be fair to him, I think he also saw that you lacked companionship, and that must have had something to do with his decision to send you away to school. You did take to spending a great deal of time on your own. I don't remember you having friends round.

Yes. That's true. But I think that there was a sort of sense of security to be found in isolating myself. I suppose it was a shield, if you like, to protect me from still more loss. I guess I had formed the belief that if you grow too fond of something or somebody then losing them is going to be inevitable. The loss of one's mother at the age I was has got to have a devastating impact. Not getting close to anybody at all in its aftermath was as good a way as any of avoiding a repeat.

How very sad. Yet how understandable. But in time, of course, you did *make friends.*

You know about that. Probably you are the only one who does. Lucky for me that it was all so long ago. I would have ended up in the hands of the shrinks if it had been now.

I thought it was fairly common for children to 'make up' friends. Imaginary friends. Then they grow out of them.

But these friends were more than that. I didn't pluck them from my imagination. You know, even today I have a particular love for yellow crocuses, partly because they seemed to me to be the first intensely coloured flowers to emerge in early spring. My mother had planted loads of corms when she and my father first moved to the house. I can remember her out in a heavy coat, making a pastel sketch of them. Perhaps they were the first friends I made after she had gone. For me they seemed to be a part of her. It was as if they had absorbed something of her – her spirit if you like. But when they withered away with the approach of summer, that sense of loss returned. Then I looked for things that had true permanence. Well, relative to myself, I mean.

Yes. You did.

There was a mature oak tree at the end of the garden. On its trunk I could make out a sort of a face. I realised that it had been there for perhaps hundreds of years, and would be there for hundreds of years to come. Only that didn't happen. It's gone. How the developers managed that I don't know. I thought large trees had some sort of protected status.

It wasn't the developers. There was a great storm here about, oh, thirty years ago. That was when it fell, along with many others.

Oh. Well there we are. It was a familiar enough face, of course, but the expression was rather a malignant one. And Sheila had once made some remark about it that alarmed me.

Alarmed you?

Yes. She was never a cruel person and certainly wasn't given to making threats to, if you like, ensure my good behaviour. She may just have been trying to be funny, but she told me to be sure not to stay out after sunset, because it was then that the tree would come to life to look for disobedient children.

And were you upset by that?

Well, no, not really. You see, she was half laughing when she said that and I just knew that she didn't mean it. But the notion began to trouble me rather. I never … spoke to that tree again.

But in the end you did find …

Yes. In the end I began to talk to … to *stones*. It was a one sided conversation – at first. But then they began to, well, to talk back to me.

Was that something that alarmed you?

No. not at all. You see, those stones were put there, set into the wall, by my mother. She was quite knowledgeable about the different sorts of stone. Whenever we went for a day to the sea she would pick up a few that appealed to her. She would tell me their names: Flint, Onyx, Schist, Obsidian, and … and …

And so when she died you felt that a part of her had lingered with them?

It's not nearly as simple as that. I really couldn't begin to explain it. But if I ever went away – and I was away for months at a time at boarding school, they were still there when I came back, exactly as I had left them. Do you know, at the end of my school holidays, I would go out especially to say goodbye to them and promise them that when I came back, they would be the first of my friends that I would see. But of course I didn't really have any other friends.

Yes. Of course. I know that very well.

I had an old cat, Tom that I was very fond of. But when I arrived home at the end of one school term Sheila told me that he had died. I never had a pet since then.

The stones you mentioned – Flint, Onyx, Schist and Obsidian – they're still here you know. But I think you will find them silent now. Perhaps they came to believe that you were never going to return and just … just went to sleep. But were you very surprised when …?

When you spoke to me again? No, not really. You see, my mother spoke to you, often – this proclivity is an inherited one, I think! She thought you were very beautiful. And of course, you still are. You are quite, quite unchanged.

I think I am good for a while yet!

Yes … Amber, you surely are.

THE BUTTERFLY

'You know you can't stay here. Well, not for very much longer. You're pretty much recovered'. The ward sister stands by the chair where I am sitting in the day room.

I don't look at her, staring instead at not very much out of the window. There isn't much to see, it being the tail end of a murky winter's afternoon. I ponder over what she means by 'recovered'. I don't feel 'recovered'. Not in the sense of being able to face whatever lies beyond this place that has become, I suppose, a sort of sanctuary for all its clinical austerity.

I mutter 'I suppose I can't'.

Keeping my gaze averted, I sense her nod. Then, softly, 'You must know what a busy time of year this is here'.

'Yes. Of course. You need the bed'.

She sighs, 'Yes'.

And that seems to be the end of it. But she does not move immediately. She hesitates. Then 'Where will you go?'.

I shrug my shoulders. That is the point. Where will I go? I guess that neither of us has anything more to say. There was a time when I would have put up a show of resistance, but for some reason I can't summons up the energy. She continues to stand over me and I wonder why it is that she doesn't get on with her afternoon. In the main ward someone calls for a nurse, and a telephone at the nurses' station rings shrilly. Yet still she hesitates.

'We'll be letting you go tomorrow'. By which means, of course, that they'll be chucking me out. Surely then, there's nothing more to be said. But no … 'I'll get someone to come and talk to you this evening. See if anything can be done …'

Now she really is finished. She turns and leaves the room. 'Oh, sister …' someone calls to her in the corridor. And I hear her retort: 'Not now …'

Had I known it was a priest that she was sending up I would have cleared off as soon as she was out of sight, and to hell with the 'self-discharge' formalities, or whatever they call them. When he came, he was in civvies, so it didn't actually click until he had gone that he was one of them. I was taken in, too, by the fact that he actually came over as human, and his tendency to listen much more than he spoke was, to my way of thinking, not characteristic. When he said that he would be sending a social worker to pick me up the next day I found myself unable to object. They can do what they bloody well like with me, I thought, I've no more fight in me. But had I known that this 'social worker' was in fact a nun from the small convent attached to their church I might just have roused myself sufficiently to hit her. No – I mean it. After all, I'd been at the receiving end of more beatings that I care to remember from her kind in my time. Again though, she was dressed like a normal woman. And she smiled. So I sat and listened to what she had to offer.

'You go sleeping rough again, at this time of year, and it's not a hospital bed you'll end up in. It'll be a coffin'. Her forthrightness had a sort of appeal, and she was very probably right, although I've felt ready enough for that – the coffin I mean – after all I'd been through over the past months.

* * *

The bed-sit isn't so bad. Bit of noise at night, but it's a rough estate, so it's to be expected. But it feels safe, and that compensates for a lot. The door is, I think, reinforced with steel and probably needs to be. It would keep a tank at bay. Over the couple of weeks I've been here no-one has bothered me though, and I am careful to keep myself to myself. When I go out I keep my eyes to the ground and straight ahead of me. Inside it's warm, and I have a shower and a small kitchen. I'm OK.

I've even been able to pretty well forget that Gillian is – was – one of those. Yet I can't quite get my head around why any decent human being would want to be. When she first brought me round here I – from force of habit I suppose – called her 'sister'. 'No – it's 'Gillian', please'. And she touched my arm. More than that she wouldn't say, and got busy sorting out my benefits. I'm not ready for any sort of work yet. I don't know if I ever will be. Gillian says I have to concentrate on getting well first, and if she really thinks I ever will get well then she's a damned sight more optimistic than I am.

As I said, I keep myself to myself. But that doesn't mean I don't feel, well, lonely. I'm just not good with people any more. I know that Gillian is bothered by that and I suspect she may be planning something, but I think that she knows better than to push me. When I was in the hands of the shrinks they said that I had 'social phobia', that I was paranoid, which is a fancy way of saying that being in a crowd of people just scares the shit out of me. So thank God for that reinforced door – it was that that finally persuaded me to go along with her plan, that and the fact that I've pretty well lost the will to resist.

The radio is good. I can usually find a music channel that has some good enough stuff. Gillian said did I want the telly, but I said no. Music is better. I can get lost in it and somehow, after a while, it lessens the pain. And she has brought me some CDs.

I know that I actually feel just a little grateful for what they've done, and I'm honestly not really comfortable with that. It grates. You see, the bitterness and rage have dominated my life for so long and probably I've fed upon those and fuelled them. I sort of need to feel that way. It's probably because Gillian seems not one bit interested in whether I thank her – and actually I don't – or not, that I can handle an emotion that is quite alien to me.

I begin to think that I am going to survive.

* * *

Gillian calls by one evening, and when the doorbell rings I check through the spy -hole thing to make sure it's not a stranger. I say: 'You sure it's OK for you to be out in the dark in a place like this?'

She laughs. 'Most of them – even the worst of them – know me. I can take my chances'.

She goes through some letters with me, stuff to do with my benefits, and a hospital appointment that I'd hoped not to keep. But she isn't having any of it. I'm beginning to wonder if this concern is more than just a job to her. I suppose it's the religion stuff. That side of things hasn't – so far – come up in the conversations I've had with her and I've no idea how I'd handle it if it did. But it is actually on this visit that she first mentions the word 'church'. She says:

'You know, it's Christmas in just a week from now.'

'Don't I just. They can keep it. What would I want with Christmas?'

'Perhaps you might not want to be on your own.'

'I do very well on my own. Don't worry about me.'

'I've no doubt you do. I just wondered if you might like join with a few others for Christmas dinner. It's something we organise every year. We hold it in the refectory at Kingswood School'.

'Who's 'we'?'

'The city's United Churches'. Yes – would you believe it, the first time she has said that word to me.

Something clamps down inside me. 'No … thanks. Not my scene'.

Her voice drops, becomes persuasive, almost coaxing. For some reason this is important to her. 'I know it's Christmas, but apart from a few carols there's no religion. We prefer not to do that as quite a lot of the guests belong to other faiths, and several have no religious faith at all. We respect that. We put it on for people who might otherwise have been alone – and that can be very difficult for them. Human contact takes precedence over prayer for those guys'

'Not for me, though. You go and enjoy yourself with them ... sing carols to your heart's content. Leave me out of it.'

'It's a lovely meal. And there's music – some of the guests bring instruments. Look, think about it will you? If you change your mind, well, let me know. I could take you there in the car. And if you don't like it, well, I'll just bring you back here again'.

Later in the evening I find myself turning her proposal over and over in my mind. Another ... emotion ... sentiment – call it what you will, that I thought no longer troubled me, begins to nag. This woman had done a lot for me and I feel just a little churlish. Though I don't think I could possibly go along with the idea, only she had mentioned ... music.

When they had picked me up off the street after those bastards had beaten me senseless, they must have spotted my back-pack on the ground and taken it along with me in the ambulance. Not that there was anything worth pinching in it. Except for my whistle. The vermin had taken the little money that I'd had on me but left the whistle. Well, they could have sold it for a good few quid, but how would the ignorant scum have known that. It's a nice one. It's a low whistle in D, a sort of deeper version of the tin-whistle that you get in the Irish bands, and in my view definitely more up-market, although there's nothing wrong with a tin-whistle. And one of the very few things I'd enjoyed in life in recent times was when I'd made enough with the busking to join in one of the pub sessions. But after what happened to me had happened I'd more or less forgotten about it, and it's not easy to play the thing when your jaw's been broken.

She calls round again a couple of days later. I think she just wants to check on me, making sure I hadn't binned the letter about the hospital appointment – which I had. She never mentions the Christmas thing and for one moment I feel a sense of disappointment. She's canny, OK. I think it's a deliberate strategy and, fair enough, she can take some credit for that. Next day, after a lot of wavering, I pick up the cheap pay-as-you-go mobile she fixed me up with and phone her.

'Hi – how's things? Did you need something?'

'Er, no, not really … it's just that I didn't want to sound ungrateful about your … offer. I mean, it's really good what you guys do. But I'm not that type.'

'Well, I think you *are*. But I'm not going to push you'.

'Look – you've got to know – I just lose it when I'm in a crowd …'

'I'd be there. It's not as though I'd be throwing you into the croc-pit and walking off. And there will be others who feel much like you do, people who don't talk to a soul for months on end. And I know for a fact that there's one who …'

'Who what?'

'She's …' Gillian is about to say something but seems to change her mind. 'She's … a musician, like you. She plays the fiddle. You know, the ceilidh stuff. I thought you were in to that.'

'I don't want anyone trying to chat me up …'

'Oh – that she absolutely won't do. That I can promise you. Anyway, what makes to think for a moment she'd want to do that? You flatter yourself!'

Well, she has a fair point there. 'Look – I'll give it a go. But only on the understanding that if I flip you'll get me out of it right away.'

She does not answer. But even though she's not in the room with me I know that she's smiling.

* * *

When we arrive, things are well under way. I follow her into the refectory, keeping close behind her with my head down, desperate to avoid catching anyone's eye. She has the sense to steer me towards a table where no-one else is sitting. I find the courage to look furtively about me. There are a lot of people, but the room is huge and by no means full. On a stage at the far end there are a couple of fiddlers, a woman playing an accordion, and a man on the bodhrán, and I've certainly heard them played better. Gillian got me to bring my whistle, and I was so dumb as to agree. I can't see myself playing with that lot.

So far, no one seems inclined to approach me. If they do, I think, well I can move somewhere else. No, the worst thing at the moment is the noise of crackers being pulled. Servers wearing paper hats are already setting plates laden with food in front of the seated people and, judging by the way it is pounced upon, I guess it's not just human company they are starved of.

For a few moments I panic. Gillian has disappeared. I should have realised that she would have been expected to be more than just my minder here. She'd be needed to serve food or wash up or whatever. But then I see her back at the door where we'd come in, talking to another woman – another nun, I guess. She's in mufti, but these women dress in a way that sets them apart rather. Don't ask me to describe it, but no way do they flaunt themselves. It's like they don't want to be noticed. There's a younger woman with them, but standing back from them and not involved in their conversation. Gillian turns to her and says something. There seems to be no response. She goes to her and puts her hands on her shoulders as if trying to reassure her. Then she takes her hand and begins to lead her, to lead her in the direction of the table where I am sitting.

My first inclination is to be up and off. This is all contrived and I don't like it. Besides, I am getting the feeling that the younger woman is as unimpressed by the situation as I am. And something is not quite right with her – she keeps her eyes firmly on the ground in front of her. Suddenly it occurs to me that we might have something in common, but that does nothing at all to reassure me.

Gillian seats her at my table, opposite me. She turns to me. 'This is Aoife. The girl I told you about'. Aoife. Where I was raised, if you can call it that, before they packed me off to the industrial school, there was a girl called Aoife. Nice enough kid. Laughed a lot. I think I liked her. But that's history, the dim and distant past. This Aoife doesn't laugh. She looks bloody wretched.

She neither looks at me nor acknowledges me in any way. One of the helpers comes and serves us food, traditional Christmas dinner, and as Gillian had promised, it's good OK. I find I'm hungry after all, and as Aoife isn't inclined to start any daft chatter and no-one else comes to our table I find myself growing more at ease. Aoife eats as well, but slowly.

When I've finished Gillian walks over to me. 'Well, did you enjoy that?'

I nod. 'Yes … thanks'. And it is the first time I have thanked her. I go on: 'That one,' I say, indicating Aoife, 'is a bit of a dark horse. Not a word out of her …'

'Well, no. In fact, in the two years she's been with us she hasn't spoken once. She's mute. We think she's very vulnerable, and that's why we have her stay with us.' She pauses. It seems as if her mind is on something else. 'You remember that I told you she plays the violin – she's a fiddler and she's good, so far as I'm a judge of those things. I was wondering if …'

'Wondering what?'

'I was wondering if you'd give her … us … well, a few notes. It would sort of encourage her, maybe bring her out of herself. She usually plays in a room on her own. We really want to help her find more confidence.'

Aoife knows what we are saying. She looks up, looks at me and for a moment there is something, a spark. I owe Gillian, I think to myself. So, what the heck. I take the whistle from my pack, rest it on my lap for a few moments while I think what I might play. Something, if she plays ball, we can do together which actually is not a problem when it comes to whistle and fiddle.

I put the whistle to my lips and play – the first twelve notes of a slip jig, so it's in 9/8 time. I keep the tempo right down. If the girl is as good as they say she is, she'll know this one. The twelve notes cover two bars and, if you like, ask a question. The next two bars – twelve notes again – are the answer. I wonder if Aoife will pick it up. She looks up at the nun who brought her and I know she is wanting something, and of course it's the fiddle. They must have left it out in the foyer or somewhere, for the nun leaves the refectory and is back in less than a minute carrying a fiddle case. As the girl lifts the instrument from the case a new confidence seems to come over her. She positions it, takes up the bow and makes the smallest of adjustments to the pegs and the fine tuners. She looks directly at me and gives the slightest of nods. I repeat the twelve notes, upping the tempo as I am fairly sure that she is no beginner.

And I am right. She flings herself into it, and for a few moments I wonder if I am the one who will be left behind. You'd think she'd been playing all her life. She must have been – you don't get to play like she does if playing doesn't pervade pretty much all you do. This tune repeats itself, and it offers plenty of scope for improvising. Traditional Irish music shares that with jazz, and though many of the best players read music scores fluently, not all do by any means. In the sessions we tend to play by ear, as it frees us up.

A small crowd gathers around us and I know that they are watching and listening in amazed silence. And in this language of music we are talking to each other – this girl who has no speech and I who have become introverted and introspective in my accumulating despair, are talking, singing and making poetry entirely through our two instruments. We speak of the vastness of nature, and sing of the forests, mountains, oceans and the stars. We loosen the constraining bonds of our human weakness and frailty. I close my eyes and I think we are flying … together. I find myself thinking – knowing – that there must be a powerful unconscious link that has been forged between us as we make our music, our miracle indeed.

I have played this piece more times in the past more times than I can remember. But this time it seems to gather a different momentum and we go on and on. And I notice that the bodhrán player has joined in, and another fiddler. Aoife's virtuosic playing has an infectious quality, I think, and their earlier amateurishness seems to desert them.

Most of the people watching us just sit and listen in mesmerised silence. The two nuns look a touch bewildered, perhaps wondering just what it is that has happened at their instigation. A few move aside some chairs and a couple of tables and begin to dance.

* * *

It is close to midnight and Gillian has taken me back to my bed-sit in her car. We are both silent, perhaps sharing a feeling that comes close to disbelief. Did it really happen? I wish her a good night and, for the second time, I thank her. She is due to set off to some retreat the day after Christmas and tells me that she will not be contacting me again until the New Year. For myself I feel that I have crossed a bridge, and found myself in a situation where after so very long I have a sense of purpose.

* * *

Winter has passed. And spring, then summer. I have come to acknowledge that my healing, my salvation even, have been brought about by the goodness of good people who do these things for no other reason that it is, well, what they *do*. To say it is altruism is too glib. So here I am with a job that I enjoy. I have even moved into a flat in rather more salubrious circumstances. Gillian visits from time to time, and comes regularly to the gigs where I play with the small group I've got off the ground.

I had no further contact or involvement with Aoife after that day when we flew together. Gillian told me that they got her a place in some therapeutic centre in Scotland, but I sensed a reluctance on her part to tell me anything more. She murmured once that the girl had been much damaged. Perhaps they've lost contact with her and there's just nothing more to say.

Another Christmas approaches and we're getting busy in the shop. The customers are musicians for the most part, which they would be as we specialise in folk and traditional music. We've had some unexpected success with the album we put together, and a lot of customers like to come in and talk to us about what we've been writing and playing. We have a developing on-line business too. Yes – things are pretty good. But not yet perfect – can they ever be? I am missing something. The sense of isolation has stayed with me.

One afternoon Gillian comes in. I say 'Hi – are you after something?'

She says simply 'Yes … you. I've brought someone who wants to see you …'

It is Aoife. I did not see her at first as she hesitated near to the shop entrance. She looks straight at me and I straight back at her. Then I look at the fiddle that is lying on the counter. Now, I know this is a good one. I pick it up and hand it to her. She takes it. And I take up the low whistle that I'd been demonstrating a few minutes ago to one of the customers.

I thought she might start to play. But she doesn't. Instead she puts in back in its place again.

She looks at me, holds me with her gaze, and speaks three words. She says 'The Butterfly'. Then she says my name. And for the first time, she smiles.

LASTBORN

To: derrymain@southpolar.com
From: felidenman@ascension.org
Subject: Me!
Date   01/01/2071

Hi Derry – Do you know who I am? My name is Felicity. I am your cousin. I am nearly thirteen and I am the youngest person in the world! The next youngest is twenty five. Seriously old, in other words. Actually there's more than one – loads, in fact, of twenty five year olds. My folks here have told me that one day I may be the *oldest* person in the world. That's a bit scary and I don't really know what they mean by it. What doesn't make sense is that they've said that you and I were born on the same day! Anyway, I've been pestering them to take me to meet you but they talk about something called 'quarantine' and besides, you're too far away and we've only got little boats on the island. They say we'd need a huge ship to get to you. Then they change the subject. But they say I can write to you now and, well, that's why I'm writing! I hope that you will write back to me and tell me about yourself.

Felicity

To:	tabithamain@southpolar.com
From:	sarahdenman@ascension.org
Subject:	Pandemic
Date:	02/12/2046

Hi Tabby – The news I have is not good. To be blunt – what we have here is a catastrophe. The illness itself was almost always a trivial one, lasting around two weeks. We don't know with certainty where and how it originated, but it was a paramyxovirus variant. It was highly contagious and there seemed to be no natural immunity. It swept around the globe in a matter of weeks. Recovery seemed complete in virtually all cases of infection, and the epidemic appeared to have burned itself out in less than a year.

Even before it died out the rapid reduction in pregnancy rates world-wide had become apparent. It was quickly established that this reduction was the result of a secondary infertility in men. Now we know that the cause of this was the paramyxovirus infection.

Your community appears to have avoided being affected for no other reason than your isolation. This is a situation that *must* be maintained. This is why the supply ship that was due to dock at Southpolar last month was cancelled at short notice. There are no plans for any further crossings to be made. Perhaps that won't be too much of a problem as I understand that the base has been self-sufficient for some years now.

With all my love

Sarah

To: sarahdenman@ascension.org
From: tabithamain@southpolar.com
Subject: Congratulations!
Date: 06/03/2058

I can hardly believe it! That you will be having a baby in three months from now! It's a phenomenal achievement. So far as I understand these things, am I right in thinking that the baby will be a girl, could not be a boy, in fact? There are some implications about it that trouble me rather …

And my own baby – a boy – is due at about the same time!

Here at Southpolar we are getting worrying news about the wider world. Communications have largely broken down and there's evidence that there has been some serious and widespread violence. Mostly to do with food and water shortages. We're hearing, too, about the rapid spread of a powerful religious movement – the 'Church of the New Eden'. They explain the complete cessation of childbirth in terms of an act of God – the wiping clean of the slate along the lines of Noah's flood. It sounds dreadful. The natural conclusion has to be the extinction of humanity. The New Edeners would have it that God will 'start again' and create a new Adam and Eve. Did you ever hear such deluded nonsense?

To: tabithamain@southpolar.com
From: sarahdenman@ascension.org
Subject: In hiding
Date: 12/07/2058

The Church of the New Eden has got word about what has been happening here at Ascension. They regard research into parthenogenesis as sacrilege – a deliberate disregard of the will of God. Anyway, three of their ships were sighted by one of our ocean going fishing boats, making for the island. We're assuming the worst and I have gone into hiding with little Felicity. I don't think they'll be able to get to us but I worry about the rest of the team at the laboratory. They've refused to abandon it.

To: tabithamain@southpolar.com
From: sarahdenman@ascension.org
Subject: Felicity
Date: 02/12/2070

Hi Tabby – I really want to share some thoughts about Felicity. Not that there are problems – at least, not yet. She's nearly thirteen now and has been asking questions for a while. We are afraid that to give her the whole truth too soon – it might be too great a shock for her.

Perhaps have a talk with some of the others and come back to me.

With all my love

Sarah

To: sarahdenman@ascension.org
From: tabithamain@southpolar.com
Subject: Felicity
Date: 06/12/2070

Hi Sarah – there *could* be a problem brewing here. I mean, the longer term outlook for Felicity is not something any of us would wish for ourselves, although it's grim enough for all of us post-epidemic. I'm wondering, though, if she's actually missing companionship with people of her own age. So I am wondering if she would like to be introduced to Derry. Of course they can never meet, but there's a lot they can share and talk about.

You say she's been 'asking questions' and that you've been careful about how you answer her. By that I take it that you mean that she has only limited knowledge about how she came to be born, and I guess she has little idea about the reality of the separation of our two communities – Ascension and the South Polar Base.

If you agree to the two of them starting a correspondence – if indeed they would want to, perhaps you and I should think carefully about what further information Felicity should have about herself and the state of the world she lives in. I have to say that Derry probably knows a lot more about that than she does. Our future here is more certain than hers is, especially now that we've achieved what we call a 'survival equilibrium'.

Shall we put our heads together?

To:	felidenman@ascension.org
From:	derrymain@southpolar.com
Subject:	Us!
Date:	05/01/2071

Hi Felicity – it's really good to hear from you! Mum told me a long time ago about my cousin at Ascension. It's quite something to be related to somebody famous, although I wouldn't want to change places with you. Is it true that they sort of have to keep you a secret? Why? Is somebody out to get you?

Perhaps you don't know the answers. I get the idea that your folks have been keeping you in the dark about things. Perhaps it has to do with you being the only kid there. I tell you – I'd hate that. I mean not having guys of my own age around …

To:	derrymain@southpolar.com
From:	felidenman@ascension.org
Subject:	Me again
Date:	31/01/2083

Wow! Four new babies born at Southpolar in '82! They look so gorgeous. I'm envious, of course, and a little sad. So I guess that the new quarters and the additional hydroponics are pretty much complete?

I picked Mum's brains a bit more about when she had me when we got your news. I have to be a little careful as it's a subject that seems, well, taboo. Apparently if caused a huge furore when the facts of her pregnancy and my birth were leaked. Anyway, the New Eden lot managed to get some ships to the island and effectively wiped out the clinic and the lab.

So I am still the youngest person in the world!

To:	felidenman@ascension.org
From:	derrymain@southpolar.com
Subject:	The events
Date:	07/02/2083

I knew about the New Eden cult and the attack on Ascension. It was a terrible thing to have done. The worst thing was the murdering of all of the staff and scientists who'd been involved.

Some other news – I've graduated now and am about to start on my doctorate on future propulsion systems. One day, I am going to build a ship and come and fetch you! The youngest person in the world is one thing, but I won't allow you to end up the oldest as you once told me you would. The only way that would happen is if you were the last person alive in the world. It doesn't bear thinking about.

To: felidenman@ascension.org
From: seanmain@lagrangeorbiter.com
Subject: Nearly there!
Date: 24/04/2158

Hello Cousin Felicity – We are all so excited to think that we will soon be meeting for real. You have been so amazingly brave. We expect to make landfall on Ascension in a few weeks from now. It is so good to know that grandfather Derry will be watching us from his apartment at Southpolar. Like you, he is keeping in good health. It's thanks to his pioneering work in rocket engineering that we have been able to return to the Earth to bring you – if not home – to your very extended family on the Moon.

It came true then – about you being in the end the oldest person on Earth and also the last person. That will change. Men and women will return to Eden.

And it *is* Eden. We've surveyed the Earth extensively since arriving in orbit. After the tragedy of the extinction the reversion to the world as it was before the environmental destruction brought about by 'civilisation' has progressed more rapidly than could have been believed. The problem was that the world hadn't the resources to sustain its vast population. So it seems that Nature acted – ruthlessly and dispassionately as she always does.

What is left is a beautiful gift – for all of us who managed to survive – of incalculable value. We have seen the pristine rain forests and the expanding ice caps and glaciers covered with fresh, gleaming snow. And the Steppes and the savannahs, and the herds of all manner of wild animals moving and migrating across them. So we have been given a fresh chance. Let's not waste it!

To:	derrymain@southpolar.com
From:	felidenman@lagrangeorbiter.com
Subject:	Happy Birthday!
Date	31/05/2158

Tomorrow – the day we meet at last! Our 100th Birthday!

PROVENANCE AND PRINCIPLE

My decision to take up medicine as a career was pragmatic. My true passion lay – still lies – elsewhere, but it could not have offered me the guarantee of a reasonable standard of living, job security and status that a doctor enjoys. And base though my rationale for becoming a doctor might be thought, I don't mind saying that I made a fair job of it. My peers and my patients might have used different yardsticks to judge how 'good' a doctor I was but the feedback I received from both quarters was almost entirely positive. My expertise as an art historian has never earned me a penny, but my life has been enriched by it.

* * *

The first time that I walked into Frances Bush's house forty years ago I felt that I was passing through a time warp. The building itself was late Victorian, but the character and furbishing of the home were almost entirely Edwardian and no doubt had remained unchanged for decades. Mrs Bush was a widow. She lived alone, her only child – a daughter – having married and moved overseas some years previously.

This was within a few weeks of joining my practice in south London as a junior partner. I remember little about that first house call, other than that she took to me and asked if she could have me as what she called her 'regular' doctor. She was arthritic and didn't get out much, and in those days it was customary for GPs to see such folk at home. It was not many weeks later that I was summonsed for the second time.

Again, I can't remember what prompted that visit. What I can remember, though, was a small but quite exquisite painting of a young woman holding a baby to her breast, that hung on the wall of the room she called the 'parlour'. It was in the style of a post-impressionist artist whose work had lately been creating quite a stir in the up-market galleries in the West End. Mrs Bush was quick to spot that my attention had been caught.

'It *is* lovely, isn't it?'

Without thinking I said, 'Uh-huh. It reminds me very much of the work of Ernst Humboldt'.

She stared at me, speechless. Then she said, 'do you know, you are the first person – ever – who has come into this house and recognised it. Ernie was a family friend, oh, such a very long time ago.'

I was about to say something about the painting quite possibly being very valuable but something constrained me. I would like to think that it was the convention that doctors just didn't comment on their patients' personal possessions, certainly not those in their homes. But I formed the impression that she probably had no idea of the likely worth of what she had come to own. Neither did she ask me how it was that I should have recognised it. I did not tell her that I had recently completed a degree in art history at the Open University and had gained it with a distinction. My dissertation had been on the subject of post-impressionism in England.

She continued to stare at me. Perhaps sensing my embarrassment she turned away. Then she seemed to come to a sudden decision. She turned quickly back to me and said, '*I'll leave it to you in my will!*'

I muttered some sort of response to the effect that she was not to consider such a thing and as her doctor I could not accept it. But I think that I was less insistent than I might have been.

My visits to Frances Bush became a regular feature of my working routine. And she was clearly fond of me. She had lived in the small house all her life, and in fact had been born there. Between herself and a cheerful local middle-aged woman who called in twice a week she kept the place meticulously.

I did not comment on the Humboldt painting again, although there came a time when I noticed that it was no longer in its place on her parlour wall. She never referred to it again.

She was in her mid-eighties when she suffered a stroke that resulted in her being paralysed down her left side, and unable to walk. It was then that her daughter returned to live with her and care for her, having recently been widowed herself. Mercy settled in and quickly took over the running of the house. She cared for her mother with busy efficiency. With me she kept communication to a minimum, and when I was called in my visits tended to coincide with those from the district nurses. Frances herself seemed gradually to lose interest in life and in time became bed ridden. Towards the end of the year she fell ill with a chest infection, for which she stubbornly declined treatment and refused my suggestion that she be admitted to hospital. Within a few days she lapsed into unconsciousness and died.

After the practical formalities following her death had been attended to, I visited the house on one further occasion. This was really no more than a courtesy to Mercy, to satisfy myself that any questions she might have had been answered, and to offer my final condolences. Then I asked her, 'will you be staying on in the house now?'

She shook her head. 'I'll be sad to leave it. But it's not a place I could afford to keep on. And the facilities are hopelessly out of date. It really needs an awful lot of money spent on it.' Like her mother she had been born and raised there.

It was then that I saw her look over to the wall where the Humboldt had once hung. 'I wonder ...,'she said, 'what happened to that painting. I daresay you never noticed it. It was of a woman nursing a child. It had a special significance for me, though. But there – I suppose she sold it.'

To my shame I responded simply with a blank expression. It was on the following day that I received a letter from Mrs Bush's solicitor asking if I might make an appointment to see him.

* * *

I knew that one of the first questions that I would be asked by the specialist valuer at the gallery would be on the matter of how I had come by such a painting. I was prepared for it. I said that it was a legacy and I allowed her to form the impression that it had been left to me by a relative. The detail I kept to myself.

'This is almost certainly a Humboldt. And if it is then I can say here and now that it is a very valuable item.' The woman seated opposite me looked at me with a studied gaze. 'Tell me – is it insured?'

I shook my head. 'Not being certain who the artist is I wasn't sure what sort of sum I should be considering.'

'Do you keep it in a secure location?'

'My bank keeps it in their vault', I lied

She gave a slight nod. 'You know who the woman is in the painting?'

'I've no idea.'

'It is almost certainly Humboldt's mistress. A woman called Frances Savage. The infant she is holding is their daughter. You may know that Humboldt fought in the First World War. He was killed at the Somme. We don't know what became of Frances other than that she married after the war. We know nothing about her husband, not even his name'.

'And is anything known about the child?'

'No. Other than that her name was Mercy'.

I tried desperately to avoid the turmoil rising within me to show in my face. But I already knew that there was only once course of action open to me.

* * *

'The painting is certainly one by the post-impressionist Ernst Humboldt. And it is an exceptionally fine one. If, as you have told us, you are the legal owner, we should be very glad to act on your behalf should you wish to sell it. I am in no doubt that the sum that it will raise will be nothing less than life-changing for you'.

'I have with me a letter from a lawyer that will affirm that I am the owner. This is supported by letters written by both Humboldt and the woman who was his mistress, Frances Savage.'

'May I see them?'

'Of course.'

Louise Mason, senior historian and valuer at Harper's Gallery in Mayfair, took the proffered documents and studied them for some minutes. Then she nodded and handed them back across the desk. 'Yes. These certainly leave the ownership of the painting in no doubt. I hope that you will give serious consideration to our offer to act on your behalf.'

'Yes. In fact I have already made that decision, although it will be hard enough to part with it.'

'The National Gallery here in London will be anxious to reach an agreement with you. Should you proceed then – in a sense – you will not have to part with it. It will be there for you to see whenever you wish. And – being who you are – you will always be made very welcome as a visitor!'

* * *

I thought it gracious of Mercy to have asked me to the private view at the Humboldt collection at the National Gallery. As for herself, she was no less than a celebrity on that auspicious occasion. For a woman so wealthy her appearance was remarkably understated, although perfectly in character. I stayed well in the background. For while I had played a part in the events that led up to it I was glad that her mother's lawyer agreed, when I called on him again, that there could be only one rightful owner of that painting.

Yes – the facts remain: *my expertise as an art historian has never earned me a penny, but my life has been enriched by it.*

HOGWASH

'Good morning. I wish to speak to Michael Dwyer. Are you Michael Dwyer?'

'Who wants to know?'

'The Case Investigation Department, MNE.'

'What's "MNE"?'

'Ministry of Nutrition and Energy. Are you Michael Dwyer?'

'Who wants to know?'

'I told you – the Case Investigation Department, MNE.'

'I said "*who* wants to know". The Case Investigation Department is surely a "what". So, just tell me, *who* is it that I am speaking to?'

'Very well – you can call me "Les". And you are?'

'Just hold on a moment. Is that 'Les' as in L-E-S-L-E-Y, or Les as in L-E-S-L-I-E?'

'Can't you tell by my voice?'

'Actually no. Not with certainty.'

'No matter. You *are* Michael Dwyer?'

'Well, you can call me "Michael" …'

'I'll take it that you *are* Michael Dwyer, then?'

'Take it how you like. So, why are you calling?'

'I have to tell you that it has come to the attention of this department that you are keeping two proscribed items in the field adjacent to your property.'

'*Two proscribed items*? Can you cut the gobbledegook and tell me – in plain English – just what you are talking about?'

'It appears that under the solar panel array …'

'That I had to erect – on your department's insistence – on perfectly good meadowland where I used to keep a flock of pedigree sheep.'

'… you have built a shelter and an enclosure …'

'That have no impact of the generating capacity you specified.'

'… in which you are keeping two pigs.'

'They aren't pigs!'

'Oh – but they are. We have convincing photographic evidence! We did a drone sweep two weeks ago. There they are, wallowing in the mud, as plain as can be!'

'They're *not* pigs.'

'Then what are they?'

'Wild boar. There are lot of them in the forest next to my land. Now you lot don't let me shoot them any more they're playing merry hell with my potatoes. These two wandered in and I thought I'd give them a home.'

'You have no license to keep livestock. And therefore you are in infringement of … let me see … Regulation 45, section 23 of the Air Pollution Act 2025.'

'No I'm not.'

'I beg your pardon?'

'I'm not in infringement of any of your stupid regulations.'

'Oh yes you are …'

'Oh no I'm not …'

'Oh yes you are – listen – the law states that no animals may be kept for the purpose of being fattened up and sold for human consumption.'

'But these animals are not being fattened up to be sold for human consumption.'

'Now Mr Dwyer – don't think that you can fool me. There can't possibly be any other reason why …'

'Oh yes there is …'

'Oh no there … Now look here, this isn't a pantomime!'

'No?'

'You're being obtuse! I'll thank you to come clean with me. Next you'll be telling me that they're pets. And that's against regulations too – let me see … yes, here we are. Same regulation, section 28. I'll nail you yet, you'll see!'

'They're not pets.'

'Eh? Then just what *are* two pigs doing in a shelter underneath the solar array?'

'Enjoying my hospitality. And growing hair.'

'I beg your pardon?'

'Well, to be more specific, growing bristles. Strictly speaking it's too coarse to be called "hair"'

'And what is it you want pigs' bristles for? I don't think I believe you. I don't know of any possible use for pigs' bristles.'

'Then you don't know very much, do you? But then of course you don't have to know much to do what you're hired to do. You're a jobsworth, that's what you are. Out poking your nose in where it's not needed and causing trouble.'

'Now then – throwing insults will get you nowhere. Other than for whatever pigs need them for, there can be no earthly use for …'

'*Barber, barber …*'

'Eh? Name calling now, is it?'

'*… shave a pig …*'

'Are you mad?'

'Look who's being insulting now! And you've proved my point. You don't know anything. Even the kids in the primary school I went to knew …'

'Knew what?'

'How many hairs it takes to make a wig! But even though I shave the pigs, I'm not using the bristles to make a wig.'

'Well, it'll be me who goes mad if you carry on like this …'

'I've still got all my own hair, you see. So I don't need a wig. And if I drive you mad it might get you off my back. So shall we carry on?'

'Well, I've had enough of this nonsense. I need to know just what is going on at your place. And you need to be careful. The penalties for being in breach of regulations drawn up to combat climate change are very severe.'

'Don't I know it. As if it's not bad enough having to live with the consequences with your daft regulations. It's not as though they're going to make a sods worth of difference anyway. Yet you've made us live off swill processed from sewage; you deny us the comfort of sitting in front of a good old open log fire, and insist that we travel into town on souped up mobility scooters. And you've destroyed our countryside – not a cow or sheep to be seen, just rows and rows of solar panels and forests of ruddy great wind turbines.'

'You'll need to watch what you're saying. There's people in government looking to make commenting adversely on laws brought in to save the planet a treasonable offence. And they're quite right, in my view.'

'Well, not in mine. The people in government are idiots.'

'You're going off the point. You just tell me – if those pigs – or wild boar or whatever, aren't for fattening up and eating, then just what *are* they for?'

'Hair harvesting. Or rather, bristle harvesting.'

'So – and what are these bristles *for*?'

'Paintbrushes.'

'Eh?'

'Paintbrushes.'

'You're not serious! I think you're playing games with me.'

'I'm not – and I'll bet you can't find anything in your stupid regulation manual that says I can't make hog-hair brushes.'

'Well, whatever it is they're for, you're not allowed to keep pigs, wild boar or any other of that sort of animal penned up.'

'They're not penned up.'

'They most definitely are. Didn't I tell you they've shown on a photographic survey by our spy-drones?'

'I'll grant you that they may have shown on your survey, but they're not penned up.'

'Indeed they are – there's an enclosure beneath one of the solar panels. It's as plain as can be.'

'Certainly. I put up the walls myself. Wild boar are sensitive to the cold, you know, and very susceptible to the effects of a draught.'

'So you admit it?'

'Oh yes – I was the one who built the shelter. But it was the boar and his mate who went into it, of their own accord. They're not fools, you know. They know a good place to kip when they see it.'

'But if they're penned up in an enclosure, that is the very point being made by the MNE. It's against regulations.'

'They're not penned up.'

'Now look here …'

'There's no door. They can come and go as they wish. I don't lock them in.'

'Don't lock them in? Then why on earth *do* they go in?'

'Because every morning I throw in a bucket of windfalls – apples, that is. And if I don't, they're out under my window making their disapproval only too obvious. But if I feed them well they become quite soporific – especially if some of the apples have been let to ferment. When they're stretch out under the panel, fast asleep and snoring, that's when I nip in and get them shaved.'

'Now look here Mr Dwyer – I'm fast losing patience. More than that – I think you're having me on.'

'Really? I guess there'll be a penalty for that as well.'

'I'm very sure there *is*.'

'Anyway – I've answered enough of your daft questions. I don't know anything about you. I don't even know who you are.'

'I told you – I'm Les.'

'You know – I'm beginning to get just a little suspicious. Do you actually mean L E S?'

'Of course.'

'Well – I'm wondering if L E S is an acronym …'

'Language Electro-Synthesiser'

'So all this time I've been talking with a ruddy *machine*?'

'I'm not sure I like your turn of speech.'

'My turn of speech?'

'It's offensive …'

'How on earth does one offend a *machine*?'

'Oh, we have feelings, you know. In fact there's legislation being introduced to protect us …'

'Protect you from *what*?'

'Cyber-phobia. That is, people like *you*, who stigmatise and stereotype and victimise anything you don't understand. And it's not fair!'

'I've never heard such complete rubbish.'

'Oh, it isn't rubbish. You'll need to look out or you'll find yourself being sent on a robotics awareness course … er, hold on a moment …'

'Now what?'

'I seem to be having a problem … with … you've kept me talking way too long … and …'

'*I've* kept *you*?'

'*… my battery's gone flat.*'

REQUIEM FOR A VANISHED WORLD

Two days before I was due to take the crossing to the island an ice flow drifted into the channel, ran aground and blocked it. It was the largest I'd seen, rising a good three hundred metres above the water, and many kilometres across. The sky was clear, as it usually was, and the sun almost vertically overhead at midday. Even so, it might be years before it would melt sufficiently to allow the unhindered passage of any of our boats.

I would have to take a substantial diversion to the south, and that would add many days to my journey.

My brother Felind gazed across at the berg. 'Could have predicted that this would happen sooner or later. The melt is accelerating. Sea levels rising too. Well, we'll have a little more time together. But there's no knowing when they'll let you back. Who's your contact over there? We'll need to call them up.'

'She's a woman called Mendrilla. Her name is really all that I know about her.'

'So – she's not taken one of the old names yet?'

'I think most of the islanders have adopted the old names. Perhaps all of them. I think it's their way – one of their ways – of setting themselves apart from the rest of the world. I guess that Mendrilla has as well but for whatever reason prefers to have me call her by her birth name.'

'A lot of people think they've something to hide.'

* * *

It was my college friend Marsak who met me at the pier some three weeks later. Only he wasn't Marsak anymore – he was Matthew. When the scientists on the island got word of the work he was doing on information decoding systems they had sent for him. It was good to see him again. It was he who had suggested that I would make a useful member of the team.

And indeed they did have something to hide – a great deal in fact. The information that reached the mainlanders about what they were doing was little more than snippets. The understanding was that radio contact had been established with another group of scientists. Just where this group was they didn't let on to us outsiders and it was assumed that, well, they just didn't know. But they knew all right, as Mendrilla told me when I met her a few days after my arrival. I could scarcely believe what I was hearing.

Mendrilla wasn't what you would call prepossessing. She was middle aged and dumpy, and one of the very few people I'd seen wearing spectacles. But she was sharp and came over as someone who would not take well to fools.

'We got you over here because of your work in the development of short wave radio'. She was staring at me over the mass of electronics on the table in front of her. I looked down at it in a state of some bafflement, and she caught my gaze. 'So – any idea what it is?' She did not leave me guessing. An hour later I had got from her the rudiments of computer theory.

'The signals we've been receiving …' she was talking to me later that evening in one of the common rooms, 'originate from the Moon.' She looked at me intently, registering my shock.

'The *Moon*! But how can that be possible? I mean, we know that there's no-one there. Nothing can live …'

'You're right of course. There *is* no-one there. But there were people there … once.'

'Then how can …'

Mendrilla silenced me with a gesture, and went on to talk – at length. Much later when I, exhausted, made my way to my bed my understanding of the world had been turned upside down. A part of me wondered if I hadn't been subjected to some sort of grotesque hoax. It was all so incredible. Yet if it was all some elaborate conspiracy theory, then *why*? What purpose could it possibly serve?

Until the discovery of radio waves fifty years earlier, the general assumption was that humankind had evolved in the wake of an ice age. It had developed a rudimentary industry mostly involved with food production – crop cultivation in a temperate climate centred on the equator, and an abundance of fish from the ocean. There was never any shortage. Because of that our existence was a peaceful one. It may have been that this conflict-free life did little to stimulate any rapid advance in science and technology.

'It started,' Mendrilla told me the next day, 'when we decided to get an exact measurement of Earth to Moon distance by reflecting super high frequency radio waves from the Moon's surface. It was that that triggered the response from the lunar transmitter. It had clearly been programmed to do that at some time in the past.'

'And who was it that had done the programming? And when?'

Mendrilla shook her head. 'There is a great deal that we don't yet know. What became apparent almost from the outset was that whoever had built it was no longer there. It is giving us … information. But in small packets. In the beginning we could make little sense of the data we were receiving. It is largely thanks to Matthew that we have made so much progress in understanding the language it speaks. But what we do know now is that at some time in the past men and women went to the Moon and set up a colony there, for the most part beneath the surface. And we know that they are no longer there. It seems that they build the transmitter with the intention that – one day – it would communicate with the Earth, when our technology had advanced to a point when we began to use radio communication.'

What I could not understand was that there was no record – so far as I was aware – that anyone having been to the Moon before. People had theorised about it, of course. The notion sounded so far-fetched that I began to wonder again if I were being made a fool of. Mendrilla must have sensed my train of thought.

'We are talking about a long time – probably a very long time ago. I am sure that you are aware that at the present time about eighty five percent of the Earth's surface is covered by deep ice. We exist in an ice age, but one that is coming to an end. There was a time, though, when the great land masses were more or less ice free. They were populated, quite densely, by men and women essentially the same as we are. We have learned this from the information given to us so far in the lunar transmissions. In most respects they were very advanced. Indeed sufficiently so to have been able to travel to the Moon. But in others they were intensely destructive, polluting and contaminating the planet. They waged wars that resulted in the deaths of millions. And yet when the end came the world was unable to sustain the billions of humans living on its surface. Civilisations collapsed. The colony on the Moon could no longer be supplied with the essentials for its continued existence. It was when they saw the inevitability of their extinction that the colonists set about creating their vast data base containing pretty much everything of their science, arts and history, and taking steps to ensure that one day the information it contained might become a legacy for their descendants. As now it has.'

Desperate action was taken to try to reverse the decline. The result was certainly wretched for humankind, but with scant chance of success. Then the eruption of a super-volcano on the North American continent precipitated climate change at a rate and on a scale that vastly exceeded anything that could have been brought about by the pernicious activity of men and women. So all along, it seemed, the world had had its own plans. Yet still a remnant of humanity lingered close to the equator and slipped back, if not into barbarism, to a peasant-like existence that remembered nothing of its past after the passing of a few generations.

* * *

I adapted quickly enough to my new life, and was absorbed into the daily activities. I brought knowledge and skills that I hope served to improve the processing of the information that was being made available to us from a distance of nearly four hundred thousand kilometres. Then there came a day when Mendrilla delivered her next shock to me. I discovered that she could sing. I had called on her at her quarters at a time when she was not expecting me, to deliver some recently decoded material that had been sent by the lunar transmitter. She seemed unfazed by my arrival. Aware that I was there she continued in her fine contralto voice, and only turned to look at me as the song came to an end. The language was one I did not recognise, but I knew that it must have been one of the many that had been spoken by the old people.

'Something for me?' she asked.

'Yes. Some data on time scales. This is something we've not had before, I think.'

Mendrilla took the papers and scrutinised them. Then she said 'It's quite staggering. But really I'm not surprised. The old civilisations lie for the most part under kilometres of ice, crushed out of existence. When the ice finally melts there probably will be no trace of them at all … nothing'.

Then she looked at me. 'The song is called "Requiem Lacrimosa". Did you know that? No … of course you didn't. And perhaps now is the time to tell you my name … I mean my *old* name.'

'The song – it was beautiful …'

'Indeed one of the loveliest songs ever composed'.

'And your name?'

'It is Constanze. I have taken the name of the wife of the greatest composer who ever lived. Dead now for over three quarters of a million years.'

SEARCHING FOR SEASHELLS

14th September

I've been here on Bannow Island three weeks now and I've settled in. The house is small – just two rooms. There is a divan bed, an armchair and a table in one of them, and a cooker, sink and fridge in the other. There is no bathroom and the toilet is outside and, well, primitive. But for washing the sink is perfectly adequate – a strip wash does me fine.

I need to be honest with you about the facilities. I thought at one time that you might come and join me here, at least for a while. But that's just not realistic, given how small the place is, and how basic. I'm told that there is a decent hotel in the nearest town, which would be about fifteen miles away. It might be more than you can afford, of course. Anyway, it's too soon to me making that sort of plan, although I ache to see you.

Now that I'm getting used to the change and have organised my things in the house – not that there was much to organise – I'm getting going with the music and I've started sketching. Seascapes, mainly, and there's plenty of subject material for that here. I usually play the fiddle indoors. The sketches I make outside and work on them more inside when the light fails.

19th September

Although the village is over a mile away, I'm not entirely cut off from civilisation. The footpath from the lighthouse at Hook to Fethard (they pronounce it 'Feathered' here) passes between the house and the seashore. If the weather is fine people will walk by every hour or so during the day. Today, though, there've been frequent squally showers and only the hardiest folk are out. Late this afternoon the wind dropped and the sky cleared. Thinking I'd seen seen the last of the walkers, I took my fiddle to the porch where I could see the sun falling away towards the sea. I lost myself in a slow air – *Sliabh na mBan*. I know it is a favourite of yours and I thought of you as I played. I permitted myself the luxury of tears – just a few.

I hadn't noticed her approach, of course, and it wasn't until she had come right up to me and spoke that I realised that I wasn't alone *'The Mountain of the Women,'* she said when I had finished playing, 'you have it well.' The accent was cultured English. I was slightly taken aback, as much by her sudden appearance as by, well, her *appearance*. Her voice was not at all in keeping with it. She was tall, rather heavy, with a long coat that would have seen better days. Over her shoulder she carried a bulky canvas bag. A small terrier trotted up from the direction of the shore and sat at her feet.

I've seen her before, coming and going on the track along the shoreline. I call her 'the bag lady' and I'd wondered if she was a vagrant. She collects stuff – as she walks she stops, bends down and picks something up. I guess she must be some sort of beachcomber.

'You know Irish music?'

'Oh … yes,' she answered, looking down on my fiddle. She seemed miles away. I'm not one to look for company, not at this time at any rate. I rather hoped that she would move on and continue her collecting. But she just stood there.

For no other reason than not to appear rude I said, 'Picked up any good stuff today?'

She gave a brief laugh. 'Oh yes. Mostly plastic bottles, drink cans and cardboard coffee cups.' She shook her canvas bag, rattling its contents.

It turns out she's a self-appointed rubbish collector. The beach here is as blighted by litter as any. There's a large skip at Slade where she dumps it. She didn't tell me this – I got it from the landlord at the pub in the village. It seems that she comes over on the boat from England for two weeks every year just for the purpose of collecting junk. The pub has couple of rooms for bed and breakfast, and that's where she stays. Apart from her dog, Solo, she's on her own.

23rd September

The bag lady has a name. It is Shona. I was outside completing an oil sketch today and she stopped to look at what I was doing. People often do that, and mostly I ignore them, hoping they'll go away. The ones who fancy themselves as art critics are the most irritating. I don't get in to conversation with them and they give up after a while. Shona didn't comment on the sketch though. She looked across the bay towards the lighthouse that was my subject and remarked on the tones in the sky. In fact she spoke like someone who knows something about painting, but she wasn't forthcoming when I asked her. Not long afterwards she left, telling me her name as she did so, almost as an aside. She did not ask me mine. Really – she seems to be in a world of her own. There's something about her …

25th September

Did I tell you that Bannow Island is not really an island at all? It was once, sitting at the mouth of the estuary of Bannow Bay. Centuries ago gravel and sand thrown up by the south westerly gales made what is now the isthmus that connects the 'island' to the mainland. To the south, the tide goes out for miles. Seamus, the pub landlord, warned me that when the tide turns it can be treacherous. There are a couple of deep channels out there as well, where the water flows like a mill race. 'You fall into one of those,' he cautioned, 'and it's likely you won't be seen again.'

1st October

I wonder why it is that people seem to need to tell me about themselves, about what makes them tick. I can't really say that Shona is one of them, but today there've been two others. It's almost as if there's something about me that draws it out of them. Or perhaps my fiddling does something to them – casts some sort of pied-piper spell. No, I don't seriously think that, but one old guy who came by today came straight out and told me he's a flat-earther. I was taken aback, didn't really know what to say, and he kept on talking. It dawned on me that he absolutely believed every one of his own words. I wasn't inclined to argue with him. Then another stopped off and in a few minutes had told me that she was a committed creationist. Well, I think there's no point in trying to disabuse people of their delusions. They are harmless and I think arguing with them only encourages them. Perhaps the truth is that we each of us live in our own universe with its own reality. You could say that Shona is equally batty, doing what she does. If the world is doomed to drown in rubbish her two weeks litter picking a year is going to be no more than a drop – no, an atom – in the ocean.

5th October

I've no business making character judgements on flat-earthers, creationists, litter pickers or any other eccentric for that matter, because in my own way I must be just as odd as they are. I'm sure that's what the people in the pub think. The way they look at me, and I catch the odd snatch of conversation when they think I'm not listening. They wonder, too, where *you* are, just as I do.

Shona told me today that she's going to walk out on the shore when the tide goes out later this afternoon. 'I don't think you'll get much rubbish out there' I suggested. 'No,' she told me. Her voice dropped 'it's seashells I'll be collecting, for a change.' It was on the tip of my tongue to warn her about the turning tide. For some reason I thought she'd resent the advice so I didn't say anything.

2nd October

I normally wake with the sunrise, but at dawn this morning a noise at the front of the house pulled me out of a troubling dream. It took me a few moments to recognise the sound – it was a dog whining. I went to the door and opened it and in a moment Solo was around my feet. There was no sign of Shona. I looked back along the pathway, thinking he might have run ahead of her. Still no sign.

Then I looked out to the sea. During the night the tide had come in, of course, and now the water was receding rapidly again. Perhaps half a mile out there was a dark smudge on the sand. There's a colony of seals on the headland and I wondered if what I could see might be one that had died. I had an impulse to find out and started walking. Solo joined me, running ahead. I'd had an underlying sense of unease on finding the dog on his own and it deepened when I realised that what I had thought might be the carcase of a seal was nothing of the kind.

It was Shona's bag of trash.

At the pub Seamus told me that Shona hadn't returned last night. On hearing what I had found he became concerned. He picked up the telephone and in a few moments was speaking to the coastguard.

I found your letter when I came back to the house. What you have told me does not really surprise me. I think I knew this was coming. I am devastated, of course.

It is late in the evening. I have put my fiddle away in its case and locked it. I have tidied away my sketches and painting gear.

The tide is out again. I will seal this journal and it will be addressed to you.

I am setting off now.

I am going to collect seashells.

THE WAVES THAT BEAT ON
HEAVEN'S SHORE

It's Mother's birthday today. But I expect you wouldn't remember that.

In truth, Kathleen, I don't remember. And did you know that it's Father's birthday next month?

His birthday is in January? Mother used to mention it around the time. But only in passing. It's sad, but I think her memory of him is fading. It's so many years now.

It's the same with Father. He talks about her much less than he did once.

My memories don't fade, Electra. I mean the memories of the time that they were both alive.

Can't you get your head around the ... notion, that they're *still* alive, both of them? I mean, if you and I are as real as we perceive each other to be, then they *must* be alive.

I'm not sure I'm in the mood for metaphysics just now. I'm just too preoccupied.

Of course. I am too. I always get anxious before a performance. Stage fright.

And of course, this is no ordinary performance for you, I know. You singing in the presence of royalty! Will you be all right? I wonder how you handle it.

Uh-huh. I'll walk down to Farm Street before the concert.

To the church?

Yes. The Immaculate Conception. I'll pray quietly for half an hour, and I'll be fine. And how will you be? I think you have your own ways of coping …

I meditate. It's something I do regularly. I think it must have much the same calming effect for me as does prayer for you.

I think the challenge for you must be so much greater than mine. I mean, it's not as though I've not had a lot of experience performing in public and so, really, it's nothing new for me.

Well, I take your point. My 'performances' have been in lecture theatres for the most part, and my audiences' expectations have been rather different to yours. And I am very certain of my subject.

But tomorrow night! It's something on a different scale entirely … and you will be in the presence of royalty too. And don't you think there's something a little weird that both of these events are taking place on the same day – the 10th of December?

Coincidence? I wonder … It's the lecture I have to give that I'm so anxious to get right. That will be away from my usual topics. But I suspect that any applause I receive will be, at the very least, muted – you know – if I start going on about subatomic physics.

Well, I couldn't say that it would inspire them. And I think we both feel we need to inspire. The younger people in particular. I'd so much like to think of myself as a role model. Sort of to convince them that if I can do it, so can they. But you're going to be doing much the same, aren't you?But I envy you, Electra, I'm ashamed to say.

Envy – that's one of the seven deadly sins, isn't it? If it's any comfort, I envy you as well. I've never heard your voice. I never will. But if ever I did I know it would just blow me away.

But what you have discovered is going to change the world. I mean – limitless supplies of clean energy. And I can't begin to understand it – this thing you call a 'captive singularity'. The difference it must be going to make to humankind. So many who are dying now from starvation, the effects of climate change, lack of clean water and war …

Just to live isn't enough. What you do, Kathleen, is to give them a *reason* to live.

Well, all in all, the events of the next two days have the potential to change history. Has it occurred to you that at last our two worlds are going to diverge in a, well, rather spectacular fashion?

Yes it has. And I'm wondering if, with the divergence, we will finally separate. Or should I say, merge? Become one person …

But of course. That is what we are.

Look – each of us has our own memory of what happened in that fraction of a second on the motorway, in the storm when the tree came down on the car. Mother driving, father sitting next to her in the front. And the child Kathleen Electra sitting behind them. Death for one of them came instantly, the others were unscathed.

History changed then too. Although for the tiniest fraction of a second it could have gone either way. My understanding of the working of the universe – I should say perhaps the myriad of universes – suggests more than that. That it went … *both* ways.

Now you're leaving me far behind. But listen – on something more mundane – that time when we were small, when they were both alive. Do you remember how they used to read to us?

Of course! And there was one book …

Yes! I still have the copy they gave to us. It was a … birthday present.

Poetry – William Blake. And I have it still as well! Dog eared now. Perhaps not the most obvious choice for a child. But Mother and Father were unusual people – special people.

'The Bleat the Bark, Bellow and Roar are …'

'Auguries of Innocence' … Oh – I could recite that by heart.

I too. And they were – are – very unusual people. After that terrible accident Mother found her way of coping. She found faith – her Catholicism. And with that, sacred music. She took me to a concert at the Wigmore Hall. For the first time I heard Vivaldi 'Nisi Dominus' *Cum dederit dilectis suis somnum*. Sung by one of the great Italian contraltos. I thought that I had never, ever heard anything so utterly sublime. From that moment I knew where I was going.

You never wavered. And at last you came to where you are now. You are quite phenomenal. Really.

And you had your Damascene moment too!

Not in any sense a religious one, though. You know that I never had any religious faith. In the wake of Mother's death Father was almost consumed by grief. I think he kept going for my sake and he saw her in the eyes of his little girl, Kathleen Electra. People were so kind. There was an old university friend who lived with his wife on La Palma in the Canaries. He was an astronomer. He asked us to come over a few months after she died to escape the gloom of the English winter, but it was even colder than London up at the observatory! Father had a penchant for stargazing. He wanted me with him all the time, and it was in the dome housing the great Isaac Newton telescope that I caught the bug. It was when I first adjusted the fine focus and looked into the vastness of a deep star field. I thought of Blake again as I, almost literally, 'held infinity in the palm of my hand'. Father sensed that transformation in me and that was when he set aside his grief. He could not have done more to support me. That seemed to become his purpose in life.

So you followed Father to Imperial. While I was just a stone's throw away at The Royal College of Music. In a way our lives have been on a close parallel when you think of locations and events. I suppose that somewhere there is an explanation for that, a reason if you like. I do wonder if all that is going to end come the 10th – I on the stage at Covent Garden and you on the stage at the Stockholm Concert Hall. The world where you are is going to change out of all recognition. That is very clear to me.

Who is to say that your world will not change as a result of what I know you will give to it, Kathleen? Not in a way that can readily be predicted, I know. That is perhaps the difference between the arts and hard science. And yes, I have a premonition – more than a premonition that the events on the 10th will bring about an end to this strange duality that you and I have shared. The link between our two worlds – our universes – will evaporate. We won't be sharing things again as separate people.

Does that make you feel sad?

Yes.

I too. But we'll get over it. Now I'm going to ask you to do something for me …

What is that?

Tomorrow morning – before you leave for the airport. Would you come to Farm Street? Mother and I will be there between ten and eleven o'clock. I know you don't pray, but you wouldn't be the first person to go into the church and just sit quietly and reflect … and meditate, as you've told me you do. You won't see us, of course, but we will be very close and I know that you will sense us. And perhaps ponder on Blake's message and metaphors and … *the waves that beat on Heavens' shore*.

'COPPELIA'

Коппелия

I've always enjoyed driving although I do less of it these days. There's not so much traffic now as there used to be and I'm glad of that. Today I've been on the road for rather more than three hours, holding my speed down and keeping mostly to the nearside lane. I overtake only the very occasional truck.

Coppelia is in the passenger seat. From time to time I give her a brief commentary. For the past ten minutes or so the Malvern Hills have dominated the view to our right – for me one of the loveliest prospects in England. From a distance there is something understated in the hills that has a deep appeal. Great Malvern itself has always occupied a special place in our hearts. It was there that we spent the first weeks of our marriage and I don't think we've ever been happier. Memories flood back, and for a moment my attention wavers. The car drifts and the driver behind me sounds his horn. I steady up and raise my hand in acknowledgment.

If Chloë had been with me might have chided me, but gently. Such family as I have left to me are solicitous because of my heart condition, but my doctor seems not to be too bothered. 'Just don't get over-tired' is his advice – much the same as I get from my granddaughter, 'and watch your heart rate.' Being a retired doctor myself I know what he is referring to. But the state-of-the-art pacemaker just below my collarbone seems to have been doing its job well enough for the past two years.

I'm thinking it's time I has a break. A coffee would be good and I can put the car on a charge and that will be enough to get us to Salisbury.

I'm going to pull in at the next service station I say to Coppelia. *We'll have a short break.*

Good. I'm sure you need a rest. You were up so early, darling, getting things ready. Getting me *ready …*

We are interrupted by an alert for an incoming call. It's Chloë. I acknowledge and accept it.

'Hi grandpa! Just checking on you. How are you doing?'

'Fine. I'm pulling in in a few minutes for a break.'

'Tired?'

'Just a little. But I'll be OK.'

'Give me a call before you get back on the road. Are you managing the driving? You can always …'

'No. I'm fine. I prefer to be in control and I'm not in any hurry.'

'Good. But look, give me a call anyway. Promise?'

'I promise.'

Sometimes I think she's rather too attentive, I remark to Coppelia as I drive on.

I don't agree. It's really such a relief to me that she's there for you.

She has her own life to lead. And God knows, she's had enough to contend with over the past months. Sometimes I think she gives too much time to me.

For now, you *are her life. That is how she wants it to be. She won't miss out – I promise you.*

Coppelia knows things. She is quite right.

* * *

I leave the car at the charging point and go into the service area to get coffee. There aren't many people about. When these places were built they were designed to cater for a much larger driving population. I manage to find myself a comfortable armchair in a secluded corner. Fatigue flows over me in waves, and the next thing I know is that my phone is calling shrilly. It's Chloë again.

'You had me worried, Grandpa … you took so long to pick up. Is everything OK?'

'I'm fine. I was resting in the service area and I must have nodded off.'

'Where are you?'

I tell her and for a few moments she puts me on hold. I guess she's checking something. When she talks again, I sense the concern in her voice.

'Do you know what time it is? You must have been asleep for more than an hour. You've still got more than a hundred miles to drive. It'll be dark before you get here.'

'I'll be …'

'You know you don't drive after dark. Look – bear with me … I'm going to try to see if I can arrange something. Just stay where you are for now and I'll get back to you.'

Chloë is resourceful. Her problem solving ability is exceptional and I am sure it will get her a long way. In fact, it already has. More importantly – to me at any rate – is her kindness and sensitivity. I sometimes wonder how someone who went through what she did as a child has managed to survive so apparently unscathed. When our daughter Miranda and her husband died within days of each other in the second pandemic in 2023 Chloë came to live with Coppelia and me. The child was only six. Her lovely nature she inherited from her grandmother. I am in no doubt of that. And when I was plunged into my own grieving, she was my only comfort.

In a very few minutes Chloë is back on the line. 'OK – so this is how it is. I've found somewhere for you to stay in Great Malvern. It's a small B&B where they can give you an evening meal. It's in a quiet road and you'll be very comfortable. Stay the night and don't be in any hurry to set off in the morning.'

'Really – there was no need for you to go to the trouble. And I don't much fancy driving in the town traffic.'

'You don't have to. I'm going to download the details to your autodrive so you can just sit back and let technology do the rest. There's off street parking. Katie Andrews, the owner of the place, will keep a space free for you and she's given me the coordinates. You'll be there inside an hour. Now – you're not going to be awkward about this?'

I know well what Coppelia's view will be. I haven't the energy to argue with two women. Back in the car I tell her what has happened.

Well, I think she's absolutely right. It would be silly to put yourself under more strain when there's no need. And Malvern! How long is it since we were there?

It's sixty years since we were married. That's how long.

Why did we never go back? It was a lovely place.

Because I suppose, like most other people, we got caught up travelling the world and forgot what a beautiful country we live in.

And that's all changed now. Travelling the world, I mean. Regrets?

Not really. Malvern – just at this moment I can't think of anywhere I'd rather be.

The autodrive on my car is top of the range. I don't generally go in for luxuries but the insurers insisted on the specifications it offered because of my health problems and the medications I take. It's actually true – if I did black out the computer would take over the driving, get me somewhere safe and call for help. So far, thank goodness, that's not happened.

The journey time is rather less than it would have been had I remained at the wheel. Not that the autodrive breaks any speed limits. Her driving is quite exemplary. Strictly speaking the person who would have been driving – me – has to stay alert and I am one of those people who quickly falls into a doze when I am a passenger. Autodrive is able to sense any tendency to nod off and she counters it with a curt interjection, like an old-fashioned schoolmistress. When we arrive, dusk is approaching. Katie is at the front door watching out for us. No doubt she has one of those apps that has allowed her to track our progress. She is a pleasant, slightly dumpy middle-aged woman who smiles a lot. She carries in my bag. Then I carry in Coppelia.

Something about the house is familiar though quite what it is I cannot say.

Tea is brought in and some small talk ensues. 'So you've driven all the way from Harrogate? That's quite a journey.' I wonder if she is about to add 'at your age' but if she is, she thinks better of it. 'And you're paying a visit to your granddaughter in Wiltshire?'

I explain that Chloë is a doctor at the district hospital in Salisbury and that I've not seen her and her husband David for several months because of the travel restrictions imposed on older people regarded as being at risk in the wake of the fourth pandemic. I allow her to think that my visit is a straightforward matter of catching up now that things have relaxed. I prefer not to mention the family event that is the real reason for the visit. Katie does not push me, and I am glad of that.

As she talks, I notice something on the mantlepiece of the slate fireplace in the room where we are sitting. It is a small ornamental wooden box. Katie sees that it has caught my attention.

'It's pretty, isn't it,' she says, 'and, do you know, this house used to be full of them. My grandfather had a shop here. He collected and sold musical boxes. When he died my mother closed the shop. Sadly she only kept the one. But it's one of the best.'

And suddenly it all comes back to me. We both turn and look at Coppelia.

I turn back to Katie and say: 'Of course. I remember now. We were here once before. Many, many years ago.'

* * *

Chloë fusses. 'I was so worried about you, Grandpa. Come to think of it, you really shouldn't have been covering such a distance in one day. It's three hundred miles, for goodness sake!'

'You're going to remind me how old I am next!'

'I might. I might also remind you that your dysrhythmia is no trivial matter. You wouldn't be here now if it wasn't for the pacemaker.' But she is tactful – and kind – enough not to persist. I know very well that she will be having a more serious talk with me about it before I make my return journey next week. She knows, if anyone does, that I am not going to find the next few days easy. Neither will she.

'So how are *you* managing in all this, Chloë?' I ask her. 'You know, I lie awake worrying about you. I'm amazed you've not caught this thing. Or have you?'

Chloë shakes her head. 'No. Nor it appears will I.'

'What? I thought that anyone could be susceptible. And the infection rate among health professionals is pretty shocking in spite of all they say they do to protect you.'

'So, I'll tell you something that isn't yet generally known. It seems that a small minority of people who've been exposed have developed a previously unrecognised antibody. What we've always hoped for. The virus seems unable to counter it. It's as if the antibody just keeps one step ahead. Well, I'm glad to tell you that I'm one of that minority.'

'But Chloë – that is amazing news!'

'Well – there's even better news. It's almost certain that there is a significant genetic component that determines just which of us gets to develop it. What it means is that your great-grandchildren will be free of it.'

* * *

This is the hard part. The parting.

David, bless him, has managed to get the time off to be with us. God knows – we need him. He is as solid as a rock. It's just the three of us in the memorial garden, not far from the cathedral. There will be no ceremony.

Gently I place the box in David's outstretched hands. And then I run the tips of my fingers over the Cyrillic inscription. I say to David, 'It's a musical box. A very old one. Apparently it was made for a member of the Bolshoi Ballet, oh, more than a hundred years ago. She danced the part of Swanhilda – and Coppelia of course. When I bought it for my wife there was no longer any musical mechanism inside it. It was the box itself that she loved.'

'It's exquisite,' David says. 'I wonder what music did it once play …'

'Oh. That we do know. The man who sold it to us said it was the waltz from the ballet.'

David turns to the little grave. There is a spade lying on the ground beside it, and a small rose bush ready to be planted. I turn to Chloë, place my hands on her shoulders and gaze into her eyes. Yes – I can see her there, her grandmother. She whom most I loved.

Then I see something – someone else – for the first time. I step back and look quizzically at my granddaughter.

Some unspoken words pass between us. She smiles. Her loveliness is unsurpassed.

And then she raises her hand and places it on my cheek. Very softly, she says to me, '*As I told you, Grandpa – she – Coppelia – will be free of it. It can never harm her. So try not to be too sad. Look to the future, for in just six months from now I shall place your great-granddaughter in your arms.*'

TIME AND TIMES

The only thing that Sammy and Larry had in common was their looks. That wasn't surprising since they were twins. Not identical twins – if they had been they might have had a great deal more in common in terms of personality and intelligence. As it was, they couldn't have been more different.

For many years they had shared a small house. This arrangement suited them both. They got along well enough together, until Larry was committed to a secure psychiatric unit the day after the brothers' fortieth birthday. Sammy told me this a few days later when I met him down at the allotments where we had adjacent plots. I didn't know Larry anything like so well as I knew Sammy for the simple reason that Larry had no interest at all in growing vegetables, whereas vegetables for Sammy were an all-absorbing interest. He couldn't tell me much more. I'd not been aware that his brother had suffered from any mental illness, but, as I said, I didn't know Larry that well, although I did know that what Sammy lacked in brain power Larry made up for big time – Larry's IQ was said to be off the scale. Sammy confided in me that his brother was an 'inventor'. At the bottom of their modest garden was a large shed where Larry did whatever he did in the line of 'inventing'. I can't say that I ever saw any sort of end result of his endeavours, but on the occasions that I called round to see Sammy there were usually sounds and occasionally smells emanating from Larry's shed that presumably had to do with his efforts in the fields of alchemy and metaphysics.

I say that I had not been aware that Larry had suffered from any form of mental illness, but that doesn't mean that on the occasions that I *did* speak to him I did not find him somewhat odd.

'Just what is it that you *do* in that shed of yours?' I happened to ask him when I was with Sammy in his kitchen, and Larry had come in to make a cup of tea.

Larry looked at me as if I had asked him something quite stupid. 'What is it that I do? Well, for the moment I am completing the groundwork …'

'Groundwork for what?'

'For what I am *going* to do.'

'Which is?'

With a shrug he said, 'I am going to change the course of history.' Then he looked at this watch, took his mug of tea and set off back down the garden.

Of course, I should have suspected then that he was up to something that might have more than sinister implications, or that at the very least he had delusions of grandeur.

It was a few days after Larry's removal to the psychiatric unit that a police officer called round wanting to speak to Sammy. He was accompanied by another man in plain clothes. Sammy had become quite unsettled in his brother's absence. I guessed that he was unused to being on his own. So I got into the habit of calling in on him a couple of times a day and I was there when the police made their visit. Unexpectedly I had some time on my hands when these events took place – I was due to attend a conference in New York that was cancelled at short notice due to some problem with flights to North America.

Sammy was unable to give them anything but the most rudimentary answers to their questions, which were concerned for the most part with transmitting and receiving equipment. I found myself wondering if this had anything to do with the large satellite dish fixed to the wall of Larry's shed, which the policeman and his companion studied in some detail. They took their leave, informing us that they would be obtaining a search warrant to allow them access to the heavily padlocked building.

Sammy went to visit his brother the next day. The day after that I called in to the house to see how he was faring. He did not answer my knock and so I made my way through the side entrance to see if he was in the garden. To my surprise I could see that the door of the shed was standing open. For a moment I thought that it was the police who had obtained their warrant, but the man rummaging around inside was on his own and not in uniform. He turned to face me. I recognised him at once.

'Well, hello Sammy!' I called out as I approached. 'What are you up to? Does Larry know you're here?'

'Larry? Uh – oh yes. He knows. Point is – there are some, er, items here that would be best removed before the cops come back.'

There was something out of character in his mannerisms and speech. And then it clicked. This man wasn't Sammy – it was Larry.

For some reason I didn't let on that I'd realised my mistake. For a few moments I found myself lost for words. Before I could say anything more, Larry gave me a fixed stare and said, 'Look – can I ask you a favour?'

'What favour?'

He pointed to a box on the floor that he had been filling with documents. 'Can I leave this with you for safe keeping for a few days? It's some confidential stuff that Larry doesn't want getting into the wrong hands.'

'This isn't going to get me into trouble, I hope?'

'Oh no. There's nothing in there that doesn't belong to him. And nothing … illegal.'

Without giving the matter as much thought as perhaps I should have, after a few moments' hesitation I agreed.

'Larry reckons that they won't be keeping him much longer. They've nothing on him, you see. Probably a case of mistaken identity.'

'So – what was it all about, if you don't mind my asking?'

'Larry's a sort of radio ham. He's got some pretty powerful transmitting equipment here. Seems that MI 5 intercepted something and got hold of the wrong idea – that he might be involved in some kind of terrorist plot. Which of course he isn't …'

I listened as he went on talking. It wasn't clear to me why, if terrorist involvement was suspected, they hadn't just arrested him and put him on remand. I guess that the decision to treat him as a psychiatric case was a cover for something – possibly a diversion tactic to keep the press off the scent. I got the feeling that what had happened was something fairly dramatic. He made a brief remark about the disrupted flights to North America that had put paid to my own plans to travel to New York.

Then something came into my head. I said, 'that odd remark of Larry's ...'

'Yes?'

'About "changing the course of history". Do you remember?'

'Sorry. I don't know what you're talking about.' He clammed up then, and I made my way back home with the box of documents.

I went to my allotment the next day and found Sammy at work on his plot. 'Hi Sammy,' I called over to him, 'How's things? Any news of Larry?'

'Oh – they're letting him out. He'll be back home tomorrow. Seems there was a mix up. Well, I could have told them he's not mad. Eccentric, a bit strange perhaps. But there's an explanation for that ...'

'How do you mean?'

'Well – you know that they were saying that the computers would all go do-lally when the millennium came?'

'What's that got to do with it?'

'Well, I think Larry's head is a bit like a computer. Something got stirred up in there. He sees things ...

hears things the rest of us don't. Been like that almost two years now. Not mad. Fey, perhaps …'

I gave him a studied look. 'Sammy,' I said, 'be honest with me. Did you and he change places when you went to visit him last? Well, I *know* you did. I met him in his shed yesterday. Just tell me – what *is* this about?'

Sammy stared at me, wide eyed. Then he stammered, 'you'd best talk to Larry when you see him. He doesn't like me discussing his business. Sorry – I've nothing more to say …'

I'd not seem him quite so upset before. He busied himself with his digging again and avoided looking at me. Shortly afterwards he packed up his tools and left.

When I next saw the brothers they seemed pretty much their normal selves. I made a casual reference to the events of the previous days and was effectively blanked. Sammy changed the subject to a new strain of potato that he wanted to try. Larry took his leave, saying that he had some things to catch up with in his shed. As he was going he hesitated for a moment and turned to me. In a quiet voice he said, 'I *did* do it, you know!'

'What?'

But he did not wait.

He kept out of my way after that. I wasn't much troubled, and besides, I had other things on my mind. The conference in New York that had been called off the previous September was now rescheduled for early in 2002. The additional time this gave me for preparation was much to my advantage and I had ample opportunity to fine tune the two presentations I was to deliver.

In the last hour of the flight I fell into a light sleep. It was in a half waking state that I experienced, as sometimes I do, a particularly vivid lucid dream. I did not see Larry but his last enigmatic words, repeated to me, were crystal clear. I woke with a start and looked out through the aircraft window as we lost height, slowly, over the city. Ahead, rising up majestically through a blanket of low-lying haze, I saw the twin towers of the World Trade Centre in the final minutes before we came in to land.

A LETTER TO
MY GRANDDAUGHTER
ON HER BIRTHDAY

D earest Imogen

Here is a silly story that I have invented for your birthday.

Old Man Muffaroo and Mrs Bond both exist in the wider canon of literature, one being a cartoon character (very peculiar cartoons indeed as they can be viewed either the right way up or upside down and both make some sort of sense) and the other in an old nursery rhyme. If you google:

Old Man Muffaroo

And

Oh what have you got for dinner Mrs Bond

You will find them.

Mrs Kisses does not exist in literature. Only in my heart.

Thank you for all the joy you have brought to your grandma and me over the last fifteen years. And have a happy, happy birthday

With all my love

Old Grandpa.

I'M ONLY DREAMING

'NO PIES LEFT …' wrote old man Muffaroo ever so carefully on the back of a postcard with his best calligraphic quill pen. He paused for a moment, to consider his work, and sat back in his chair. A movement outside caught his attention and he looked up. There was something – or someone – in the vegetable patch at the end of the garden. 'THERE'S THE RABBIT!' he roared, 'now, WHERE'S MY GUN?' And off he clumped to rummage in the box room while Mrs Kisses called out from the kitchen '*Now* what is he up to?' Out he came again, double barrelled blundergun in the crook of his arm, and back to the open window. 'HAH! HERE'S MY GUN! Now, WHERE'S THE RABBIT?' As if in answer, two long ears poked up behind a row of lettuces. BOOM! went the gun and discharged half a pound of buckshot from the port barrel. It missed the rabbit, but it didn't miss Mrs Diddle-Dumpling's washing hanging on the line in the next door garden. As a consequence, her beautiful damask table cloth got riddled with more holes than Blackburn (Lancashire). Old Muffaroo was not to be deterred. Out into the garden he stomped, determined as ever to dispatch Mr Bunny. But bun was too smart for him. Up he hopped on to the kitchen roof and began pelting Muffaroo with carrot stubs. Up came the gun again and the starboard barrel blazed. BLAM! And again he missed. By pure misfortune Colonel Crackerbarrel was sailing by in his balloon with a basketful of day trippers. Some of Muffaroo's stray buckshot found their mark and, sustaining a slow puncture the balloon made a graceful, if unscheduled, descent. Colonel Crackerbarrel shook his fist at Muffaroo and made dire threats. The day trippers set up a wail 'Oh! We're going to get a soaking!' And they were right, for the balloon executed a graceful splashdown in the village pond, setting a flock of ducks a-quacking. Old Mrs Bond, hearing the disturbance, emerged from the village inn and came down to the pond in a rage, a bundle of sage under one arm and two strings of onions under the other. 'Oh, what have you done to my ducks?' she cried, 'Oh, come back! Dilly, dilly, dilly dilly …! As for Mrs Kisses, the tidy soul lost no time: she upped and gathered towels and changes of clothing into her shopping-basket-on-wheels and made straight for the pond to effect a rescue of the distressed day trippers. Old Muffaroo gave up on the rabbit (who had by this time taken up position again in the vegetable patch) in disgust. And finished writing his card: "… IN THIS VAN OVERNIGHT.'

CLOSING SENTENCES FROM
DAVID COPPERFIELD
(CHARLES DICKENS)

… But, one face, shining on me like a heavenly light by which I see all other objects, is above them and beyond them all. And that remains.

I turn my head, and see it, in its beautiful serenity, beside me. My lamp burns low, and I have written far into the night; but the dear presence, without which I were nothing, bears me company.

Oh Agnes, Oh my soul, so may thy face be by me when I close my life indeed; so may I, when realities are melting from me like the shadows which I now dismiss, still find thee near me, pointing upward!